A Second Christmas Wish

A Second Christmas Wish

Kathryn Freeman

Where heroes are like chocolate – irresistible!

Copyright © 2016 Kathryn Freeman

Published 2016 by Choc Lit Limited
Penrose House, Crawley Drive, Camberley, Surrey GU15 2AB, UK
www.choc-lit.com

A CIP catalogue record for this book is available
from the British Library

ISBN 978-1-78189-398-2

Printed and bound by Clays Ltd

To those of you kind enough to be reading this book, I wish you a very Happy Christmas. May your mince pies be warm, your tree not shed its needles and all your wishes be answered.

Acknowledgements

My deep and heartfelt thanks to Choc Lit. It's their
wonderful Tasting Panel who passed *A Second
Christmas Wish* for publication, their wise editor
who pummelled it into shape, their clever cover
designer who gave it the Christmas sparkle.

And Choc Lit who were kind enough to put
their name on the front cover next to mine.

A special thank you to the Tasting Panel readers who
read and enjoyed *A Second Christmas Wish* and made
this possible: Rebecca A, Hrund, Dimitra, Stacey R,
Alison B, Linda Sp, Jackie M, Anne W, Katie P,
Gill L, Kim L, Debbie J, Sue T, Betty, Alison S.

Prologue

The dining room was so silent Melissa could hear her knife scraping the plate as she cut through the turkey. Why didn't Lawrence talk to his parents, for goodness' sake? Why did he just sit there, his face like thunder?

Her eyes scanned to her in-laws. Attractive yet cold, aloof. Perhaps it was no wonder Lawrence couldn't talk to them. His parents belonged to an era when the Lord and Lady of the manor ruled their household with a rod of iron. When guests who stepped out of line were silenced with a sharp tongue and a stern look. When children were seen and not heard.

Lawrence was fast turning into them.

Next to her, William started to become restless, kicking his legs under the table, shifting about in his seat.

'Finish your meal, darling,' she whispered.

He shook his head. 'Not hungry.'

Lawrence's black eyes darted across the table at them and William immediately froze. Melissa touched his small hand reassuringly. 'Okay, if you're sure you've had enough you need to sit patiently while everyone else finishes.'

'He's got the appetite of a sparrow,' Lawrence's mother stated witheringly. 'He should be made to eat his meal.'

Melissa bit the inside of her cheek and fought for control. 'It's Christmas day. William should be allowed to do whatever he wants on such a special day, don't you think?'

'If you give children an inch, they'll take a mile,' she retorted, then glanced over towards her son. 'You're very quiet, Lawrence. The turkey not to your satisfaction?'

1

Lawrence clattered his knife and fork onto his plate and drained the contents of his third glass of wine. 'I have no appetite for dry turkey,' he announced, shooting Melissa a cutting glance.

'I'm sorry,' she whispered, then bit her lip, angry with herself for being so timid. 'Perhaps if you put some more gravy on it?'

'Drown overcooked turkey with lumpy gravy?'

She felt tears prick. Did he have to be so rude to her in front of his parents? In front of their son?

'Manners,' his father scolded. 'What's got into you today?'

Lawrence reached for the wine bottle and refilled his glass. 'I'll tell you what's got into me. My darling wife announced a few days ago that she's leaving me.'

Melissa's heart bounced inside her rib cage. Oh no. She'd begged him not to raise the subject today. She'd wanted to give William a Christmas to remember – for the right reasons. 'I don't think today is the time to discuss this,' she said, unable to stop her voice from shaking.

'Why not?'

She turned to William, who was hanging his head, staring at his lap. 'Because Christmas is a time for smiling. For having fun. Especially when you're nearly five.'

'And are you having fun, William?' Lawrence asked his son coldly.

William's head shot up. 'Yes.'

Lawrence continued to glare. 'Is that how you've been taught to address your elders?'

'Yes, Sir.'

'And what constitutes fun in your book?'

Confusion flickered over William's face and Melissa reached for his hand again, this time holding onto it. 'Your

2

father just wants to know which part you've enjoyed most today.'

For a brief moment his eyes filled with joy. 'Opening my presents from Father Christmas.'

Lawrence snorted. 'Father Christmas, eh?'

'Yes, Sir.'

'You seriously believe one man goes round to all the children in the world delivering presents in one day?'

Melissa inhaled sharply. 'Don't,' she hissed. 'Please, I beg you, don't ruin this day for him.'

'Ruin it?' Lawrence thrust his glass onto the table with such force some of the wine spilt, forming a blood-red stain on the white tablecloth. 'I rather think you're the one who's ruining things.' His eyes flicked over to William who looked impossibly small on the large antique chair. 'Let me save you a lot of heartache later in life, son. Love, rather like Father Christmas, doesn't exist.'

'He does,' William shouted, shifting agitatedly in his chair. Melissa had never heard him answer his father back, ever.

'If you believe that, then you're as big a fool as I am.'

William started to cry and, as he scrambled desperately off his chair, he sent his plate clattering to the floor.

'You bloody idiot,' Lawrence bellowed.

Melissa slid off her chair and scooped her sobbing son into her arms. 'You're the idiot, Lawrence,' she replied as evenly as she could. 'Mr and Mrs Raven,' she nodded over to her in-laws, 'I'll leave your son to entertain you. I'm going to take William upstairs.'

She spent the rest of the day playing games with William in his playroom. Because it was a far better way to spend Christmas afternoon than sitting with his stuffy parents,

Melissa almost felt like thanking Lawrence for his petulant outburst at the dinner table. Almost. But she would never forgive him for taking the magic out of the day for William. Though she'd tried to reassure him Father Christmas did exist – that his father thought he was being funny saying he didn't – she wasn't sure William believed her.

When he was finally asleep in bed, Melissa walked hesitantly back downstairs. She found Lawrence sitting by himself in the lounge, staring into the fire. With the crackle of the logs, the cosy glow of the flames and the fresh smell of the pine tree she and William had carefully decorated, the scene should have brought her a warm, fuzzy Christmas feeling. It didn't.

The man on the sofa was too cold, the atmosphere far too tense.

'Decided to come back down, have we?' Lawrence stood and walked towards her, his dark eyes glittering menacingly.

'You upset your son today,' she accused, fighting for calm though her heart was hammering. 'How could you do that?'

Irritation flickered across his face. 'You mollycoddle him too much. He's turning into a real mummy's boy, frightened of his own shadow. He needs toughening up.'

'He's a few days away from being five. ' She dared to look up at him. 'I asked you not to discuss the separation today. It wasn't the right time.'

'I beg to differ. My parents had a right to know.' He bent his head and she caught the smell of stale wine on his breath, mingling with his exotic aftershave. 'I still find you incredibly attractive, Melissa.'

The words – ones she'd heard often over the years – were almost a purr. Once she'd believed them. Now she knew it was his way of keeping control. One minute charming, the next cruel, it made sure he kept her unbalanced. 'And you're still trying to manipulate me,' she retorted, twisting her body away from the confines of his. 'I won't be pushed or pressured by you anymore.' Back ramrod straight, she raised her chin. 'You got away with it when I was young and naïve. Now I'm old enough to fight back.'

Lawrence took a step away, his long hair falling away from his sharp features. 'How is telling my wife she's attractive trying to manipulate her?'

'You blow hot and cold, and I'm tired of second guessing your mood. Tired of feeling on edge all the time, wondering how you're going to react to me. How you're going to treat your son.'

His lip curled. 'You make me sound like an ogre. Have I ever hit you, hurt you?'

'Physically, no.' Damn, her voice had started to tremble. She took in a deep breath before speaking again. 'You had an affair, Lawrence. Did you really think that wouldn't hurt me?'

He laughed harshly. 'That was ages ago and there were reasons for that. Reasons I've explained and you accepted.'

'It doesn't mean I forgot, or forgave. I can't trust you any more. I can't trust your mood, your fidelity, your treatment of William. I want out.'

'So you've already told me.' Reaching out a hand, he ran his finger down her cheek. 'Do you remember the day we first met? You were modelling my new range and I'd never seen a more exquisite creature, yet when I went to introduce myself you were so unsure, so shy. I knew right then you were not only going to be a superstar, you were going to be my wife.'

'And you made sure of both.' Her life had changed almost overnight. He'd thrust her into the limelight, turning her from a painfully shy, unheard of young model into Melissa

Raven, supermodel and wife to the hottest designer in the country. 'I'm grateful for what you gave me,' she added, moving away from his touch. 'But now I want to live my own life, not one made for me.'

He sighed, dropping his hand and swivelling dramatically on his heel before settling elegantly onto the sofa. 'It's a mistake,' he barked coldly. 'Without me backing you, your career will tumble.'

'You think I care that much about wearing clothes and smiling for the camera?'

He glared back. 'You will, when the glamorous lifestyle you've enjoyed comes to an abrupt end. Still, it's your loss. I'm not going to beg you to stay.'

Chewing on her bottom lip, she fought for the courage to ask the most important question. 'Will you want joint custody of William?'

His dark eyes widened in surprise, and then he started to laugh. 'Of course not. We both know I never wanted the boy.' Then his features turned sharp. 'But for appearance' sake I'll want to see him now and again.'

'Fine.'

Joy flared at the knowledge he wasn't going to fight her for William and for a brief moment she wanted to put her arms around Lawrence. Thank him for letting her have her son. But one look into his eerie dark eyes and the impulse died. 'I'm going up to my room.'

Those eyes watched her carefully. 'It's Christmas day. Surely you aren't going to leave your husband alone on such a ... what did you call it? Ah yes, such a *special* day.'

Though she wanted to escape upstairs, she didn't. Out of habit, and a desire to keep the peace, Melissa did what her husband asked of her. She spent the rest of Christmas evening with him.

Later that night though, as she opened the door to her bedroom – the one she'd moved into last week, next door to William and at the other end of the corridor to Lawrence – she promised herself next year it would be different. She and William would spend Christmas in their own house.

And with a bit of luck, away from Lawrence's oppressive, controlling presence, they might both learn to loosen up and live a little.

Chapter One

At the knock on the door, Melissa sighed and grabbed at the bag of sweets she'd left on the side. Halloween seemed to be the only time they ever received visitors. Tentatively she opened the door.

When she saw who was there, all she wanted to do was slam it shut again.

'Lawrence.'

He gave her a twisted smile. 'Melissa.'

She should ask him in, she thought, then dismissed the idea. She was done being subservient to Lawrence. It was nearly three years since she'd left him. Now she did what she wanted, not what was wanted of her. 'What brings you here?'

'Aren't you going to invite me in, first?'

'No. I repeat, what are you doing here?'

He sighed dramatically. 'Fine, if we must discuss private matters on your doorstep. The reason I'm here, my darling Melissa, is to ask to see my son over the Christmas holiday.'

Every cell in her body seemed to freeze. Right now she bitterly regretted her decision to let Lawrence know where she'd moved to. At the time she'd harboured a crazy hope that he might change once she'd left him. Might wake up to realise how lucky he was to have such a beautiful son and want to build a proper relationship with him, one borne of love and patience, not disinterest and domination.

The last few years had only proved how delusional she'd been.

'Christmas?' she finally managed. 'How do you expect me to plan that far ahead? I haven't even thought about it yet.'

'Which is why I'm telling you now. I'll be spending a lot of my time in the States over the next month, but I'm back in England for Christmas. Evangeline wants to meet him.'

'Evangeline?' Her mind instantly recalled the dark-haired woman she'd shared both a catwalk and a husband with. Evangeline hadn't smiled because it caused wrinkles, and hadn't talked to the other models because she thought she was above them all. 'Why her?'

'What do you mean, why her?'

'Why would she want to see William?'

'Because he's my son.'

Melissa registered the implication, that Lawrence was now dating the super bitch, and felt nothing. No anger, no bitterness, no jealousy. Just a calm *nothing*. She almost smiled. Almost. 'Why do *you* want to see William?'

Lawrence gave her one of his arrogant smirks. 'Don't most fathers want to see their sons? Especially over Christmas?'

'You're not most fathers. In fact, you've barely been one at all.'

'Come now, you're being cruel.' He gave a dismissive shake of his head. 'It's not my fault I've had to spend most of the last few years out of the country. Let's just say I want to make up for lost time.'

'You want to update your image more like.' She knew her ex-husband, and the world of fashion he was driven by. As one of the country's leading designers he was constantly setting new trends, many of which continued into his personal life. When she'd first met him he'd been the sophisticated bachelor. A party-animal, enjoying his freedom following a strict upbringing. When he'd married her, he'd morphed into the glamorous, attentive husband. At least as far as the media were concerned. Since their divorce, his star had started to wane. 'Is William the latest attempt to prop up your dwindling image? Are you trying for super dad?'

'Sarcasm doesn't suit you.' Scorn filled his features, making him appear cruel.

'Well, whatever your reason, you can't take him away for a few days. He hardly knows you. It would terrify him.'

'Still frightened of his own shadow?'

Her hand clutched tighter onto the door handle. 'William is a shy, sensitive seven-year-old who needs love and support. Not a fickle father who bullies him.'

Lawrence's mouth hardened. 'You're exaggerating. I simply instilled some much-needed discipline into him. And besides, it's my right to see him.'

'Just as it's my duty as a mother to do what's best for him. God, Lawrence, you've only bothered to see him once since I left you.' And that stilted afternoon would remain with her for a lifetime. 'If you want to build a relationship with him, I can't stop you. But you'll do it my way, or not at all.' Melissa marvelled at how calm she sounded. He'd never know by the tone of her voice how much she shook inside. How terrified she was that Lawrence would simply push her aside and take William away.

'And what is your way?' Lawrence asked, leaning his shoulder against the wall, his hands loosely shoved into his pockets.

'We all go out together, at a time and place of my choosing.'

Lawrence snorted. 'Oh my dear Melissa, I hardly think you're in a position to dictate terms. The custody agreement clearly stated I would have access to him when I wanted.' His dark eyes skimmed over her face, scrutinising, assessing. 'You're harder than the shy girl I married. It doesn't suit you.' Straightening, he carefully secured his flamboyant wine-coloured fedora onto his head. 'I'll be in touch.'

Melissa waited until he'd driven off before slamming the door and collapsing on the bottom stair. God, how she wished he were right, and she had become a tougher version of the girl he'd married. If she had, she wouldn't feel this absolute terror whenever she saw him. At twenty-eight she might have learnt to act confidently, but inside she was still intimidated by him, and she hated herself for it.

'Mum, are you okay?' William stood at the top of the stairs, his dark hair spiked up at awkward angles and his round grey eyes looking worried.

Forcing a wide smile onto her face, Melissa stood and beckoned him down. 'Of course I am. Come on young man, I've got something I want to talk to you about while I make the tea.'

Wariness added to the worried look in his eyes. 'Is it about Dad?'

Her heart squeezed painfully. 'Why do you ask?'

'That was him just now.'

She wondered how much he'd heard – clearly enough to make him worry. Taking hold of his hand, she gave it a quick squeeze. 'Your dad just needed a quick word with me, that's all. Now come into the kitchen because I want to tell you about these tennis lessons I'm trying to set up for you.'

'Simon plays tennis.'

Relieved that the tension had disappeared from his face, Melissa laughed. 'I know. How would you like to play, too?'

He wrinkled his nose. 'But it's winter. People don't play tennis in the winter.'

'Ah, that's where you're wrong. If you play indoor tennis, you can play all year round. I used to love playing when I was younger.'

William shrugged. 'I dunno.'

She stifled a sigh. William was always so reticent about trying anything new. 'Well, the tennis player I used to love watching, who happens to be Simon's uncle, runs a tennis centre with courts inside, so you can play even when it's snowing.' And while her experience with Lawrence had left her distrustful of men, especially rich, successful, overly confident men, she wasn't averse to the idea of drooling over Daniel McCormick from afar.

'Is it going to snow?' Latching onto the last part of her sentence, William's eyes shone with something close to delight. 'I want it to snow for Christmas.'

'That's a while away yet.' Smiling, she dipped down to kiss the top of his head. 'But who knows, by then you might have to walk through the snow to play tennis. Maybe strap the rackets onto the bottom of your feet to help you.'

He started to giggle and the sound warmed her heart. She only wished she heard it more often.

Sitting in the café in his tennis academy, Daniel eyed his sister over his coffee cup. 'Let me get this straight. You're asking me to find a space in my coaching programme for the shy seven-year-old son of your friend. I'm expected to be warm and friendly to them both, but under no circumstances come onto her?'

Alice smiled sweetly back at him. 'I always knew you were good at assimilating information. Come on, you can find little William a space, can't you? She'll pay, you know. She isn't poor. And Simon will love having his friend in the same group.'

Daniel sighed and reached his hands behind his back to stretch out his shoulders. Injury had forced him to give up his professional tennis career several years ago and every now and again he felt a twinge in his right shoulder where they'd had to operate. It became worse when he tensed up, like he was now. *Sisters*. 'I'm pretty sure I can find William a place, yes. But assuming the mother is as lovely as you're saying, why am I not allowed to chat her up? She's single, isn't she?'

Alice shifted back against her chair. They shared looks – dark hair and brown eyes – but not temperament. Where he was calm and patient, Alice was impetuous. Where he was laid-back and easy going, unless he was on a tennis court, Alice was gregarious and at times temperamental. Daniel was thirty-three and still single. Alice, older by three years, was onto her third husband.

'We're talking about Melissa Raven, Daniel. Haven't you heard of her?'

Daniel searched his mind, but came up blank. 'Should I have?'

Alice let out an exasperated sigh. 'She was the face of the Raven fashion label for years. Surely you've heard of Raven? You've probably got a suit made by them somewhere in your wardrobe and you're just too ignorant to know it.'

'Hey, if we're going to start trading fashion insults I can think of a few horrors you've worn over the years. I still remember that fluorescent-green dress.'

She gave him the traditional sister put down – sticking her tongue out at him. 'I was just trying to tell you that Melissa was a famous model and that Lawrence Raven, the world-renowned designer, was her husband.'

'I take it they're divorced?'

'Yes, and she goes by her maiden name of Stanford now. I've only known her for two years, since William and Simon became friends at school, but long enough to know she doesn't like talking about her marriage. I think she went through a pretty bad time and still carries a lot of pain and mistrust. She tells me she's sworn off men.'

Pushing his empty cup away, Daniel raised a dark eyebrow. 'If that's the case, neither of you have anything to fear from me.'

'Oh no, I know you too well. You won't be able to stop from trying to charm the socks off her. She's just your type.'

'First, I don't try and charm. I charm. Second, what do you mean, my type? I wasn't aware I had a type.'

Alice smirked. 'Not in the traditional sense of blonde versus brunette, no. But you do always hanker after women who are both gorgeous and smart. Then you get let down because that combination are usually also arrogant and pushy, which you hate. Melissa is stunning, clever, but actually quite shy.'

Feeling slightly irritated now, Daniel glanced at his watch. 'Much as I'd love to carry on discussing your version of what I might find attractive, I'm afraid I've got to dash.' He rose from the table, unfurling long, muscular legs encased in navy track suit bottoms. At six and a half feet tall, he dwarfed most people he met, including his sister. Bending down, he placed a kiss on her cheek. 'Tell this friend of yours that she and William can come by next week. And I promise to keep my hands off her.' He walked away a few steps before looking over his shoulder and giving Alice a wink. 'At least for now.'

Chapter Two

The moment Daniel caught sight of the two women and two boys walking through the reception area towards him, he swore softly. He hated it when his sister was right. Even from a distance, and having not yet spoken to her, Daniel knew the tall, slender blonde walking alongside Alice was most definitely his type. She walked with the easy grace he'd expect from an ex-catwalk model. Her head held high, her elegant frame fluid in its movement. As they came closer he could make out the striking angularity of her face. It shouldn't work, he thought as his sister waved at him. Melissa's mouth was too full, her grey eyes too large, her cheekbones too sharp. Yet as she came to a halt in front of him, Daniel could only stare. Of course it worked. The combination was stunning.

'Daniel, meet Melissa and her son, William.' He was only dimly aware of Alice making the introductions. His eyes, his mind, his focus, were all on Melissa.

'Uncle Daniel, I'm going to beat you today.'

The sight of his nephew, Simon, leaping up and down in front of him, knocked Daniel out of his trance and he grabbed the boy by his legs, dangling him upside down. 'What did you say?' he remarked gruffly, swinging him slowly from side to side.

'I said I'm going to beat you,' Simon giggled from his upside down position.

In a routine he'd begun when Simon was just a toddler, Daniel slowly raised his nephew up and down. 'Who's the best tennis player in the family?' he growled, allowing Simon's face to come perilously close to the floor.

'You are,' Simon squealed, clearly ready to come back to earth.

As he carefully put his nephew back on his feet, Daniel glanced at the quiet boy standing next to Melissa. 'Do you think you're going to beat me, William?' he asked, grinning down at him.

William shrank back, clutching tighter to his mother's hand. 'No, Sir,' he replied quietly, his eyes watchful and unsure.

'Is that because you don't want to be dangled by your feet?' Daniel prompted, his voice more gentle this time. William was one nervous little boy.

'Yes,' William whispered.

Daniel searched for the beginnings of a smile on the boy's serious young face, but wasn't sure he could find one. 'Very wise. Perhaps Simon here will learn some sense from you.' He ruffled his nephew's hair before turning back to William's mother. 'Now is probably a good time to mention that I don't hang all the children here by their feet. Only family members.'

'I'm glad to hear it.'

For a moment Daniel stared into her clear grey eyes but then her lids lowered and she dropped her gaze to the floor.

Damn, he'd embarrassed her.

'Have you bought me a new racket yet?' His nephew piped up, breaking the slightly awkward silence.

'Simon,' Alice admonished. 'I know it's only Daniel, but that was still rude.'

'Thank you, I think.' He smiled wryly at his sister before turning back to Simon. 'Why would I want to buy you a new racket?'

'Because it's nearly Christmas.'

'Okay, I'll bite. Even though we're only just in November,

why would I want to buy you a racket because it's *nearly* Christmas?'

'Because you buy me a tennis racket *every* Christmas.'

As Simon's face lit up with laughter at his own joke, Daniel bit back a smile. 'Maybe this year I'm going to be less predictable.'

'Nah. I like you being pre … whatever. I get an awesome racket.'

More laughter, this time with Simon and Alice joining in. When his eyes shifted over to Melissa though, she was looking everywhere but at them, as if she felt out of place.

As the laughter died down, she cleared her throat. 'Thank you for finding a space for William. I know you're fully booked, so I really appreciate you letting him join.'

'No problem.' He couldn't seem to stop staring at her. If Alice was right, and the lady had sworn off men, it was a crying shame.

'Shall I go with the boys and get them changed while you talk to Melissa about the set-up?' Alice's glare said it all. *No flirting, no asking her out.*

'Yes, ma'am,' he replied, both to her verbal command and the unspoken one. Turning to Melissa, he gave her an encouraging smile. 'If you'd like to follow me?'

Her eyes flickered to him and then to her son. Wary about being alone with him, or wary of letting her son out of her sight? 'We'll catch up with William and Simon on the court in a minute,' he reassured, though if it was being alone with him that had her all het up, that was unlikely to help. Still, she followed him as he led her down the corridor, which had to be a start.

Melissa followed behind the giant of a man who was her friend's brother. He seemed friendly and easy-going

17

enough, but she couldn't help feeling slightly uneasy. She wanted to be flattered by the admiring looks Daniel had just been giving her – after all, she'd had a crush on this man for years – but instead all she felt was uncomfortable. She simply wasn't interested in becoming the focus of any male attention. Even from one who looked every inch as attractive in the flesh as he had done on the television.

Daniel opened the door to a large office dominated by a black desk with an in-tray in danger of buckling under the weight of its contents. To the side of the desk was a glass-fronted display cabinet and inside it row upon row of gleaming silver trophies.

'Are all those yours?' She nodded over to the trophy cabinet.

He gave her a grin she'd have described as sheepish, had it not been on the face of a strapping six and a half foot athlete. 'Yeah. I know it's a bit corny to have trophies on display, but I figured they looked better here than on my mantelpiece at home.' He laughed at himself. 'Besides, I worked blood, sweat and tears to win the damn things. I reckon I owe it to myself to show them off once in a while.'

'Yes, you do.' She'd watched him win a fair few of them.

While Daniel moved round to sit at his desk, Melissa slipped cautiously into the black leather chair facing him. In his tennis playing days the man sitting across from her had been known as a handsome charmer and it wasn't hard to see why. The combination of rippling athleticism, dark good looks, compelling brown eyes and a dazzling smile was hard to ignore.

'Is it something I said?'

She blinked. 'Sorry?'

'You're staring at me. Don't get me wrong, I'm not averse

to having a woman stare at me, but in this case I get the feeling it's not because you like what you see.'

'Oh no, it's not that at all.' His lips twitched and she realised how that sounded. 'What I mean is … well, to be honest I was thinking how relaxed and easy-going you were. Then I remembered how you used that charm on court to sucker the competition.'

He let out a startled laugh. 'I did?'

'You know you did. One minute you were entertaining the crowds with a wise-crack. The next you'd turn deadly and rip your opponent to shreds. I believe they nicknamed you the Laughing Assassin.'

He laughed, coughed and laughed again. 'Oh boy. I hadn't realised you were a tennis fan.'

She felt herself starting to blush, which hadn't happened to her in years. 'I wasn't just a tennis fan,' she admitted. 'I was a Daniel McCormick fan.'

His gaze crashed into hers and for a moment she was transfixed by his deep brown eyes. An almost forgotten feeling of attraction tugged at her, warming her skin, tickling her senses.

'Has William ever played tennis?'

Grateful for the safer topic, she smiled. 'No, not really. I've been out on the local courts a few times and tried to help him hit the ball, but he hasn't received any proper coaching.'

'Did he enjoy it?'

She watched him pick up a pencil and twirl it through his long, tanned fingers.

'Melissa?'

Shaking herself, she focused back on the conversation. 'Sorry, yes, William does enjoy tennis. That's why, when I mentioned it to Alice, she offered to speak to you.' She decided to leave it at that, even though it wasn't just an improvement in William's tennis skills she was hoping for from the academy.

'He's quite shy, isn't he?'

'Yes.' She sounded abrupt and defensive but couldn't help it. The question put her on edge.

Daniel's dark eyebrows rose up a fraction. 'It was just an observation. I didn't mean to imply it was a bad thing.'

'I know.' She sighed and took a moment to remind herself this stranger was also her friend's brother.

'I understand you and his father are divorced?'

'We are, yes.' She wondered how much more Alice had told him, and felt her posture slowly stiffening.

Daniel narrowed his eyes, his expression hard to read. 'Does he still see William?'

Abruptly her chin shot up. How much more did he really need to know? He was only going to give her son tennis lessons, after all. 'Sorry, but I'm not sure that's any of your business.'

Daniel took the barbed retort on the chin. 'Fair enough. Is there anything else you do want to tell me? I'm afraid you're going to have to fill out some forms. Just the usual stuff, name and address, any allergies or illnesses we should be aware of. Emergency contact.' He smiled at her look of alarm. 'I can assure you we've only had to use that once, when one of the mums forgot to pick up her daughter because she thought the session finished an hour later.'

'William's pretty healthy. No illnesses, no allergies.' Just a fear of his arrogant, overbearing father, she added to herself. But that would go in time, now it was just the two of them. Already she'd seen an improvement. It was an extra reason not to let another man into her life again. It simply wasn't worth the risk.

'Excellent. If you could fill these in for me while you're waiting for us.' He pushed a couple of forms at her. 'Then the only thing left to do is see him play tennis.'

He stood and once again Melissa was struck by his size. Quickly she got to her feet, though even with her model height she felt dwarfed by him. It wasn't just his physique that intimidated though. It was his air of confidence, of sureness. His *presence*.

More aware of him than she wanted to be, she followed him out of his office.

Enjoying a drink in the café opposite the courts, Melissa found her eyes constantly straying towards the young tennis players William had joined. She was acutely aware of how he hung back, even though his best friend, Simon, was there. The group, a mixture of boys and girls, all seemed determined to prove to Daniel that they were the best. All except for William. His shyness, in direct contrast to the confident children around him, was almost painful to watch.

'He'll soon settle in when he gets to know Daniel and the other children better,' Alice remarked gently.

'Yes, I know.' It didn't stop her worrying, though. Happy wasn't a word that sprung to mind when she watched him. Oh he laughed when he was with her, but his quietness around others was wrong. She worried it was more a reflection of his state of mind, than his true character.

Daniel changed the exercise, getting the children to throw a ball at each other and catch it on the bounce. He demonstrated with one of the girls, pulling comic faces when she dropped it, much to the amusement of his young audience. Clearly his brand of easy charm worked equally well with children as it did with adults.

'Does he miss the tennis?' she asked Alice, intrigued that a top ranking professional could find contentment teaching basic tennis skills to children.

'You wouldn't think it to watch him, or to talk to him.' She paused, eyes on her brother. 'There were a few weeks, right after he knew his career was over, when he was very down. It was heart-breaking to see.' Briefly her face filled with sadness. 'But then he pulled himself together and focused all his energies on taking his career in another direction. I don't know if he still yearns for what might have been. I only know that he's put his heart and soul into these academies and is rightfully proud of what he's achieved.' Alice turned to her. 'He's a good man, Melissa. He would suit you very well.'

Melissa almost dropped her cup. 'Oh no you don't. I've already told you, I'm not interested in another relationship. The scars from the last one are far too raw, for both me and William.'

Alice merely shrugged and took a sip of her drink. 'Don't worry, I heard you and I won't be doing any stirring. It doesn't stop me thinking you're wrong, though. And we are coming into the season of goodwill to all men.'

Melissa groaned. 'Don't remind me. I've never really enjoyed Christmas, but after Lawrence's sudden appearance on my doorstep last week, I've started to dread it. I expect I'll spend most of December terrified he'll try to see William again. I ran out of goodwill towards that particular man a long time ago.'

Alice looked at her sharply. 'Did he make any threats?'

'No, not in the sense you mean. He just made it clear that he wanted to see his son over Christmas, which is odd because the last time he saw either of us was nearly two years ago, on William's sixth birthday.'

'He's not what you'd call a doting father then,' Alice remarked dryly.

'Not at all. William's birthday was … awful.' No words could adequately convey how distressing and difficult the few hours had been. Seeing her son change from happy in the morning, to tense and miserable in front of his father.

'Are you going to let him see William?'

'I told him he could only see him if I was there, too.'

'And was he happy with that?'

'No.' She sighed. 'Truth is, neither am I. I don't want Lawrence seeing William at all. He'll only intimidate him. And me.'

Alice squeezed her hand. 'It'll sort itself out. As Lawrence didn't bother to see William last Christmas, I can't imagine he'll try very hard this time. Don't worry.'

But asking a worrier not to worry was easier said than done.

Chapter Three

A few days after William's first lesson, Melissa parked outside the front of the tennis centre again and turned off the engine. William sat quietly in the back. He hadn't said a word, not since she'd told him he was going to have an extra coaching session this evening, just him and Daniel.

'Here we are then,' she remarked easily. 'Let's go and get you changed.'

Head bent, William clicked off his seat belt. 'Will Simon be there?'

Melissa bit back a sigh. 'No, I've already told you, Simon won't be there today. Daniel thought it would be good to give you a few extra lessons so you can quickly catch up with the others.'

''Cos I'm rubbish,' William muttered under his breath.

She shot round to face him. 'That's not true at all. The others have been having lessons for longer than you. If you have a few extra sessions, you'll be up to their standard in no time.' Reaching out, she squeezed his hand. 'Come on buddy. You never know, you could be a future Wimbledon champion in the making.'

William glanced at her from under his long dark lashes. 'Could I drive a Ferrari, like Daniel?'

'I guess so,' she replied slowly, opening the door for him. 'How do you know Daniel has a Ferrari?'

'That's what Simon said. He said Daniel was the best player in the world. Was he really?'

'Yes, for one year he was. But then he got hurt and had to give it up.' She raised William's chin up so she could look

24

him in the eye. 'So you see, you're getting coaching from the best. How can you fail to improve?'

William changed quickly and together they wandered over to the courts to wait for Daniel. It wasn't long before he came into view, sauntering towards them with the loose stride of a confident man. Though outside it was grey and cold, inside it felt like spring – and the sight of Daniel's long, tanned limbs stretching beneath his white tennis shorts made it look like spring, too. She was immediately reminded of those days when, as a tennis fan, she'd ogled his legs, enjoying watching the play of his muscles as he'd run and lunged. With a small sigh of reminiscence she hauled her eyes up to his face instead. With his slightly ruffled dark hair, chocolate-brown eyes and broad grin, it was no less appealing.

'Good to see you both again.' He slipped them an easy smile. 'It's always a relief when people come back for the second time. It means we must be doing something right.' With a nimbleness at odds with his height, he crouched down to speak to William. 'How are you feeling? Ready to show me how much you remembered from Monday?'

William have him a hesitant nod. 'Yes, Sir.'

'Okay then. How about if we play on this court and your mum watches from the café, like last time?'

Another nod, this time slightly less sure.

'If you prefer I can stay and watch you from the side of the court.' Melissa smiled reassuringly at William.

Daniel gave her a sharp look. 'Can I have quick word?' he asked, guiding her out of William's earshot. 'Look, it's going to be much better for William if you don't hang around.'

'I know that's what you prefer, but he's nervous around men.' She winced at her shrill tone. 'Sorry, I realise I sound like an over-protective mother, but he'll settle faster if I stay for a while.'

'He won't,' he countered bluntly. 'It will make him worse. Trust me, he'll be fine as soon as you're out of the way. I'll have him doing so many drills he won't have time to be scared. Even of me.' He levelled her a look. 'So now it comes down to whether you trust me or not.'

'Of course I trust you—'

'Then we're in agreement,' Daniel interrupted, grinning disarmingly.

Annoyance hummed through her. 'It seems your sneakiness isn't reserved for your tennis matches.'

He laughed, brown eyes dancing with amusement, but didn't contradict her. Instead he draped a casual arm around William's shoulders and led him towards the service line. 'Have you ever played basketball?' she heard him asking before they drifted out of ear shot.

Melissa kept her eye on them as she walked off the court, but not once did William turn around to check where she was.

Daniel was enjoying his session with William. At some point during the warm-up games and the chats he'd instigated during them, the boy had forgotten to be shy. He'd also begun to demonstrate an uncanny eye for the ball.

'You know you could be a really good tennis player if you're willing to stick with it,' he told him as they collected the balls up after the final exercise.

'Yeah, sure.' William focused on tipping two balls from his racket into the ball carrier.

'You don't believe me?'

His head shot up guiltily. 'Yes, Sir, I believe you.'

'That's good.' When his head began to drop again, Daniel tapped him on the shoulder to regain his attention. 'You've got a good eye and fast feet. Those are two things you can't learn. The rest is only technique and practice.'

William took his time to consider this. 'Will I be as good as you when I'm older?'

Laughter rumbled in Daniel's chest. 'Maybe. It depends how badly you want it.' He took hold of William's racket and pressed the strings. 'It would help if you had a decent racket. Perhaps next month you can ask Father Christmas for one.'

William's face immediately shuttered. 'He doesn't exist.'

'Who told you that?'

'My dad.'

Daniel already disliked Lawrence Raven from the few hints Alice had dropped about Melissa's ex. Now he wanted to punch his lights out. 'So your dad's the world expert on Father Christmas, is he?'

William frowned. 'I don't know.'

'Tell me, what does your mum say about Father Christmas?'

'She says he's real.'

'Clever lady. And do you get any presents on Christmas Day?'

'Yes. She says they're from Father Christmas, but I reckon they're from her.'

Daniel hoisted his tennis bag over his left shoulder – the right still bugged him now and again – and picked up the ball carrier. 'Strikes me you need some evidence to decide who's right, your mum or your dad. How about you write to Father Christmas and ask for a racket, but don't tell your mum about it? If you get one on Christmas day, you'll have your answer.'

Slowly the corners of William's mouth lifted and he nodded. 'Thank you, Sir.'

'And now we know each other I think you should stop calling me Sir, don't you? Call me Daniel, coach, or Oh Mighty One if you like, but not Sir.' As William's face at last

27

broke into a full-blown grin Daniel felt an odd little squeeze on his heart. Inside the quiet shell there was clearly a playful little boy trying to come out. 'Come on, let's go and find your mum.'

It wasn't hard to spot Melissa in the café. Only one woman immediately caught his eye. She was dressed simply in a loose black long-sleeved top, tied at one corner, and well-fitting jeans but it wasn't what she wore. It was how she wore it. Class, style, call it whatever you wanted. She had it in spades.

'Mum, Daniel says I'm going to be as good as him when I'm older.' William rushed over to his mother, his voice bubbling with excitement.

'Hey, wait up. I think I only said maybe.' He caught Melissa's eye over her son's shoulder and watched as a small smile crossed her face. If he had to guess, he'd say it wasn't founded in humour though, but in relief. It begged the question, was it him she was so mistrustful of, or the male species in general?

'I'm thirsty.' William tugged on her arm, breaking their eye contact.

She reached into her slim black purse and handed him some coins. 'Here you go. See what you can find in the drinks machine.' After watching him trot off, she turned back to Daniel. 'He seems to have enjoyed himself. Thank you.'

'No problem.' He was going to leave it at that, but something William had said while they'd been talking niggled at him. 'I think he's worried about having to see his father again.'

The blood drained from her face. 'I think I already told you that William's father was none of your business.'

Anger fizzed up his spine. 'What's that supposed to mean?'

'It means that going behind my back and grilling my son for details because you can't get them from me, is, well …' She tailed off, visibly shaking. 'Bloody rude,' she finished off. 'And pretty low.'

'I asked William if he had any plans for Christmas yet,' he returned evenly, fighting for calm. 'He chose to tell me he thought he might be seeing his dad, and that he didn't want to. I hadn't realised small talk with your son was banned. My mistake.'

More angry than he could remember feeling in a very long time, Daniel stalked off towards his office, making sure he gave William a quick wave before he disappeared. It wasn't the boy's fault his mother was so touchy. What the hell did Melissa think he was? Some sort of child molester who took pleasure from tormenting small boys? Well she could damn well find someone else to coach her son. He'd had it with her.

Fuming, he plonked himself down on his office chair and began to systematically rip open his post with unrestrained force. His wild movements caused his hand to bang into the pile of paperwork on his in-tray, toppling it onto the floor.

'Shit.'

'I'm sorry.'

His eyes flickered between the carnage on the floor and the woman standing awkwardly in his doorway. As they settled on her troubled face, the anger slowly defused. 'Okay.'

'Can I come in?' she asked hesitantly. 'William is having his drink outside and …' She wrung her hands together. 'I'd like the chance to explain.'

'Be my guest.' Part of him wanted to stay cross with her. At least then he wouldn't feel this need to hold her and make everything right.

'I know you didn't grill William about his father,' she began as she sat down opposite him.

'You couldn't find any thumb screws?'

She managed a slight smile. 'William doesn't even talk to me about his father, so I doubt, even with the thumb screws, he would have discussed it with you if he hadn't wanted to.' She paused, fidgeting again with her hands, crossing and then uncrossing her legs. 'That's why it was such a shock to find that he'd told you something he hasn't told me.'

The words came out in a rush as emotion caught at her throat. How could she explain to someone so in control of his life as Daniel, that she felt such a failure?

'Sometimes children don't say things to the people they love, because they don't want to upset them,' Daniel said quietly. 'It doesn't make it your fault.'

The kindness in his eyes shattered all her carefully built control and a loud sob erupted from deep inside her as tears flowed down her cheeks. 'Look at me, blubbering like a fool.' Reaching for her handbag she fumbled around for a tissue as tears splattered onto the leather. Come on, come on. Where were they?

Daniel calmly handed her a box from the top of his desk. He smiled at her look of surprise. 'It's my emergency box. It isn't the first time someone's needed a tissue, though usually it's for sticky fingers or runny noses. And the recipients are under ten.'

She took it gratefully. 'Thank you. I'll be okay in a minute.' Dabbing at her eyes, she tried not to be aware of Daniel watching her. 'Sorry. I must look a state.'

'You look beautiful,' he murmured.

Her heart faltered, then fluttered gently; like wings of a butterfly, experimenting after a long imprisonment in the cocoon. He's just being kind, she told herself. And inhaled a steadying breath. 'I think I owe you an explanation about William's father.'

Daniel's eyes drifted to her lips and for a heart-stopping moment she wondered if he was thinking of kissing her. But then his expression turned carefully blank. 'You don't owe me anything. I'm just your son's tennis coach.'

It was hard to imagine him being *just* anything. 'You're also the man who's drawn more smiles out of him in the last hour than most people have managed in the last month.'

Once again their eyes met and Melissa wondered briefly what it would be like to lose herself in those dark brown depths. Would it feel tight and claustrophobic? Or warm and easy? Like bathing in a vat of melted chocolate.

'Mum, I've finished my drink now.'

The sight of William in the doorway snapped her guiltily out of her daydream. 'Sorry darling, I'm coming. Go and grab your things.' She smiled apologetically at Daniel. 'Perhaps another time?'

'Maybe I could buy you lunch? Or dinner? I'm a far better listener when I'm being fed.'

He smiled, his eyes crinkling at the corners. It was a smile no female could help but respond to and her own insides seemed to melt in agreement. Dinner with Daniel McCormick was out of the question though. Far too intimate. Far too dangerous. 'Lunch,' she agreed. 'And I'm buying. My way of thanking you for your help.'

'I look forward to it,' he drawled, standing and walking round the desk to clasp her hand. He held it a tad too long to be professional, but not long enough for any panic to set in.

And the tingle from it stayed with her all the way to the car.

Chapter Four

Driving to her lunch date with Daniel the following week, Melissa tried to recall any of the reasons why she'd thought this was a good idea; she could only think of reasons why it wasn't. The fashion show she was working towards was only two weeks away and she still had far too much to finish off. It might be early November but Christmas was fast approaching and she hadn't done anything towards it yet. The biggest reason of all – she hardly knew Daniel. How could she tell the very personal details of her failed marriage to a virtual stranger?

And then there was that *other* reason. The one that had kept her awake last night. Daniel, with his drop dead gorgeous looks, powerful athleticism and mesmerising charm, could easily knock a woman off her feet. Even a woman with both feet firmly planted on the ground.

When she reached the restaurant Daniel was already there, laughing with the waitress. He'd dispensed with his usual sports attire and was wearing casual chino trousers and a denim blue shirt. From the enchanted look on the waitress's face, he'd made another conquest.

'Melissa.' As he caught sight of her he stood and kissed her cheek. It was done with such casualness, such confidence, she wasn't aware it was happening until she inhaled the tang of his citrus cologne. Felt the press of his warm, sensuous lips.

Feeling unbalanced, she slipped gratefully onto the chair, nodding over at his glass. 'As I promised to pay, I'm sort of hoping you haven't ordered the most expensive wine on the menu.'

He grinned but shook his head. 'I stuck with sparkling water. Wine and tennis aren't a good combination. At least not in that order.'

'Do you play every day?'

'Most days. The coaching isn't really playing, but generally I have a knock about with one of the other coaches during down time, or in the evening.' He took a sip of his water. 'I like to keep my hand in. What about you? Do you play?'

Laughter shot out of her. 'Oh no, at least not in the usual meaning of the word. I can hit the ball, but that's as far as it goes. My style definitely leaves a lot to be desired.'

'I could improve it,' he replied easily, but the way his eyes remained riveted on her face left her flustered. How many women had fallen for that dark, smouldering look?

'I think one tennis star in the family is enough for now.' She closed that avenue of conversation by opening up her menu, taking the time to study it carefully even though she knew full well what she was going to have. Since she'd stopped modelling she'd discovered a taste for club sandwiches. Full of carbohydrate and dripping with taste. Perfect.

'Speaking of tennis stars, I forgot to tell you I think William would like a racket for Christmas.'

'Oh?' She wasn't surprised at the choice, more at the fact that Daniel seemed to have prised yet another piece of information from the usually painfully shy William.

'As a matter of fact we had a bit of a talk about Christmas, and about how he doesn't believe in Father Christmas. He told me he thinks his mum buys his presents.'

Melissa's heart sunk. 'Oh no. I thought I'd managed to convince him otherwise.'

'I'm sure the battle isn't lost. I ... um, took it on myself to suggest he write to Father Christmas and ask for a racket, but not tell you. That way, if he did get one for Christmas, he'd have his answer about whether the fat guy in the red suit did exist.'

He flashed her a grin and Melissa instinctively smiled back. He was too hard to resist. 'I guess that means I'm buying a racket.'

'I guess it does.' He hesitated a moment, then swore softly. 'Sorry, I didn't think about that. I can get one for you at cost, if it helps.'

She took pity on him. 'It's fine. William doesn't ask for big flashy presents, at least he hasn't yet. I'm sure I can run to a racket, though I wouldn't mind your help in choosing one.'

'Deal.'

They ordered quickly, Daniel surprising her with his choice of the chicken and avocado salad. When she raised her eyebrows, he shot her another lazy grin. 'It's alright for you ex-models to pig out. We athletes have to stay in shape.' He jokingly patted his utterly flat stomach. 'When did you stop modelling and start eating carb-laden meals?'

'How did you know I was a model?' she returned and then shook her head. 'Of course, from Alice. You probably already know more than I care to think about my life.'

Daniel smiled. 'My sister is actually a lot more discreet than you think. I know you're single but were once married to Lawrence Raven, who apparently I should have heard of, though fashion isn't my strong suit. If it can't be worn on a tennis court, I'm not that interested. I also know that you used to be a model, but now you're a designer.' He held up his hand. 'No, wait. Alice would string me up for that. You're a *shit-hot* designer, her words. But that's the sum total of my knowledge on the life and times of Melissa Raven, now Stanford.'

'Well, you seem to have covered the basics,' Melissa murmured. It felt uncomfortable knowing she'd been discussed, but she didn't doubt he'd told her the truth. He had a way of looking at her, direct and honest, that made her feel she could trust him.

'Alice didn't tell me why you divorced.'

'No, well.' She toyed with the edge of her napkin. 'That's hard for me to talk about.' Oh boy, why was she being so coy? Wasn't she here to tell Daniel a bit about Lawrence so he would understand William better? And in the process, wouldn't it also help him understand *her*?

'You don't have to tell me anything, you know.' His quiet, measured voice cut through her chaotic thoughts. 'I'm sure we could find plenty of other very interesting things to discuss.'

She caught the flirtation in his voice and wondered what might upset her equilibrium more: discussing her ex husband, or being subjected to a full dose of Daniel's seductive charm. 'I promised I would talk about it, and I will.' She reached for her glass and took a steadying gulp of water. 'I married Lawrence when I was very young. A painfully shy seventeen-year-old.'

Daniel hoped his shock didn't show. Luckily the waitress chose that moment to deliver their meals. 'What did your parents have to say about that?' he asked when they were alone again.

'I suspect they were just glad to get me off their hands. They weren't exactly your average doting parents.' She stared down at her club sandwich. 'I spent more of my time at boarding school than I did at home.'

'Ouch.' He grimaced in sympathy, thinking of his own very close family. 'That must have been tough. No wonder you fell for the first man to offer you affection.' At the surprise in her eyes he quirked a brow. 'Don't tell me, you didn't think jocks could do perception?'

Her cheeks flushed slightly. 'Sorry.'

'I'm wounded but I can probably manage to eat through the pain.' He speared at a lettuce leaf. 'Please, carry on.' When he received a small smile he mentally chalked up another point.

'In retrospect, marrying Lawrence was definitely not the smartest move on my part, but at the time he seemed perfect.' Her stunning light eyes looked briefly into his before settling at a point just past his shoulder. 'We met when I was modelling his new range. I was bowled over by him, I guess you could say. He was a designer at the top of his game, wealthy, powerful and charismatic. He was twice my age and I saw that as a positive; he was mature and experienced. The complete opposite to me. He actually seemed interested in me. Not just my face, or my body, but me. When he offered to change my life, I jumped at the chance. It had been pretty underwhelming up till then.'

Daniel crunched on his salad though he could barely taste it. His mind was filled with images of her as a seventeen-year-old girl. Lonely and vulnerable. 'Did you love him?'

'Wow, you don't beat about the bush with your questions, do you?'

'Not when I'm interested in the subject matter.' She stilled, the wariness back in her expression, and Daniel kicked himself. 'Look, I'm a nosey sod so I'm going to ask lots of questions; it's in my nature. Feel free to ignore those you don't want to answer. I won't walk off in a huff. Not when you've offered to buy the lunch.'

Her features relaxed again. 'Good to know.' Then she sighed, a gentle exhalation of breath that seemed to come from deep inside her. 'It's in my nature not to answer questions, but as that won't help us move forward I'll try and be as honest as I can. So, back to your question. Did I love Lawrence? In the beginning, I think I did. At least it was the strongest emotion I'd ever felt for anybody. My parents were too distant to love. Lawrence was easy, at least at first,' she qualified. 'He dazzled me, you know? I was overawed by him, under his spell. He took me under his wing, helped me in my career, took me to far-flung places I'd only ever dreamt of visiting. He made me feel cherished, at least for a while. That's until I began to see a different side to him, a crueller side.' The words had clearly tumbled out more quickly than she'd wanted because she immediately stared down at her plate.

'Did he ever hurt you?'

'No.' He was surprised how relieved that single word made him feel. 'Lawrence was moody, domineering and overbearing but never violent.' Finally her eyes rose back up to his. 'He treated me much like he would a child. I was someone he could order about at his whim. Of course when I was newly married I was too in awe of him, too grateful, to do anything other than what he said. That changed when I became pregnant with William.'

Daniel eyed her shrewdly. 'And how did the fashion designer take to having his model becoming pregnant?'

'As you've already guessed—'

'Because I'm surprisingly perceptive,' he cut in, trying to defuse some of the tension he could see she was feeling.

'Because you're so perceptive,' she agreed, her lips curving slightly. 'Lawrence wasn't happy about me being pregnant. Not happy at all.'

Immediately her expression tightened and he instinctively reached across the table to clasp her hand. 'I'm sorry.' A useless statement, but he didn't know how else to politely convey how gutted he felt for her. All the other phrases that came to mind contained explicit four letter words.

'Thank you.' Her slender hand remained under his for long enough for his heart to thump, but then she seemed to realise the connection and quickly tugged it away, resting it on her lap.

Swallowing a sigh, reminding himself of his promise to his sister, Daniel took another sip of water. 'You can stop this conversation at any time, you know, I won't mind. In fact if you want, you can ask me about tennis. I'll rabbit on for hours, no problem.'

She gave him a slight smile. 'But then I wouldn't have achieved what I came here to do.'

'And what was that?'

'Help you to understand my son.'

The words put him firmly in his place, dashing any hopes he'd had that at least part of her had accepted his invite because she'd actually wanted to have lunch with him. With his sister's warning still tripping alarm bells in his brain though, this way was probably best. 'Okay, you were telling me how your husband wasn't exactly over the moon to find out you were pregnant.'

'That's putting it mildly. He wanted me to have an abortion.'

He couldn't help but wince. 'Wow, that must have hurt.'

'It did. More than anything else he'd ever done.' She paused then and he noticed how her hand trembled slightly as she reached for her glass and took a long drink. 'For once in my life I actually stood up to him and refused.'

'It wasn't just your life you were standing up for,' he murmured.

'No, it wasn't.' Unconsciously she brushed a hand over her stomach. 'Lawrence threatened to leave but I went ahead and had William anyway. Needless to say he wasn't there for the birth but you know what? I didn't care. My husband went to the US to show his collection, and I was left alone to enjoy my new son.'

As she spoke the words her features softened and Daniel found he could picture her, serenely cuddling her newborn child. 'I take it that wasn't the end of your marriage though?'

'Not on paper, no.' She let out a short laugh. 'My goodness, why am I telling you all this? I haven't told it to anyone in so much detail, not even Alice.'

'Because I'm a good listener?'

'Perhaps, though I think you're also doing that thing you used to do on the tennis court. Lulling me with your effortless charm.'

He grinned. 'Charm like mine takes a lot of effort. And I promise I won't go on and ... what did you call it ... rip you to shreds?'

'Good, because I had enough of that with Lawrence.'

The light that had shone briefly in her eyes dimmed once more. Daniel wanted to tell her he'd heard enough, then spend the rest of the meal making her laugh. Selfishly he also wanted to hear the rest of her story. 'So what happened when Lawrence came back from America?'

'Predictably he didn't want anything to do with William, though he was keen to pick up where we'd left off in terms of our marriage. There were ...' She trailed off, taking a breath, before starting up again. 'Let's just say there were other complications in our marriage, besides how hurt I was over his reaction to his son. In time I started modelling again, but now there was a baby to look after and it changed things. It also changed me.'

'How so?' He finished his last mouthful of salad, noting she'd only eaten half her sandwich.

'I wasn't the naïve young girl he'd first married. I was a mother now, responsible for another life besides my own. I was less willing to be controlled.'

'Did you consider leaving Lawrence?'

She sighed and shook her head, causing her blonde hair to flow over her shoulders. 'It sounds so stupid now but at the time, despite everything, I wanted to make the marriage work. Lawrence had let me down, true, but I still remembered how wonderful he'd been in those early days, how much he'd given me. I wanted that love and security back. I also wanted William to have a father.'

'Did they start to bond?'

Her laugh was short and humourless. 'No. Lawrence showed no signs of being paternal. He simply wasn't interested in his son. By the time William started school I realised staying in the marriage was doing both of us more harm than good.' She pushed aside the half eaten sandwich. 'Having a father who takes no notice of you, other than to shout when you do something wrong, is far worse than having no father at all. As is having a husband who thinks he can control your every move. My biggest regret is that I didn't come to my senses sooner. I let my son down,' she added, her voice catching.

His heart aching for her, Daniel leant back against his chair. If he ever got his hands on Lawrence, he didn't think he'd be able to hold back. 'It was his father who let William down,' he told her firmly. 'Has William seen anything of Lawrence since your divorce?'

She smiled slightly. 'You asked me this before, and I think I snapped your head off.'

He laughed. 'You were a bit curt, yes. And it is still none of my business.'

'It isn't, is it?' But just when he thought she was going to clam up, she spoke again. 'Lawrence came round on William's sixth birthday, which falls just after Christmas; December the twenty-ninth. I'm sure it was more out of duty than a desire to see his son – a hang over from Lawrence's strict upbringing – but either way it was a disaster. William was terrified and Lawrence didn't know how to talk to him. In an effort to get them chatting I told William to show his father some of his school work. Sadly when he did, his dad seemed to think it was funny to point out all William's mistakes. Words spelt incorrectly, a drawing of a house where he'd forgotten to include the door.'

'What a bastard,' Daniel muttered, unable to help himself.

Her small smile indicated she didn't seem to mind. 'Exactly. After that he disappeared from our lives, no cards, no phone calls. Nothing until a few weeks ago when he dropped by the house and told me he wants to see William over the Christmas holidays so he can get to know him more.'

'I take it you doubt his motives?' Daniel nodded at the waitress as she asked if they wanted any coffee.

'You bet I do. At one time I would have given anything for Lawrence to show some interest in William. Now I know there's a reason for him wanting to see his son, and whatever it is, it isn't because he wants to be a proper father.' Her eyes glinted with anger. 'It makes me so cross that he thinks he can just waltz back into our lives as if the last few years haven't happened. Once more he's trying to dictate to me.'

God, Daniel thought, she's even more glorious when she's worked up. 'You're not going to let him though, are you?'

'Too right I'm not. I respect that, as William's father, Lawrence has rights, but William has rights, too. He's terrified of him. When we were still married William would clam up and hide behind my legs whenever Lawrence came into the room. How can I let my son spend time alone with a man he fears, even if he is his father? I won't let it happen.'

Daniel found he could only guess at the depth of sadness swirling in her eyes. 'So that's why William's worried,' he murmured, putting the pieces together. 'I take it you've told him his father wants to see him again?'

'I want to be honest with my son, so I've mentioned the possibility that they might meet, though I've also reassured him that if it does happen, I'll be there, too.'

Because she looked so torn, half defensive, half worried, Daniel reached across the table to touch her hand in reassurance. 'It's the right thing to do. It sounds like this is just a whim. Clearly Lawrence doesn't love his son. Next month he'll have a different whim and leave you both in peace.'

'I hope so. I'm not a great fan of Christmas but I was just beginning to look forward to this one. With this hanging over me now, I can't.'

'What's Christmas done to deserve your dislike?'

'Never lived up to expectations?' Her eyes left his, glancing down to where Daniel still had his hand over hers. In a flash she withdrew it. 'I can't believe I've spent all this time talking about me. I *hate* talking about me.' She shook her head. 'I'm so embarrassed.'

'Don't be. I enjoyed listening to you. How about we do this again, only next time you get your own back and quiz me about my life story?'

She bit into her lip, her eyes not quite meeting his. 'No, sorry, we can't do this again.'

'If it's the topic that's putting you off, we can change it.'

Her answering smile was edged with sadness. 'I'm sure your life story is an interesting one. I just don't want to give you the wrong idea.'

'Wrong idea about what? It's only lunch,' he countered, feeling slightly peeved. Sure, he wasn't meant to be chasing her, but couldn't a guy have lunch with an attractive woman without it automatically meaning something more?

'I can't see you settling for just a lunch.' The moment she said the words her cheeks reddened. 'Oh wow, that sounds so arrogant. I didn't mean it like that. You might not even be attracted to me.'

He decided it wasn't flirting to answer her question honestly. 'Oh I am. I'm very attracted.'

'Right then.' She drew in a shaky breath and busied herself folding up her napkin, placing it onto the table with unsteady hands.

Daniel sighed, cursing himself. He'd pushed too much. Gone and done exactly what he'd promised Alice he wouldn't. 'Okay, no harm done.' He slapped a bright smile on his face. 'My ego's taken a slight bruising but I'm sure it will mend in time.'

Her eyes darted back up to his. 'Thank you.'

'Even though we won't be having any more lunches together, I would like to be your friend.'

Her eyes flooded with something that looked a lot like relief. 'I'd like that. In fact what I need more than anything at the moment is a friend.'

'Friends it is then. And as my friend, I'll let you pick up the bill.'

Finally she laughed and Daniel mentally assigned himself a small victory. But as they walked out of the restaurant, he was already debating how long it would take his good intentions to begin to slip. It was hard for a man to see a single, beautiful woman and not chase after her. Especially a man used to enjoying the company of women.

Chapter Five

It was the end of November and the Christmas adverts were on the television. They filled Melissa's lounge with images of happy families gathered round a huge table, smiling as the mum, in her jaunty paper hat, deposited a massive turkey in the centre.

It was nothing like the Christmases she remembered. As a child she'd suffered stilted conversation around a formal dining table, just her and her parents. In the early years with Lawrence they'd taken off to the Caribbean, which had been glorious but not exactly Christmas. Latterly she'd done the family bit with his parents, but couldn't ever remember smiling as she'd tried to juggle cooking the turkey with looking after a fussy baby. All under the disapproving eye of her mother-in-law. As for the Christmas dinner she'd had with him just before their divorce ... she broke out in a cold sweat just thinking about how awful that had been.

The last two years it had been just her and William. She'd debated contacting her parents, but what was the point? They weren't interested, never had been. They'd attended her wedding and sent her a congratulations card over William's birth but that was the extent of their contact since she'd left home. She'd learnt to harden herself to their indifference, but she'd hurt for William when it became clear they had no interest in their grandson either.

Instead she'd cooked a small turkey for William and herself, bought crackers and encouraged him to put on a paper hat.

And she had enjoyed herself on those days more than all the previous Christmases combined.

'Hurry up, Mum. We're going to be late.'

Guiltily Melissa snapped off the television. 'I'm coming, sweetheart.'

What a difference a few weeks had made. From the nervous little boy who hadn't wanted to go to tennis lessons, William was now almost pushing her out of the door. Idly she wondered if she was creating a monster. At least if she was, he was a happy one. Daniel had been proven right; the extra lessons he'd given William had not only improved his game but his confidence and enjoyment of it, too. And on the subject of improved confidence ...

'You never told me, did you get a part in the school play?' she asked as they climbed into the car.

'Yeah.'

'You don't sound very excited about it.'

Forcefully he clicked in his seatbelt. 'I'm a taxi driver.'

She bit down on her lip to stop from laughing. 'Umm, where does the taxi driver come in to the nativity?'

He looked at her as if she was stupid. 'He drives Mary and Joseph to the hotel.'

'Oh, I see.' She turned on the engine and pulled out into the road. 'What happened to the donkey?'

He shrugged his shoulders. 'Dunno.'

'Do you get to say any lines?'

'Two.'

As he was hardly brimming with enthusiasm, Melissa let it go.

Twenty minutes later they dashed through the heavy rain and into the dry warmth of the tennis academy. 'We're early,' she told William as she shrugged off her coat, the rain leaving puddles on the floor.

'So we're not late.' He shot her his heart-melting gappy smile – his front teeth had dropped out a month ago and the replacements were only slowly coming through. 'Look, there's Daniel.'

She pretended surprise, though she'd noticed him as soon as they'd walked through the door. A tall athletic frame encased in white shorts and T-shirt, he was talking to the receptionist. She in turn was staring dreamily back at him. Typical.

He caught their eye and waved over at them. 'Hey, William. Managed to get your mum here on time today I see. Well done.'

By her side, William giggled. Ahead of her Daniel gave her a smile that reached right into his eyes and bathed her in a warm glow. Since their lunch he'd been true to his word. Friendly but not flirtatious, he treated her no differently from any of the other mothers. Melissa told herself she was relieved.

With a quick wave at her, William dashed off to join the group already on court. Melissa meandered on down to the café where she ordered her customary latte and settled down with the other parents to watch the session. It had become something of a tradition.

'Popcorn!'

The deep boom of Daniel's voice carried over to them and she watched as he lifted a racket laden with tennis balls into the air. When he dropped it back down the children scattered, desperate to catch a ball as it fell. In the thick of it all was William. No longer the one hanging back, he blended easily with others now, his eyes bright, his face wreathed in smiles.

'I see William's really coming out of his shell,' one of the mothers remarked with a smile. 'He's changed so much over the last few weeks.'

'Hasn't he just,' another agreed. 'You'd better watch out,

Melissa. Pretty soon you'll be wishing for that quiet, shy lad again.'

Melissa laughed delightedly. 'There's no fear of that. I'm happy with having a normal, boisterous boy. Oh, and speaking of boisterous children, I know this seems ridiculously early warning, but William turns eight on December the twenty-ninth and I'd like to give him a party. We'll send out invitations nearer the time but with all the chaos of Christmas coming before it, it would be great if you could put the date in your diaries now?'

'Fantastic. Something for the little monsters to look forward to in the post-Christmas melt down.' Trisha grinned. She was the mother of the loudest boy Melissa had ever met. He made Simon seem angelic. 'Can't be an easy time for you though,' she continued. 'Presents, followed by more presents.'

Melissa smiled ruefully. 'Exactly. If I had my time again I'd plan it much better.'

'Maybe you can with your next one.'

The words, kindly meant, caught at her heart. She would never have another child, she realised sadly. Unless she was prepared to go through sperm donation, a child meant allowing another man in her life. She couldn't see that ever happening.

Alice gave her a sympathetic look and swiftly moved the conversation on.

Melissa let the banter flow over her and it didn't seem long before the young group were walking back from the court. Catching herself staring at Daniel, or more precisely at his legs, she forced herself to look away. The last thing she wanted to do was give off any wrong signals.

'Would the parents of Claire, Jenny, Simon and William

stay back for a moment please?' Daniel asked as he approached the group.

His eyes met hers and Melissa felt a pulse of awareness zip through her body. She waited for him to drop his gaze but he didn't. Instead it continued to burn into hers with an intensity that made her breath catch.

Daniel knew he was staring at Melissa for longer than he should. He also knew his eyes were telling her everything he felt. How attractive he found her. How much he wanted her. He'd tried, boy had he tried, to think of her as only a friend. As just one of the mothers. But he was failing, fast. It didn't seem to matter that she wasn't interested. He was powerless to stop the bolts of desire that shot through him whenever he saw her.

He wanted to take away the pain she still carried in her eyes. To make her laugh.

And to take her to bed.

Pretty soon he was going to have to ignore her request and go after what he wanted.

With a huge effort of will he dragged himself out of the role of potential lover and back into that of tennis coach. 'I know this weekend we'll only be dipping our toes into December, but there's a Christmas tennis competition against a few of the local clubs,' he told the group, careful not to catch Melissa's eye again. 'I'd love your children to take part.'

'I'm not sure Christmas and tennis really go together,' Alice drawled.

'What, you've never played tennis with baubles?' Everyone laughed, except for Melissa who only managed a weak smile. He pushed his concern aside. 'Thankfully the balls we'll use will be real, though to keep with the spirit of the season the players and coaches will be asked to wear a silly hat. Last year it was reindeer horns. This year I believe the theme is elf.' He tried not to think how he'd look in pointed green hat. 'The day is all about having fun, but it's also a great opportunity to play a competitive game against kids of a similar age. What do you think?'

His question was met with a babble of excited agreement, though Melissa remained ominously quiet. What was going through that mind of hers now? Biting back a sigh he handed out the details of when and where the match would be played, all too aware that she avoided his eyes.

As the other parents slowly drifted away, the tension between him and Melissa tightened until it was pinging back and forth like a billiard ball on speed.

Alice cleared her throat. 'I'll take the boys to the changing room.'

He didn't notice them go. 'What is it? What's wrong?'

She took a small but obvious step back from him. 'Tell me honestly. Are you asking William to play this match because you think he's got the ability, or because you want to get into my good books?'

His jaw almost hit the floor. 'What on earth?'

'I saw the way you looked at me just now, and it wasn't the way a friend looks at another friend.' Her voice trembled slightly but she held his gaze. 'There are more experienced players than William for you to choose from.'

He swore softly. 'Do you really think that's the type of man I am? Prepared to push a young boy forward into something he's not capable of, just because I want to date his mother?' He struggled to hide his hurt. Struggled and failed. 'Don't bother replying. You've already answered. I'll find another boy for the tournament.'

Grabbing at the ball carrier he stalked away, the metal

hinges rattling with every stride. By God he needed to get some distance between himself and Melissa. A whole heap of distance.

'Wait, Daniel, I'm sorry.'

He stopped but didn't turn round. Couldn't, because then she'd see how damn upset he was.

'That was stupid of me. I know you wouldn't do that,' she continued, placing a hand gently on his arm. 'I'm really sorry.'

Still smarting, he stared down at where her slender fingers rested on his forearm, their touch scorching his skin. 'For the record, I've never used a child to get to a woman. I don't generally have a problem getting the opposite sex to go out with me.'

She withdrew her hand and let out a nervous sounding laugh. 'No, I'm sure you don't.'

'Then why say it?'

Her clear grey eyes blinked up at him. 'I panicked. You gave me that long, smouldering look and then …' She let out a long sigh, twisting her hands. 'I wanted to be sure you were picking William on merit. For his sake.'

Daniel chose to focus on the second part of her sentence. 'Are you watching the same child I am?'

'I'm pretty sure I know my own son.' It relieved him to hear some humour in her voice.

'Then you should be aware that he's already up to the level of the others and pretty soon he'll be overtaking them. Perhaps even overtaking my nephew, though I doubt Alice will be happy about that.'

'Is he really that good?' She held up her hand before he could answer. 'Sorry, I know you just said he was, and now it looks like I'm doubting you again which I don't mean to, but—'

'Relax.' He smiled to soften his words. 'He really is very good for his age. I'm not saying he's going to be a professional tennis player in life, but he's got a fabulous eye and if he keeps it up he'll reach a high standard.'

For a brief moment pleasure flooded her face, but then she frowned, chewing on her bottom lip. 'But what if he loses? What if all the wonderful confidence he's gained disappears as quickly as it arrived?'

'What if he wins?' he countered softly. 'What if, either way, he enjoys himself?'

His eyes searched hers and Melissa found herself staring into them, mesmerised. He was so confident, so sure of himself and of life. How could he possibly understand her and her pathetic neuroses? 'You're right. It's just … it's hard for me. I want to be positive but somehow the glass always seems half empty. I worry, especially when it comes to William.'

'You're a mother. It's your job to worry. I'm his tennis coach. It's my job to make sure he learns to love the game. Tennis isn't about the forehands and the backhands, it's about the competition. Pitting yourself against another opponent and seeing if you have the skills to beat him.'

She laughed, relieved things were normal between them again. 'You sound like a gladiator.'

He let rip one of his dazzling smiles. 'I suppose I do see it as a modern day gladiator show. The roar of the crowd. Two opponents and their weapons, both playing for glory. Neither prepared to give an inch.'

'We're talking about a tennis match between seven and eight year olds,' she protested, laughter bubbling. 'I hope there'll be no bloodshed.'

'I can promise you no blood will be spilt. Except maybe mine after you've thumped me because William's come off the court crying and determined never to play tennis again.'

Because his chuckle was sexy and contagious, Melissa found herself joining in. It felt good, like breaking out of the confines of a cold, dark box and staring into the sunshine.

'What are you two up to?'

She almost jumped at the sound of Alice's voice. For a few brief seconds she'd forgotten all about her son. Forgotten about everything but Daniel and how his eyes had danced with hers while they'd laughed.

'I was telling Melissa she can hit me if William doesn't enjoy the competition,' Daniel answered, glancing over at William. 'Can she hit hard, do you think?'

Her son considered the question carefully. 'I reckon she can, if she's cross.'

Daniel shivered dramatically. 'Oh boy. Promise me you'll enjoy the game, buddy. There's a lot riding on it. I rather like the shape of my nose and I don't fancy getting it broken.'

William giggled all the way to the car. The tennis lessons were changing him, she thought as she smiled fondly down at him. Her, too. She felt … happier, lighter, more at ease.

So much so that the thought of spending more time with someone as attractive as Daniel didn't seem quite so frightening anymore.

Chapter Six

Finally they eased into December and Melissa was amused to find the man in the house opposite standing on his stepladder, stringing lights around his tree. There was keen, she thought wryly, and there was mad. It may be the first of December, but there wouldn't be any lights put up in the Stanford house today. Firstly because she didn't feel Christmassy yet, and secondly because it was the day of William's tennis tournament. Alice had been right. Christmas and tennis really didn't go together.

And yet ... if Christmas was actually about the goodwill, the camaraderie, the fun, then perhaps they *were* perfect partners, because she looked forward to William's tennis days nearly as much as he did.

It didn't mean she wasn't nervous about today though. Was Daniel pushing her son too soon?

'Have you thought about what you want to ask Father Christmas for yet?' she asked in a bid to distract herself from what was to come.

Sitting on the window ledge, his eyes fixed on the street, watching out for Simon and Daniel, William shrugged. 'Sort of.'

'Sort of?'

Momentarily he strayed from his lookout duty. 'I know one thing I want.'

'Only one?'

He gave her a thoughtful look. 'I'm still thinking.'

'Okay, just make sure you let me see the letter you're writing him before you send it off.'

'Maybe.'

Her heart jumped. 'What do you mean, maybe? Aren't you going to show it to me?'

He darted her a cheeky grin. 'It's between me and Father Christmas.'

Oh boy, she had no answer to that. Perhaps Daniel's great idea of getting William to write to Father Christmas wasn't so great after all. 'How's the Christmas play going?'

'I have to sit in a pretend car.'

His voice was filled with such disgust she couldn't help but smile. 'That's what happens in plays. The actors and audience have to use their imagination.'

'I suppose.' His attention drifted back to the window. 'They're here!'

Melissa watched as a powerful black four-wheel drive parked up in front of their house. Belatedly she realised she'd been so set on getting William ready she hadn't sorted herself out. 'Go and answer the door,' she pleaded. 'I just need to find my boots.'

She was dimly aware of the door being opened. Of her son asking Daniel why he hadn't brought his Ferrari and Daniel's answering chuckle. 'It's only got two seats. I figured your Mum and Simon didn't want to sit on the roof.'

His deep voice drifted into the under stairs cupboard where her favourite boots were so far eluding her. Why oh why hadn't she got the flipping things out earlier? 'Hello, Daniel,' she called, 'I'll be there in a minute.' One day, she would be ready on time. One day.

Finally she spied them, hiding between the wellington boots and the vacuum cleaner. Clutching at them as if they were the last turkey in the shop on Christmas Eve, she ran to the front door and careered to a halt.

She'd forgotten how stunning he was, she thought wildly. And how tall.

'How are the nerves holding up?'

His eyes glinted in a way that made her knees tremble. Grateful for the excuse to sit, she parked herself on the bottom stair and focused on putting on her boots. 'How can you guess I'm nervous?'

'It's a common fault for most mothers. Why do you think Alice isn't coming today?'

Boots on, Melissa stood and peered out at the car where Simon and William were sitting in the back, talking animatedly. 'I thought she had to take her daughter to dance practice?'

'That's true, but it's also an excuse. The first match she watched Simon play I thought she was going to detonate. She was so desperate to shout and stomp, but knew she couldn't. Anything other than a sporting round of applause is strictly discouraged,' he added as he opened the passenger door for her. 'Shouting and screaming just isn't tennis.'

Melissa laughed as she put on her seat belt. 'I've seen a few of your matches. There was plenty of screaming.'

He waggled his dark eyebrows at her. 'I think you'll find that's an entirely different sort of screaming.'

Shooting her a quicksilver grin he drove off, his hands steady and sure on the wheel. Did he do *everything* with that same confident ease? The thought brought a hot flush to her cheeks and she glanced quickly out of her window, willing it to fade. What on earth was wrong with her?

When she was sure she had herself in check, she stole another glance at him. He was casual today in jeans, a navy T-shirt and a soft brown leather jacket. He wasn't up there with the latest cutting trend, but he wore what suited him, and wore it with assurance and panache.

'See anything you like?' he asked with a cocky grin, holding her eyes as they stopped at a red light.

Melissa blushed to the roots of her hair. 'I was just admiring the way you wear your clothes,' she admitted.

'Ah.' His eyes left hers and returned to the road. 'Do you think I could have a career on the catwalk then?'

'No. You're way too big, in every sense.' At his raised eyebrow, she rolled her eyes. 'I mean you're too tall, your shoulders are too broad, your thighs too muscular. You have to be gangling to be a model, even a male model.'

'Was it tough, not eating?'

'Not really. I'd always been tall and skinny as a child, so I never really had to watch what I ate. After I had William the pounds were harder to shift but it wasn't often I had to worry about my weight because for most of that time I was ...' She glanced over her shoulder to check William wasn't listening. '... miserable,' she admitted quietly. 'I don't comfort eat. When I'm unhappy I don't have much of an appetite.'

'You must have it back again. I've noticed some pretty cute curves. Not that I've been looking,' he added, though his poor attempt to hide a grin said otherwise.

A few weeks ago his compliment would have frightened her. Now it left her tongue-tied and pleasurably giddy.

Thankfully he didn't follow up his comment, instead turning his attention to William and Simon, giving them a run down of the opposition they'd be facing. 'They're smaller clubs than ours,' he told them as he turned into the car park. 'But very snooty with it. Call me shallow, but I hope we give them a good thumping.'

Simon sniggered. 'You're not supposed to say that.'

He turned off the engine and twisted to face his nephew. 'That's me speaking as your uncle. When we get inside, I'll be your super polite coach.'

They waited in the lobby for the other two players to arrive and when they'd all changed Daniel encouraged them into a huddle, hunching down so he was on their level. Melissa and the other parents stood back a little so they could still hear but weren't interfering.

'Right guys, you'll each play in two singles matches and one doubles match, but it will be short sets. Who can tell me why we play tennis matches?'

'To win!' Simon shouted. Daniel laughed and ruffled his nephew's hair.

'Exactly right, and don't let anybody tell you any differently. When you go out on court you play to win, otherwise there's no point in playing. But it's important to realise that you aren't going to win every match. In fact sometimes you might go for a long time without winning. Don't let that put you off. You never look back, only forward. Forget the last match you played, the last point you played. It is the next one that's the most important. And no matter what stage of the game you're at, play every point to win it.' He smiled. 'Now, who can remember the second reason we play matches?'

'To have fun.'

'Excellent, William. We play to win, but we also play to have fun because it's the fun you'll remember when you go home tonight. So, go out, do your best and enjoy it.'

As the players ran excitedly down the corridor and onto the court Melissa felt her heart leap into her chest. At the last minute Daniel turned round and winked at her. 'Remember, polite applause only. And if you have cause to hit me, please wait until we're home so I don't bleed all over the car.'

Their club won the competition *and* William enjoyed

himself. Daniel was both relieved and smugly satisfied when he drove them home.

He glanced in his rear-view mirror and grinned at the sight of his nephew and William still in their red and green pointed elf hats, their cheeks a matching shade of red. 'Nice hats, boys.'

They sniggered. 'Yours is worse.'

Melissa shot him a look from under her lashes. Her lips twitched.

He pulled to a stop at a traffic light and checked his image in the mirror. The bell on top of his green felt hat tinkled as he shifted his head. 'Somebody told me today that she admired the way I wore my clothes,' he remarked evenly.

Melissa tried to stifle a giggle, but then obviously gave up and began to laugh. It was a refreshingly uninhibited sound, throaty, sexy. A sound destined to warm a man's heart and send heat pulsing through his blood. Quickly he moved the conversation on. 'Are you boys getting excited about Christmas now?'

'Yes!' Simon shouted gleefully. 'I opened the first door on my Advent calendar today. It was a bell.'

'And I guess that's exciting because it was made of chocolate?'

In his mirror he saw his nephew nod vigorously. 'At Christmas you get to eat chocolate every day before school.'

'I think Christmas is about more than the amount of chocolate you can stuff in your mouth,' Daniel said dryly. 'What about you, William? Which bit of Christmas are you looking forward to?'

'Presents,' he replied with a slightly sheepish smile.

Daniel glanced across at Melissa. 'Looks like you and Alice don't have to bother buying a tree, or putting up decorations, or cooking a turkey, or watching any Christmas films, or—'

'But we want them as well,' Simon shouted back, digging William in the ribs. 'Don't we.'

They continued to shout out other things they were looking forward to – including snow ball fights, chocolate logs and no more school – right up to the moment he parked outside Melissa's pretty terraced house.

'Would you like to come in for a celebratory drink?'

She glanced shyly over at him and immediately his pulse quickened. He knew she was just being friendly, but try telling that to his body. 'I thought my reward for William coming back happy was to not get a bloodied nose?'

'What can I say?' Her lips curved in a warm, happy smile. 'Today I'm feeling generous.'

'In that case a drink would be great, thanks.' No way was he turning that offer down, even though he'd agreed to go back to the club for a knock-about with one of the trainers. 'I'll just check Alice doesn't want Simon back straight away.'

As the others went into the house, Daniel made a quick call to his sister who reassured him he could keep Simon as long as he wanted, the longer the better. Next he sent a quick grovelling text to John, promising he'd play tomorrow instead, before dashing inside. Ignoring the thumps and shrieks from the room upstairs, presumably where William and Simon had camped out, he entered the small living room. As he'd expect from a woman of style, it was elegant yet comfortable. Nothing matched; each item of furniture was different and perhaps individually didn't really fit in the room, but collectively it worked. Much like Melissa, he mused. Her features shouldn't work, but when you took in the whole woman they didn't just work, they grabbed you by the throat and made every other woman fade into the background.

He watched as she carefully set two cups on the coffee table before sitting on the opposite armchair and tucking her long legs under her, each movement fluid and graceful.

'You're beautiful.' The words were out of his mouth before he could think of stopping them.

To his utter surprise, she flushed scarlet.

'Melissa, you were one of the world's top models. How can you blush when I tell you you're beautiful?'

The vulnerability in her face shocked him. 'You have a way of saying it as if you really mean it, and yet I know my face is all angles. It photographs well, that's all.'

Daniel took a swig of his tea and shook his head. 'It's a hobby of mine, studying beautiful women. Since I met you, I haven't been able to take my eyes off you. It's that simple.'

He watched as the embarrassment slowly gave way to fear and mentally cursed it.

'Daniel, you promised—'

'I would play it your way,' he cut in. 'And I am. I will. Telling you you're beautiful is just a fact. I'm not saying it because I'm trying to seduce you. Not yet, anyway.'

She picked nervously at some non-existent fluff on her trousers. 'You talk as if you plan on seducing me in the future.'

He grinned at her over the rim of his cup, deciding it was only fair to warn her of the way his thoughts were moving. 'I do.'

A pulse began to hammer in her throat. 'That isn't funny. I didn't tell you about my previous relationship lightly. I told you so you would understand where I'm coming from. I'm not interested in getting involved.'

'Do you see me laughing?' he asked quietly. 'I'm attracted

to you, and I believe the feeling is mutual. I want you. I promised to play it your way and I'm trying to keep my promise but I need to warn you. I play to win.'

Though he didn't think she was aware of it, her back straightened. 'If we're dishing out warnings, I have one of my own. I won't be bullied or bossed around anymore. Not by anyone.'

He acknowledged the steel beneath her words. 'Understood. Have you heard from Lawrence recently?'

She smiled slightly. 'That was a neat lead-in and no, he's been thankfully quiet so far.'

'Good. Perhaps this Christmas will manage to exceed your expectations for a change.'

'I hope so.'

They talked for a little while longer but Daniel was conscious that his nephew was upstairs and the day had already been a long one. Taking a final swig of his tea, he rose to his feet. 'I'd better get Simon home before he and William destroy your beautiful house.'

He shouted up and a reluctant Simon trudged down the stairs, followed by a bright-eyed and slightly pink-cheeked William. 'Here.' He handed his keys to Simon. 'Go and get the trophy out of the car for William.'

William's eyes stood out on stalks. 'What?'

'You helped to win it, didn't you? It's only fair you get to keep it for a bit.'

'Me?'

Daniel chuckled. 'Yes, you. I figured you should all take it in turns, three months each. As it was your first tournament, you can start.' William's face burst into a grin and as they scampered off down the path to open the car, Daniel turned back to Melissa. 'Thanks for the drink.'

'Thank you for today.'

He inclined his head. 'My pleasure.'

'Not just for taking us to the match,' she added, 'but for asking William to play. You were right.'

He smiled. 'I generally am.' Then, because he couldn't resist, and because he was a devil, he bent to kiss her. Just on the cheek, but enough to make his point.

He wouldn't be warned off.

Chapter Seven

Melissa sat back on her sofa, shattered. Her small show had been a triumph, even if she did say so herself. She'd never be an internationally renowned designer, not like Lawrence. Even if she had the talent, which she wasn't convinced of, she didn't have the all-consuming passion and drive that such an aspiration needed. But she loved fashion, loved what she did, and was more than happy to remain a small, respected label, known for its soft, flowing fabrics.

She rested her head against the plush cushions, savouring the few moments of peace before Alice brought William back. How lucky to find a friend who was not only willing to look after her son, but happy to do so. Smiling to herself she stretched out on the sofa. And promptly fell asleep.

She awoke to the sound of the door bell, followed by the shrieks of two noisy boys.

'Come on in.' William and Simon tumbled through the door, followed more sedately by Alice. She managed to catch a fleeting kiss from her son before he darted upstairs with his friend.

'Any chance of a drink for your child minder?' Alice asked, already walking towards the kitchen.

'A drink is the least you deserve. You have no idea how much you looking after William means to me. It's not just knowing he's with someone I like and trust, but knowing he's happy, too. It takes away the guilt. I'm truly grateful.' She stopped and gave Alice a fierce hug.

'Whoa, no problem. He's not exactly hard work, you know. In fact it's easier having him over than not. Simon leaves his sister alone when William's around, which means a far more harmonious household.' Alice stood back and studied her. 'So, was it a success? Am I going to see trousers and tops by Melissa in all the high street stores?'

Melissa smiled and went to fill up the kettle. 'I sincerely hope not. I aim to have a discreet, classy label. Items for the discerning lady.'

'Like me?'

'Exactly like you,' she agreed with a chuckle, adding teabags to two bright pink mugs. Mugs she'd been careful not to bring out for Daniel. 'And thank you for asking, yes, it was a success. We'll know better when the critics come out and the orders come in, but there were a lot of complimentary noises.'

'Fantastic. I've always wanted a famous friend.' Alice accepted the mug of tea and wandered into the lounge.

'I would have thought you'd had enough with a famous brother,' Melissa remarked, following after her.

'What can I say? I like to surround myself with talent. That way nobody notices I haven't got any.'

Melissa wagged a finger at her. 'You have lots of talent. You just haven't decided what to do with it yet.'

'Umm, I'll have to remember that line. Anyway, speaking of talent, have you decided whether you're going to your Christmas party yet? If you're up for Best New Designer award, you really should go, you know.'

Melissa sat back on her favourite armchair and cupped the mug with her hands. When she'd first heard she'd been nominated for 'Best Newcomer', announced at the annual Fashion Designers' Christmas party, she'd been unbelievably flattered and filled with enthusiasm for going. 'I've not replied yet. I know I should go, but since I heard Lawrence will be the guest speaker ...' She trailed off, unwilling to say the truth out in the open. She was scared of bumping into him. He'd not contacted her since his last visit and she was quietly hoping he would forget all about his desire to see his son.

'Are you really going to give up the chance of collecting an award just to avoid him? Miss out on the glowing tributes? The publicity?'

She sighed. 'When you put it like that, I know it would be stupid not to go. I've worked damn hard for it. The chances are I won't win, but just think how fabulous it would be if I did?' Briefly she allowed herself the vanity of imagining walking up on stage to rapturous applause. 'I don't suppose you fancy going with me? You know, hold my hand. Give me a shove if my name gets called out?'

'Protect you from Lawrence?' Alice added shrewdly.

'Maybe, if it calls for it.'

Putting down her cup, Alice regarded her thoughtfully. 'What you need isn't a female friend, but a male one. The tall, strong, dashing type who could scare Lawrence away with a blink of his eye.' She paused and grinned. 'I know just the man.'

Melissa hastily swallowed her mouthful of tea. 'Oh no. Going to a fashion event would be the last thing Daniel would want to do. One rung below a trip to the dentist, I expect.'

'Ha. He's never worried about the dentist. In fact he dated one for a while. I'm sure that's why he's got such sparkling teeth.'

'Still, I don't want to trouble him.' It was too easy to picture herself on his arm. To imagine how confident she would feel with him at her side. 'I'll think about it over the weekend and maybe find enough courage from somewhere to go by myself.' With a gesture to the noise of drums she could hear from above, Melissa changed the subject. 'Why is it boys only want to learn a musical instrument that makes enough of a din to rattle the walls?'

Alice laughed, and the conversation moved on.

A few hours later, having settled William into bed, Melissa was surprised by a knock on the door. Cautiously she peeked through the curtain only to find Daniel standing on the pavement. He'd obviously come straight from the tennis centre and still wore his tracksuit bottoms and trademark white T-shirt beneath a bulky sports jacket.

'This is a surprise.' Melissa opened the door and stood by to let him in.

'Any food on offer for a hungry tennis coach?' he asked, bending to give her a light kiss on the cheek. Just as it had the last time, her cheek tingled from the feel of his lips.

As he stepped inside and shut the door behind him, the hallway felt instantly cramped.

'I've already eaten with William, but there's some left if you want it.' He was confusing her. He'd never visited unannounced before. Was he changing tactics now? The thought made her jumpy. She enjoyed seeing him – more than she wanted to admit – but then he pushed that little too far, or stared that little too long, and all her fears came crashing back.

'Leftovers. Excellent.' It took her a second to realise Daniel was walking through to the kitchen. He pulled out a stool by the breakfast bar and perched on it, looking perfectly at home. His legs were so long he didn't even have to hitch himself up. 'I'll have whatever you've got. And while you're warming it up, you can tell me about this Christmas party you've been invited to.'

Instantly the purpose of his visit became blindingly clear. 'Alice has been speaking to you.'

*

Daniel watched Melissa's grey eyes turn cool and struggled not to grin. In one chilling look she managed to convey that the party was her business, not his. And that she planned on dealing with it her way. 'Alice told me you're up for an award, yes,' he returned easily, watching as she scooped the left over fish pie onto a plate and into the microwave. 'It must be really gratifying to know your talent has been recognised by your peers.'

'It would be gratifying were I to win it. Which is highly unlikely.'

She busied herself with finding some cutlery, carefully avoiding his eyes. It was a bit like a game of cat and mouse, he thought, amused. She knew why he was here, but was clearly going to pretend otherwise. 'Still, just to be nominated is a great honour,' he pressed. 'You've got to get a kick out of that, surely?'

Melissa placed the plate of food in front of him. 'Yes,' she replied slowly. 'I do.'

'So it would be crazy not to go to the Christmas party, wouldn't it? To see what some of that recognition feels like?'

She heaved out a sigh and sat on the stool opposite him. 'Are you really going to do this?'

'Do what?' he asked innocently.

'Chip away at me with all your talk. Wear me down until I admit you're right.'

'I won't have to, if you admit it now.'

She threw her hands up in the air. 'Okay, okay. You and Alice are both right. I'll go to the damn party.'

Delighted to have won so easily, he took a mouthful of the fish pie. 'Mmm, this is good.' He swallowed it down. 'I'll come with you.'

He spoke the words casually, in the same tone he'd used

to compliment her on the pie, but she froze like a hare in the headlamps just the same. 'I don't believe you're invited.'

'Then invite me.'

'You make it sound so simple.'

'It is.'

'No, it isn't.' Her agitation showed in the way her hands found things to do. Wipe at a mark on the already spotless worktop. Rearrange the perfectly arranged fruit in the fruit bowl. 'You're very kind. Alice is very kind to put you up to this, but I'm not weak and helpless. Not any more. I can manage on my own.'

'I know you can. I just thought it might be more fun if you had company.' He played his charm card. 'Besides, I reckon I'd enjoy it. I love a good party.'

Surprise, followed by amusement raced across her features. 'You're kidding.'

'Why do you say that? If you're anything to go by, spending an evening in the company of a host of glamorous designers could be just up my street.' He took a final forkful of the pie. 'It's your choice, Melissa. The offer is there, should you wish to accept it.'

She rested her chin in her hands, her elbows on the breakfast bar. 'I know what you did there, twisting it round so now it looks like I would be doing you a favour, when really we both know it's the other way round.'

'There are no favours here. I'd like to spend an evening with you. Full stop.'

Her breath hitched and for a second he wondered if she was still going to turn him down. But then she smiled. 'Okay then. I'd really like it if you came to the party with me.'

He couldn't help himself. He grinned like a cat who'd just prised a bowl of cream from its frugal owner. 'There you go. That wasn't so bad, was it?' Then his grin slipped a little as he considered what he'd actually let himself in for. 'Is there a dress code I should be aware of? Do I have to wear one of your creations?'

Melissa stared at him wide-eyed for a moment, then burst into a fit of giggles. The sight of her bent over, laughing uncontrollably, did crazy things to his heart, even if the laughter did appear to be at his expense. 'A suit is fine,' she finally managed. 'Umm, have you got any clue what I design?'

She had him there. 'No. Maybe you'd better show me so I can talk intelligently about patterns and style and … buttons.' Oh boy, he was really out of his depth here. 'Or whatever it is designers talk about,' he added for good measure.

Melissa slipped off the stool and walked round the breakfast bar so she was standing in front of him. 'What do you see when you look at me?'

Daniel eyed her appreciatively. 'One gorgeous, classy babe.'

Briefly she raised her eyes to the ceiling. 'Thank you, but we were talking about clothes. More specifically, the clothes I design. I'm wearing some.'

And now he could see why she'd laughed at him. He'd look bloody daft in what she was wearing. She on the other hand … looked amazing.

Having been given a legitimate excuse, Daniel took his time to study her. He started with her top, which was made of some silky fabric that draped seductively over her breasts and was tied in a bow just above the waist of her trousers. His eyes lowered, taking in the floaty trousers that hugged her trim waist, emphasised her cute backside, and finally cascaded over her long legs to the floor. 'Elegance and sophistication are two words that spring immediately to mind. What I can't work out is whether it's the clothes making the body look hot, or the hot body that's showing off the clothes.'

Her cheeks coloured and her eyelids immediately shuttered over her eyes, making it impossible for him to read what she thought of his remark. He was damned if he was going to apologise for being honest, though.

She cleared her throat. 'That's the general idea. A really good design should have you wondering exactly that. Thank you.'

He stood and moved towards her, catching hold of the material and running it through his hands. A snap of desire pulsed through him, hot and needy. Instinctively he pulled her towards him, running his hands appreciatively up and down her arms.

'Daniel ...' Her voice was a throaty whisper.

He ached to touch her more. To haul her against him and feel how those smooth, toned curves fitted with his hard angles. But as he looked into her eyes he saw not just desire, but fear. Cursing her ex-husband, he broke away. 'Thanks for the tea. I'd better be going.'

He turned and walked towards the door. Away from her, away from temptation.

Chapter Eight

It was the evening of the Fashion Council Christmas party. Carefully Daniel parked his Ferrari outside Melissa's house. He figured at least his wheels had style, even if the rest of him didn't. To him, much as a spade was a spade, a suit was a suit. He knew enough to know whether it fitted him or not and thankfully had enough money he could shop at stores that helped him put outfits together. His interest ended there. Still, maybe after tonight he'd feel differently.

He rang on the bell and Melissa opened the door almost immediately. Stupidly, he wasn't prepared for the vision in front of him. Was it her beauty, her class or her vulnerability that cut him off at his knees? 'Wow,' was all his numbed brain could manage.

Un-stylish and monosyllabic his compliment might have been, but she looked pleased with it nonetheless. 'Thank you. And yes, it is one of my own designs.'

Made of the soft draping material that appeared to be her signature, the long layered dress she wore cascaded softly over her body. In a vivid scarlet, it reflected against her skin, giving her cheeks a soft blush. Daniel thrust his hands into his trouser pockets in a protective measure, though he wasn't sure it would be enough to stop him from reaching out and kissing her. Hell, he wouldn't stop at kissing, either. But it wasn't what Melissa wanted from him.

'William is over at Alice's already. He's having a sleep over, so we're good to go.' She paused, her eyes sliding over him. 'You know you look pretty good yourself. You can really wear a suit.'

He almost felt himself blushing. 'Thank you, though it's

only fair I should warn you I'm a jock at heart. I see a jacket on a rail and I might pick it up. I see a racket on a rail and I'll not only pick it up, I'll practise shadow moves, pluck at the strings, twirl it in my hand and, if it's really exceptional, I might even buy it lunch.'

She let out a soft laugh as she bent to pick up her shawl. 'Duly noted. And speaking of rackets, I've got a bit of a problem with William's letter to Father Christmas. When I spoke to him about it last he told me he's got one wish, which I presume is the racket, but he's also thinking of a second wish. And he's adamant he's not going to show me the letter.'

'Ah.' Why had he not thought of that? 'How about I ask him about it at training next week? Maybe he'll show the letter to me, or at least tell me what he's thinking.'

'I hope so. I'd hate Father Christmas to disappoint him. It's only a few weeks to go and if the other thing he wants is one of those over-hyped, impossible to get toys the shops always run out of—'

'I'll use the famous McCormick charm and wheedle it out of him,' he cut in.

She rolled her eyes. 'Thank you.'

'So, have you got any plans for Christmas yet? Do you usually see family?' The moment he said it the lingering amusement drained from her face and Daniel wanted to retract the second part of his question.

'No.' She fussed with her shawl, draping it round her shoulders. 'I don't have any brothers and sisters and the last time I spent Christmas with my parents was when I was sixteen. It was a chore for all of us.'

'Sorry, I remember you saying they were pretty distant. That was a tactless question. I didn't mean to put a damper on the evening.' Determined to be a better date from now on, he held out his arm with a flourish. 'Would you do me the honour of accompanying me to a Christmas fashion extravaganza, Ms Melissa?' He opened her front door and nodded over to his car, which looked pretty damn good under the street light. 'Your carriage awaits.'

He was gratified to see her jaw drop. 'So, you really do have a Ferrari.'

'I do indeed. I'm a walking sportsman cliché.'

She laughed softly. 'In that case Prince Charming, I'll be delighted to go to the ball with you.'

The party was held in a swanky London hotel and as Melissa stepped inside she felt a flutter of anticipation. A giant Christmas tree filled the lobby and silver and purple decorations glittered against the lights. For the first time she began to feel a prickle of Christmas spirit. The season might not hold many fond memories for her but now was the time to put all that behind her and look forward.

Clutching at Daniel's arm she shared a brief smile with him before raising her chin, squaring her shoulders and walking through to the ballroom – and straight into a mass of people. Immediately she faltered, her heart thumping hard against her ribs. Daniel squeezed her arm and continued to lead her through.

'I need a drink,' she whispered, and he laughed.

'A pint of Dutch courage it is.'

Daniel's presence, his unswerving confidence, had a steadying influence on her and slowly she started to relax. Stupidly she'd thought of herself as the new girl, but now she realised she might be new to design, but to fashion she was an old hand. A smile of recognition here, a small wave of hello there, and it wasn't long before designers and other people she'd worked with in the past came to talk to them.

Of course having Daniel by her side, looking incredible in his dark navy suit and pale pink shirt, drew many interested eyes, too.

Including one pair she'd hoped not to have to look into.

'Melissa.' Lawrence nodded as he approached her, a slender dark-haired woman with a hard face and endless legs hanging onto his arm. A woman she recognised only too well.

As if sensing trouble the others slipped away, leaving just the four of them. Involuntarily Melissa shivered. A beat later Daniel's arm slid protectively around her waist.

'Lawrence, this is Daniel.' She turned to Daniel, who stood straight and tall by her side. 'Daniel, this is Lawrence, my ex husband.'

The two men exchanged a formal handshake.

'This is Evangeline. My fiancé.'

Melissa experienced a jolt of surprise. How had she missed hearing of their engagement? Clearly sensing her shock, Lawrence smiled smoothly. 'There'll be an announcement in the press shortly.'

'Well, congratulations.' She forced herself to smile at the soon to be Mrs Raven. She'd expected to feel sympathy for the next woman Lawrence lured into his clutches, but this one deserved everything that was coming to her.

'I hear you're up for the newcomer award.'

As Lawrence's piercing black eyes glittered back at her she focused on the warmth of Daniel's arm against her back, his rock solid presence by her side. 'And I hear you're the guest speaker.'

He looks almost weedy next to Daniel, she thought on a bubble of laughter. While Daniel's skin glowed with a healthy vitality, Lawrence, now in his late forties, looked pale and his skin was beginning to sag. Daniel's hair was short, thick and healthy. Lawrence's hair was long and where it had once flowed dramatically over his shoulders like a black curtain, now it was going grey and thinning.

Just as she was starting to enjoy the comparison, Lawrence brought her crashing back to earth. 'We need to talk about when I'm going to see William.' His eyes bored into hers. 'I haven't forgotten, you know.'

Automatically she stiffened. 'I'm not prepared to discuss that here.'

'When then?'

Daniel's hand pressed into her side, reassuring her. Steadying her. 'I'm not going to be pushed into giving a time now.'

'You can't stop him from seeing his son, Melissa,' Evangeline cut in.

'I've never stopped him,' Melissa countered coldly, anger fizzing through her, burning through the nerves. 'He's chosen not to see William.'

'How often *have* you seen your son in recent years, Lawrence?' Daniel's voice was mild and reasonable but Melissa heard the edge.

From the way his eyes narrowed, so did Lawrence. 'Not as often as I'd have liked.'

'Is that because Melissa has prevented you from seeing him?' Again, the tone was measured, the question polite.

Lawrence hesitated. 'No,' he replied shortly. 'Sadly my work schedule has been such that I've been abroad a lot recently.'

'But I presume you've had contact? Phoned, Skyped, sent postcards?'

Irritation flooded into Lawrence's eyes.

'You don't have to listen to this boorish man, darling.'

Evangeline tugged at Lawrence's arm. 'Your relationship with your son is none of his business.'

Daniel's answering smile was cold and humourless. 'I agree. I do think a lawyer would be very interested to know how much of an effort Lawrence has made with his son though. If, indeed, he wants to go to all that bother to see William again?'

A muscle twitched in Lawrence's jaw and his mouth twisted cruelly. 'So says the tennis player.'

'Ah.' Daniel arched his eyebrow. 'Were you a fan?'

Anger flashed across Lawrence's features. He had the look of a man who wanted to throw a punch, but knew he couldn't. The place was too public, his opponent over a decade younger, and infinitely stronger. Without uttering a reply, he grabbed Evangeline by the arm and marched away.

'It would seem I've upset your ex husband,' Daniel mused, watching them stalk off.

Feeling a rush of relief, mixed in with a whole heap of gratitude, Melissa reached up and kissed him on the cheek. 'Thank you. That was beautifully done.'

'My pleasure. Let's just hope it's the last you'll hear from him. Ever.' His expression turned serious. 'Do you have a good lawyer?'

She sighed, feeling foolish. 'No. I wasn't all that interested in the divorce settlement. As long as I had custody of William I really didn't care what else happened. Lawrence suggested a lawyer and I went along with him because it seemed the easiest thing to do.' She shuddered. 'I certainly wouldn't want to use him again.'

Daniel squeezed her waist and moved towards the bar. 'I'll put you in touch with Peter Price. He's a good man as well as being a damn fine lawyer. If he can't take care of it, he'll know a man who can. Now, I think a glass of champagne is called for.'

'And the best newcomer is ...' As the compere opened the silver envelope, Melissa thought her heart was going to fly right out of her chest. Oh God, was it being too greedy to ask that it be her name? She was already doing so well, she didn't need the award.

And yet still she gripped her hands together. She didn't need it, but oh, how she *wanted* it.

'Melissa Stanford.'

She froze, utterly numb. Had she imagined it? Surely she had.

Strong hands gripped hers. 'Get your beautiful arse up on that stage.'

Blinking she spun to face Daniel. One glance at the huge grin on his face and she knew she'd done it. She'd gone and won the bloody award.

Laughing, crying, she rose unsteadily to her feet.

The rest of the evening was a blur of champagne and smiles. Of pressing hands, congratulations and so many compliments her head was spinning by the end of it. When she was finally on the way home, cocooned in the soft leather of the Ferrari and slightly drunk on champagne, very giddy with delight, she felt wonderfully, gloriously, happy.

'What's so funny?'

She glanced sideways at her handsome companion. 'I'm not laughing.'

'Maybe not, but you're making a sort of humming, giggling sound.'

'I think that's because I'm a bit tipsy.'

'Ah.' He slid her a smile. 'It's not because you're reliving the moment they read out the name of the best newcomer?'

She hiccupped. 'Maybe.' There weren't many moments in her life when she could remember being as happy as this. Only the birth of William sprang to mind and even that had been tough because she'd had nobody to share it with. Tonight, she'd had Daniel.

'Feeling pretty pleased with yourself, huh?'

She eyed him under her lashes. 'As a matter of fact, I am. I won an award, faced Lawrence without bursting into tears and now I'm going home in a gorgeous supercar driven by a reasonably attractive man.'

He barked out a laugh. 'Surely the driver warrants the gorgeous status, too. It's only fair.'

His eyes sparkled, his grin flashed and Melissa felt her breath come out in a rush. 'Okay. I'm being driven home in a gorgeous supercar by an almost equally gorgeous man.'

Daniel shook his head, muttering under his breath. 'Upstaged by my car? What's the world coming to?'

A short while later he parked outside her house and cut the engine. As he turned towards her the moonlight bounced off the sharp planes of his cheekbones, making him appear dangerously attractive. 'Are you going to invite me in?'

She wasn't so drunk that she misread the burning intent in his eyes. The sensible thing to do was to say no, but for once she'd had enough of being sensible. She didn't want the evening to end and if that meant playing with fire for a short while, then she was up for it. 'Sure,' she replied with an ease she didn't altogether feel. 'I think I can muster up a cup of coffee for a man who's just driven me home in a Ferrari.'

Daniel chuckled and eased out of the car. 'Flash sports car. It gets the girls every time.'

Melissa gently pushed the car door shut. 'I said you could get a cup of coffee. It doesn't imply that you get the girl.'

Draping a casual arm around her shoulders, he walked them up to the steps. 'Message received. Though you can't blame a man for trying.' He kissed her lightly on the forehead. 'I won't give up trying.'

Flustered, Melissa fumbled with the keys. His strong hand covered hers, plucking them out from her fingers and swiftly opening the door. 'You haven't had as much to drink as me,' she mumbled in defence as she weaved her way in.

'True. Alcohol and Ferraris don't mix.'

She smiled. 'You said that when we went out for lunch together. Only then it was tennis and alcohol not mixing.'

'Always good for the male ego to know his date was listening.' Daniel shrugged off his jacket and walked through to the sitting room where he draped it carelessly over the back of the sofa.

'It wasn't a date,' Melissa reminded him, watching as he undid the top button of his shirt and yanked down his tie. 'Why don't you make yourself at home,' she remarked with a heavy dose of sarcasm.

'I intend to,' he replied with a cocky grin.

Leaving him to make himself comfortable on her sofa, she went to make his coffee. Realising she wasn't quite as steady on her feet as she should be, she pulled out a second cup. Now she'd invited him in, it was probably wise to keep her wits about her.

When she headed back into the sitting room she found him nestled back against the sofa, shirt sleeves rolled up, top few buttons undone and one leg casually crossed over the other. He looked entirely relaxed and utterly gorgeous.

Placing the cups on the coffee table she perched on the other end of the sofa. 'Phew, what an evening.'

Eyes that had looked sleepy sprang open and suddenly Melissa was very aware that they were alone. There was no little boy upstairs to act as chaperone.

Daniel shifted his large body, moving deliberately closer to her, and her breath hitched. And that was before she stared into his eyes. Dark, like Lawrence's, but there the similarity ended. Daniel's weren't cold or hard but gentle and seductive. Blazing with a promise that had her shivering with arousal.

'Come here,' he ordered softly, reaching out an arm to draw her towards him.

Instinctively she did as he asked.

'You can feel this chemistry between us just as well as I can.' His warm breath fluttered against her neck as he ran a slow finger down her cheek. 'I think it's time we moved from being just friends.'

She drew in a deep, shaky breath. 'I'm not sure I can.'

His finger moved to her lips, tracing their outline with seductive gentleness. 'Surely you're not going to let a bastard like Lawrence stop you from being with another man again?'

'Yes, no ... maybe.' Her brain wouldn't work. Champagne, or Daniel?

He placed the softest of kisses on her lips and her bones started to melt. 'We would be good together, you and I,' he whispered lazily, intense brown eyes locked onto hers.

She could have pushed him away at that moment. He left her the gap to do so, but she chose not to. Seconds later the choice was taken away from her as his lips swooped on hers. Like a predator finding its prey, his mouth hit its target and all gentleness vanished. With heat and passion he devoured her, pushing her back against the sofa as his tongue plundered. Champagne fog was replaced with a sexual haze and she was aware only of the hard lines of his body and the fierce heat radiating from it.

His hand crept under her dress, the warm, slightly calloused palm unerringly finding her breast. As it fluttered over her nipple, the sudden sensation of skin on skin jolted her out of her trance. 'God, Daniel, no.' She pushed at his rock-like chest.

Instantly he sprang back, breathing heavily. 'Christ, Melissa.' He shut his eyes and fell back against the sofa. 'I'm not sure how much longer I can keep doing this.'

'This?' Her breath was as shallow as his.

Slowly he opened his eyes. 'Being with you but not being able to touch you. It's killing me.'

The tortured look in his eloquent eyes told her he wasn't exaggerating. Oh God, why couldn't she be a normal woman? One who could just lie back and enjoy a handsome man making love to her? She wanted it, she knew she did. But she was too scared of where it might lead.

Daniel rubbed a hand over his face, making her heart ache. He'd been so wonderful tonight. So patient with her over the last few months. She shouldn't have given in to temptation and let him kiss her, it hadn't been fair of her to give him such mixed signals. But oh, how she'd enjoyed it. 'I'm sorry, Daniel. I just can't.'

He let out a short laugh. 'You can, Melissa. You choose not to.'

His words needled, creeping under her skin and rubbing at old wounds. 'You don't understand. How can you? You've never been hurt before. You don't know what it feels like.' The emotion of the evening, the joyous high to the wretched low, was too much. She burst into a flood of tears.

*

Watching her, Daniel felt wretched. She'd been so happy, and now he'd gone and ruined it. What the hell was wrong with him? 'Shh.' Taking her in his arms, he cradled her against his chest. 'I'm sorry I pushed. It's in my nature, I guess. I see what I want and I go for it. Perhaps if you told me what you're so scared of, it would help me to understand, though I can't promise to back off. You're too damn appealing.'

For a few heartbeats there was silence, and he wondered if that was all he was going to get. But then he felt her lips move lightly against his chest. 'I'm scared of getting it wrong again,' she mumbled. 'Of falling for a man I believe to be one thing, only for him to turn out to be someone else entirely.'

He let out a long, deep sigh. 'So you're going to put us all in the same *bastard* box are you?'

'No, of course not.' She lifted her head, cheeks glistening with tears. 'But you have to understand, for a long time, Lawrence was my everything. Friend, lover, husband, family. I thought he was someone I could trust. A man who would love me, protect me, cherish me.' With a quick flick of her hand she wiped at the tears. 'He only wanted to own me though, to control me. When I didn't conform, when I became pregnant and wouldn't have an abortion, he decided to punish me. He … he had an affair.' The words sounded so raw, he ached for her. 'Not a discreet one either, but a blatant, slap-in-the-face affair. With the same blasted woman he's now engaged to.' Her grey eyes blazed with anger, though the hurt lying beneath it was all too visible.

'That floozy he was with tonight?'

Her small smile told him she appreciated his description. 'Yes, and believe me, she's welcome to him. His rationale, he kindly explained later, was that since I'd ruined my body against his wishes, it was his right to sleep with someone else. Someone he still found attractive.'

Instinctively his arms tightened around her, as if he were trying to shield her when of course it was far too late for that. 'Hell, he really did a number on you, didn't he?' He ran his hand up and down her arm, trying to soothe even though he knew the hurt was already far too ingrained. 'I don't know what to say. What he did wasn't just cruel, it was stupid. Most men, and that definitely includes me, would be proud to watch their wife growing rounder with their child.'

When she remained silent, her eyes downcast, seemingly lost in her terrible memories, he tried a different angle. 'You were right when you said I've not been hurt, at least not in the sense you mean. I do know what it's like to love something and lose it though. When I knew I couldn't play professional tennis again, I thought my life was over. Part of me wanted it to be over.' He reached for her chin, holding her eyes on his. 'I didn't want to pick up a racket ever again, but I did and I've never regretted it.'

'You're stronger than I am.'

He shook his head. 'No. I was lucky enough to have the backing of people who loved me. It was my family who helped me through it, telling me over and over not to give up on the sport I loved. I could learn to love it again, they insisted, but in a different way. And I have.'

'You can't equate tennis with a failed marriage.'

'Can't you? Doesn't this all come back to fear? You fear getting involved in another relationship will lead to you being hurt. I feared staying around the game I loved, but not being able to play it at the top level again, would hurt me.'

Her expression appeared distant as she considered his words. 'I don't only have myself to be fearful for. There's

William, too. I damaged him by staying too long in a relationship that went sour. I don't know if I have the strength or will to try again.'

For a long while Daniel remained silent, stroking her hair, holding her close. His heart ached to see her so upset, but he also worried for himself, too. His feelings were growing steadily deeper every time he saw her, yet the closer he got, the more she pushed him away. And if she didn't even have the will to try …

Heaving out a sigh he kissed the top of her head. 'Time for me to go home.'

She stirred against him, but didn't raise her head from its snug position against his chest.

He tried again. 'Melissa? Wake up sleepy head. I have to go home.'

'Oh.' Slowly she raised her head, looking up at him with clouded grey eyes. He felt another tug on his heart. 'Sorry, I got too comfortable.' She eased herself into a sitting position and immediately he felt the loss of her warmth.

'I'm glad I've been of some use this evening,' he returned dryly. 'Even if it wasn't the use I'd hoped for.'

Instantly her eyes darted away from him. 'No. I'm sorry.'

He exhaled slowly and planted a kiss on her forehead. 'It's me who's sorry. I'm a patient man, usually. But I need to warn you, I'm a determined one, too. I won't give up.'

She surprised him then by cupping his face and giving him a quick kiss on the lips. 'I hope you don't.' Her voice held an almost desperate edge. 'I can't make any promises, but …' her eyes found his. 'I like having you in my life, Daniel.'

Hope instantly surged through him, making his heart leap wildly. 'I like having you in mine, too.' Before he could say or do anything stupid to ruin the moment, he rose to his feet. 'Goodnight. Sweet dreams.'

Picking up his jacket, he let himself out.

He didn't drive off straight away. For a while he sat in his car, thinking about the evening. Thinking about Melissa walking upstairs to her bed, alone. It hadn't ended as he'd planned but there would be other evenings. He would make sure of it.

Chapter Nine

As Daniel collected up the equipment from the evening's coaching session, he noticed Simon and William hanging back, waiting for him.

'What's up? Haven't you got homes to go to?'

They darted looks at each other and he experienced a twinge of unease. What were they cooking up now?

'Go on, ask him.' Simon jabbed William in the ribs.

William looked quickly up at Daniel, flushed to his hairline, then scooted his eyes down to the ground, shaking his head.

Daniel's heart went out to him. He couldn't remember ever being shy, but it didn't stop him empathising. 'Simon, why don't you go and find your mum?' Silently he indicated to his nephew to beat it. When he did, Daniel crouched down in front of William. 'What is it you wanted to ask me? I'm sure whatever it is, I won't mind you asking. Can't promise I'll do anything about it, mind.'

William bit his lip and glanced shyly up at him. 'Can I go in your Ferrari one day. Please. Sir?'

Daniel laughed out his relief. He'd worried William might ask something about his interest in his mother – he didn't have a clue how perceptive seven year old boys were – but a question about his car he could easily handle. 'Sure you can. In fact, I've got it with me today. Why don't we have a word with your mum and see if I can give you a ride home now?'

A huge smile spread across his often far too serious little face. 'Really?'

'Yes, really, though you have to promise to stop with the Sir.'

He watched as William raced off towards Melissa, pulling on her arm to get her attention. After a few glances in his direction, they both walked over towards him.

'It looks like my lift home isn't good enough,' she remarked, her smile taking the edge off her words.

'What can I say? Boys and their toys.' He glanced over at the balls and cones still on the court. 'I've just got to finish up here. Why don't you go home and William and I will follow you back in a short while.'

Melissa put an arm around her son. 'Is that okay with you, sweetie?'

William nodded vigorously.

'Do you want to wait for me in reception, buddy? I'll be with you in a minute.'

William scampered off to where Simon and Alice were still standing. Daniel grinned as he watched the boys high five each other.

'Okay then, I guess I'll see you at home.'

The quiet voice drew his attention back the woman he'd not stopped thinking about since the award ceremony two days ago. 'I guess you will.'

She chewed awkwardly on her bottom lip. 'Daniel, I know I don't have to say this, but you will ...'

'Drive carefully? Make sure he's strapped in?' Daniel finished for her as he collected all his bits together, stuffing them into his holdall.

She gave him an embarrassed smile. 'Sorry, yes, I know you will. It's just ... it feels odd leaving him with someone else.'

'Do you ask Alice to drive carefully?'

Her eyes flashed guiltily. 'No. But she doesn't drive a Ferrari and, well, she's not a man.'

'I see. So it's the male species you don't trust, and not me in particular?' They both knew he wasn't just talking about looking after William now.

'It's not specific to you, no. William has always been so shy with men,' she continued, ignoring his underlying question. 'It's a big step for him to willingly go home with you on his own.'

'I suspect it has more to do with the car than me.' Together they walked up to the reception area where William was now sitting by himself, swinging his legs.

'The car is a big draw, yes, but he wouldn't have asked if he didn't like and trust you.'

'And I'm not about to abuse that trust,' he reassured, coming to a stop next to William. 'I'll drive with the utmost care, obeying the speed limit at all times.' He glanced over at his young charge, who pulled a face. 'We might have to race a few cars off at the lights though, just to make sure he gets the proper Ferrari experience.'

William giggled and his mother shook her head. 'Okay, okay. I'll leave you to it.' With only a slight flicker of unease in her eyes, she waved goodbye. 'See you at home.'

Daniel rummaged around in his sports jacket and found his keys, handing them over to William. 'There you go. You can open her up for me.'

The car was parked in the first space just outside the entrance. There had to be some perks to being the boss.

'How do you know she's a girl?'

'Because she's gorgeous to look at but expensive to run.'

William nodded sagely, though Daniel doubted he really understood.

'Do you fancy a car like this one day?' he asked as they settled inside, checking William was securely strapped in.

Something he'd have done regardless of the reminder. He pressed the start button and the engine roared.

Next to him, William beamed. 'Yes.'

'Perhaps when you're older you can put it on that Christmas list of yours.' And wasn't that a neat lead in. 'Have you sent it off yet? Christmas is only a few weeks away.'

'I'm doing it tonight.'

Daniel threaded the Ferrari out of the car park and onto the road. 'Are you asking for the racket?'

'The racket and one other thing.'

Bugger. 'Are you going to tell me what the other *thing* is?' he enquired as casually as he could.

William just shot him a sly smile. 'That's between me and Father Christmas.'

'I see.' It looked like his famed McCormick charm was fading. 'How's school? Is it all parties and games as you wind down for Christmas?'

He shook his head. 'We've got to do the nativity.'

'Ah yes, I'd forgotten about that.' He slid the boy a glance. 'Have you got a good part?'

'It's okay. But I have to drive a car made out of cardboard.'

Daniel fought to hide his laughter. 'Oh dear. What do you do in this car?'

'Take Joseph and Mary to Bethlehem.'

'Wow. That's quite a journey in a cardboard car.'

'It'd be quicker in a Ferrari.'

Daniel burst into laughter. 'True. And then there would still be spaces left in the inn and they wouldn't have to sleep in a stable.'

William giggled and Daniel smiled back, his mind flickering through a possibility. 'Simon's in this nativity too, yes?'

'He's Joseph.'

'So he also has to go in the back of the cardboard car huh?'

'Yeah,' William replied disgustedly.

'Well I'd better make sure I get myself a ticket to watch.'

'You're going to come?'

At William's look of utter surprise Daniel found himself laughing again. 'Hey, don't sound so surprised. Adults like to watch kids' nativity plays. It's all part of the build-up to Christmas.'

'It'll mostly be rubbish.'

Daniel shook his head, chuckling to himself. God, the boy cracked him up. At last he was coming out of his shell. And it seemed the real William had a pretty wicked sense of humour.

Forty minutes after she'd got home, Melissa finally heard the deep rumble of the Ferrari. It had been just long enough for her to begin to worry, but just short enough to prevent her from reaching for the phone to call Daniel. Wouldn't *that* have been an embarrassing conversation? The poor guy was already irked that she didn't trust him, even though he'd done nothing to suggest he wasn't a thoroughly decent, honourable guy. One she couldn't only trust with her son but perhaps, if she ever felt brave enough, herself.

William launched himself into the house, words he'd obviously just learnt, like acceleration and horsepower, flying out of his mouth with the confidence of a boy who thought he knew what he was talking about.

'Sorry we're late.' Daniel followed behind, shoving his keys into his pocket. 'I thought it was a bit dull going the usual route home, so we made a diversion onto the motorway. It let William feel a bit of speed.' At her slightly alarmed look, he raised his eyebrows. 'All very legal, honest.'

'Mum,' William pulled at her arm. 'Daniel says he's going to come and watch the school play.'

'He is?' She felt a spike of unwanted panic. Nativity plays were for families, not friends. Not even friends who'd shared a kiss.

'If you or Alice wouldn't mind getting me a ticket,' Daniel added quickly.

Her fear slowly deflated. Of course. Daniel was going to watch his nephew. 'I can get you one. They restrict it to two per family.' She shrugged. 'I only need one.'

Daniel leant nonchalantly against the front door, the hint of a smile on his face. 'Are you sure you don't mind me coming?'

'Of course I don't.'

'At least not now you've remembered my nephew is in the play, too.'

She smiled guiltily. 'Okay, yes. That makes it ... easier.'

'He wants to see the cardboard car,' William interrupted. 'I've told him it's going to be rubbish.'

Daniel let out one of his lazy, infinitely sexy chuckles. 'It's hard to turn down a billing like that.'

William smiled shyly back at him. Melissa knew he didn't really understand why Daniel was laughing, but she also knew to her son the *why* didn't really matter. It was enough that he was.

'Come on Mr Cardboard Taxi driver,' she said, hugging his shoulders. 'It's time for you to get your pyjamas on. I'll be up there in a minute.'

The moment William was out of sight, Daniel took a deliberate step towards her. Recognising the gleam in his eyes, her pulse rocketed and she took a deliberate step back.

Daniel merely grinned and closed the space between them.

She could hear the pounding of her heart in her ears as his lips descended. Swallowing her gasp, she tasted his hunger. And her answering need.

As abruptly as it had begun, the kiss ended. She was still coming to terms with her reaction to it when Daniel let himself out.

The following morning she bumped into Alice at the school gates.

'Just the lady I wanted to see,' Alice remarked, giving her a quick hug.

'Oh?'

'Two things. Firstly, I'm planning a New Year's Eve party this year and I want you to come. William is invited too, so there's no excuse.'

The look she gave her reminded Melissa of her brother. Fiercely determined. 'It would appear I'm coming then.'

'Excellent.' Obviously satisfied that she'd won so easily, Alice linked arms with her as they walked back to the car park together. 'Secondly, I wanted to check you're okay with what Daniel's trying to do at the school play.'

'Yes, he told me he wants to come and watch. I'm happy to get him a ticket so it doesn't come out of your allocation.'

She hesitated a moment. 'That's all he's told you?'

'Yes. Why, is there something else I should know?'

Alice squeezed her arm. 'No. Though watching the boys isn't the only reason Daniel wants to go to the play, and you know it.'

'Do I?'

'Yes, you do. My brother is smitten with you. Even you have to admit that.'

With Alice hanging on to her arm, Melissa was unable to hide from her piercing, all-knowing look. 'What do you mean, even me?' she asked, in a bid to deflect the conversation from Daniel.

'Melissa the ice maiden. Guaranteed to scare off any man who dares to approach her. Except, it seems, my brother.' Alice halted and turned to face her, eyes full of blatant curiosity.

'That simply isn't true. We're just friends.'

Melissa raised an eyebrow. 'Forgive me if I admit to a degree of scepticism at the thought of my brother in a purely platonic friendship with a beautiful woman.'

'No, you don't understand. It has to be that way. We can only be friends.' She heard, and hated, the desperation in her voice.

'Oh, Melissa.' Alice sighed and wrapped an arm around her. 'Have you got time to come back with me for a quick drink? I think we need to talk.'

She considered the mountain of work waiting for her back at her studio. Also the Christmas cards waiting to be written and the decorations still in her loft. But there was no doubt she was getting herself into a bit of a state about Daniel. 'A drink and a chat sounds good. I'll follow you back. I've got an interview with a fashion editor at eleven, but other than that I can bunk off for a while.' She smiled. 'I love being my own boss.'

Melissa followed Alice the short distance to her elegant town house. She had to give her friend her due; she actually waited until they'd settled down in the large sitting room, coffee in hand, before starting her inquisition.

'Why are you so scared of Daniel?' she asked outright, just as Melissa took her first sip.

The question was direct enough to make her jerk, almost spilling her coffee. 'Don't I get a gentle lead in question?'

'You never get to the truth if you pussy foot around the problem,' Alice replied smugly. 'Come on, no evasion. Talk to me.'

Sighing, Melissa accepted the inevitable. 'You know why. I'm scared of getting hurt again. I know he turned out to be a bastard, but I loved Lawrence. I put a lot of effort into our marriage and I failed.' She looked down at her cup. 'If I'd only let myself down it wouldn't be so bad, but I let William down as well.'

Alice snorted. 'I love you to bits, but you couldn't be more wrong about this. For a start, the only person who let William down was Lawrence. Secondly, you didn't fail. You married Lawrence in good faith. How were you to know he'd change once you were together?'

'I should have seen it. If I hadn't been so giddy with love, I would have seen through him.'

'Okay, so you made a mistake. An entirely understandable mistake, considering your background. And the fact that you were only seventeen, for goodness' sake. You were inexperienced, perhaps a bit naïve, but women in love make mistakes all the time. Look at me. I'm onto my third marriage.' She smiled, but then her face turned serious. 'The first two lasted barely a year. Like you, I was young and probably foolish. But if I'd done what you're doing and never risked another relationship, I wouldn't be where I am now. Blissfully happy with Richard. Who, I might add, I married when I was twenty-nine. Not dissimilar from your age now, I believe.'

Melissa twisted the coffee cup in her hands, taking comfort from the warmth. 'I understand what you're saying, but you didn't have children when you divorced the other times. It makes a difference. Especially when I see how much it affected William.'

'It wasn't the divorce that affected William, it was his father,' Alice corrected. 'Lawrence intimidated him. You're older and wiser now and you've learnt from that mistake. You'll never fall in love with another man like Lawrence.' Alice put down her cup and fixed her with one of her no-nonsense stares. 'I know I'm biased, but Daniel is a good man. No, he's far more than that, he's an exceptional man. He won't hurt you. Not you, or William. Have you ever heard any bad press about him?'

Melissa paused to think. 'No, I haven't.'

'That isn't just a lucky accident. It's because he treats people properly. Particularly women.' Warming to her theme, Alice sat forward on the sofa. 'Yes, he's had several relationships, and yes I know he ended them when they became too serious for him, but he treated them all with respect. Nobody ever got hurt.'

It wasn't hard for Melissa to imagine Daniel letting a woman down gently. He might be a big bear of a man but he wasn't afraid to show his compassionate side. 'I can see he's a good man,' she replied honestly. 'And of course I'm attracted to him. Who wouldn't be? Handsome, charming, rich. He even drives the flash car.'

'Don't tell me you judge a man by the car he drives. That I won't believe.'

Melissa laughed. 'I don't, though it helped him pass William's test.' Putting down her cup, she rose to her feet. 'It's because I like Daniel so much, both what I can see on the outside and on the inside, that I'm so wary.' Taking in a deep breath, she admitted the truth to both of them. 'He's a man I could easily lose my heart to Alice, and that scares the living daylights out of me.'

She wasn't aware of how much she needed the hug until Alice supplied it. 'Okay, I hear what you're saying, but love shouldn't be something you fear. It should be something you cherish. If you spend the rest of your life never allowing yourself to fall in love again, it will only be half a life.'

Tears pooled in her eyes and Melissa frantically blinked them away. 'Maybe.'

The conversation gave Melissa plenty to think about on the way back to her studio. She couldn't help but feel that the McCormick siblings were, however charmingly, ganging up on her.

Chapter Ten

When Daniel had done a reccy of the school last week he'd discovered to his delight that the school hall was located to one side and had a double door fire exit into the playground. It was an exit just wide enough to squeeze a car through.

At least he hoped it was.

William and Simon, who'd been given special permission to leave their class to say hello to him, jumped up and down, clapping their hands as Daniel carefully manoeuvred his beloved Ferrari through the doors, exhaling in relief as he made it.

'Better than the cardboard taxi?' he asked as he climbed out. Of course as a two-seater convertible it wasn't exactly taxi material. Poor Mary and Joseph were going to have to sit on the boot.

'A squillion times better,' Simon squealed. 'This play is going to rock.'

Daniel cast his eye over towards William, who was staring at the car, touching it with his hand. 'How about you, William? Is this taxi more to your liking?'

'Yes, Sir,' he whispered. Then he raised his head and gave him the most heart-stopping grin. 'Awesome.'

'Yes, *Daniel*,' he chastised gently. 'Or, if you prefer, yes, Tennis Legend. Or even Oh Great One.'

William giggled before turning his attention back to the Ferrari. Daniel turned his to the woman next to him, headmistress Cindy Stevens. She'd come to watch him drive the car in, no doubt terrified to death he'd crash it into the stage. 'Thanks for agreeing to this.'

She put a hand to her mouth, laughing. 'Oh no, it's us who should be thanking you. The children will be so excited when they see it. The parents, too, especially the dads. It's very kind of you.'

She's so *young*, Daniel thought. Wasn't it a sign of growing old when head teachers looked younger than you did?

'Can we practise getting in and out?' Simon asked, opening the Ferrari door.

Daniel chuckled. 'You know exactly how to get into it, you've done it often enough. And I'm sure you'll have a dress rehearsal later today.'

'We certainly will,' Cindy Stevens confirmed. 'Mary and Joseph will need to practise sitting on the back so they don't slip off when we do it for real tomorrow.' She turned to him and ... was she fluttering her eyes? Or was it his imagination? 'You're sure you don't mind them clambering over your gorgeous car?'

'Simon assures me he'll show Mary how to clamber *carefully*.' And no, he wasn't going to think about that part. Instead he was going to focus on how thrilled his nephew had been when he'd told him what he was planning. And the joy on William's face as he'd watched the Ferrari driving in.

Cindy Stevens gave him another of her warm, and yes, definitely *flirtatious* smiles. 'I can assure you we'll take good care of it.'

'It's a girl car,' William said quietly. 'Isn't it, Daniel?'

Cindy laughed. 'Oh, then we'll take good care of her, won't we boys? Now, I think it's time you headed back to your classrooms.'

They were almost out of the hall when William suddenly stopped and turned round. 'Thank you, Daniel.'

And suddenly Daniel didn't care if Mary dented the bonnet as she climbed onto it, or if little Toby smeared his greasy fingers all over the shiny paintwork. It would be worth it for that moment.

The following day Melissa couldn't believe the excited boy she was taking back to school for his nativity was the same boy who'd been so dismissive of it earlier in the week.

'I thought you said the play was going to be rubbish,' she remarked as she parked up.

'It was.' William gave her the secretive smile that seemed to be his trademark recently.

'So why are you so happy about being in it now?'

'You'll see.'

She supposed she'd have to content herself with that. And the fact that her shy son couldn't wait to play his part in the nativity he'd scorned a few weeks ago.

She spotted Daniel sitting on one of the chairs in the school reception area, his head bent over his phone, and her heart gave its customary flutter.

'What are you doing here so early?' she asked as they walked towards him. 'The play doesn't start for half an hour.'

He unfurled his long legs and stood up. 'Well, hello.'

In her determination to play it cool, she'd forgotten that part. Stupid. 'Sorry, hello.' Why was it suddenly so hard to get her words out? 'I was just surprised to see you here so soon.'

'Ah. Cindy ...' He grinned down at William. 'That's Ms Stevens to you ... well, she wanted to talk to me about some stuff.'

'Stuff?'

His eyes didn't quite meet hers. 'Yeah. I think I've been roped in to do some tennis lessons at the school next term.'

She found she wanted to giggle. 'Oh dear. But I'm sure the kids will be grateful.'

'Umm. It's not the kids I'm worried about.'

Before she had a chance to quiz him on his rather obscure reply, William tugged Daniel's arm. 'She doesn't know,' he whispered, though it was loud enough for Melissa to overhear.

Daniel glanced over at her, his eyes amused. 'Okay. I won't ruin the surprise.'

Her heart stuttered as she looked from Daniel to her son. Oh dear. She'd been so careful about not letting her own feelings for Daniel develop too deeply, she'd been oblivious to William's. His eyes shone, his cheeks were flushed and he bore all the signs of hero worship. How had he moved from wariness to adulation so quickly? 'What surprise?' she managed finally.

William gave her another sneaky smile. 'Not telling.' Then he dashed off to his classroom before she had a chance to even wish him luck.

'He seems so much happier about this play now.' She observed, giving Daniel a long, meaningful look.

'Yes, he does.'

His eyes danced back at her and once again Melissa's heart seemed to stop beating for a moment. This is too easy, she thought in a panic. Sharing secrets with her son. Coming to watch the nativity together. It's what families did, but Daniel was only a friend.

'Melissa?' He reached to touch her cheek. 'What's wrong? You've gone quiet on me.'

'Sorry.' She swallowed, forcing the tendrils of fear to

the back of her mind. 'I'm just nervous. It's the first time William's had any lines to say in a play.'

Daniel cupped her face in his large, warm hand. 'He'll ace it.'

Her heart did a slow somersault and her eyes didn't seem to want to leave his. Almost imperceptibly his fingers tightened and he dropped his gaze to her mouth.

'There you are.'

At the sound of Alice's voice, Melissa jumped and Daniel dropped his hand to his side, but not before he'd given her a rueful smile.

'We were waiting for you.' Melissa tried to find her voice. 'I thought it would be more fun to sit together.'

'I doubt it'll be fun wherever we sit,' Richard grumbled behind Alice. 'An hour and a half of watching a bunch of seven-year-olds mumble or forget their lines. It's hardly entertainment.'

Alice gave her husband a sharp dig. 'Keep your voice down,' she hissed. 'Some parents are actually looking forward to this.'

They trooped into the hall and filed into a row near the back. The chairs were small and Melissa was acutely conscious of Daniel's large frame sitting next to her. As his muscular thigh pressed firmly against hers, it sent a ripple of heat through her.

'How wonderful to see such a keen audience.' The head teacher's voice floated over to them and Melissa glanced up to find Ms Stevens smiling down ... at Daniel. 'But as our guest of honour, we've saved Mr McCormick a seat at the front.'

A flush crept over Daniel's cheeks and Melissa had to stifle a giggle. She'd never seen him look anything other than fully in control. 'Umm, thank you, but I'm here with my sister.'

Ms Stevens wasn't having that. 'Oh, I'm sure she won't mind you watching from the front.'

Sitting on the other side of her, Melissa could feel Alice shaking with suppressed laughter. 'Not at all,' Alice replied agreeably. 'Guests of honour should definitely sit in the front row.'

Daniel shot his sister a murderous look, muttering, 'you're dead meat,' under his breath before following Ms Stevens down to the front.

'Well, look at that,' Alice murmured. 'It looks like our Cindy Stevens has a crush on my brother.'

'Yes.' Melissa didn't find the situation quite so funny when she saw Ms Stevens patting Daniel's arm and smiling into his eyes. 'Why is he the guest of honour?'

Alice shrugged, avoiding her eyes. 'He didn't come to last year's play. Perhaps she's just realised who he is.'

Melissa wasn't sure she believed her friend, but she kept quiet and tried not to watch as Daniel bent his head to listen to something else Ms Stevens was telling him. By the time the lights dimmed for the start of the play she found she was gritting her teeth. Didn't the Head realise she was fawning over Daniel? And it was making her look ridiculous?

Daniel was fed up. Sure, he had a great view of the stage, but where he'd been looking forward to an hour of having Melissa's body tucked against his, now he was left sitting next to the head teacher. He hadn't wanted to do that when he'd been at school and, sweet as Cindy Stevens was, he didn't want to do it now.

But then Simon walked onto the stage, and Daniel forgot all about where he was sitting. Wow, his nephew was good, he thought with a touch of smugness and a heap of pride. Of course he'd always been confident, so to hear him deliver his lines in a strong, clear voice shouldn't have been that much of a surprise, but still. His chest puffed a little.

As Mary and Joseph discussed their need to go to Bethlehem, Daniel sat straighter in his chair. He didn't want to miss this. Four children tugged at a large sheet and suddenly a beam of light – pretty cool for a primary school production – fell on his Ferrari.

The crowd gasped, then clapped, but Daniel didn't notice. His eyes were glued to William as he opened the car door and stepped onto the stage to join Simon (Joseph) and Mary.

'I've got a pick up for Mary and Joseph. No surname.' His voice wobbled a little but the words were clear and Daniel felt his chest swell even further. When William caught his eye and gave him a shy smile, he feared it might burst.

'That's us,' Simon replied. 'Can you take us to Bethlehem?'

William slowly scratched his chin. 'No problem. My taxi can get you there super fast.' The audience chuckled and William and Simon shared a grin. 'But you'll be lucky to get a room … mate.' Daniel held is breath as William frowned, then said in a rush. 'It's packed because of the census.'

His hands itched to clap, but he settled for watching the grin on William's face as he showed his passengers onto the car, and then leapt into the drivers seat.

The rest of the play plodded along. Words were occasionally forgotten, some costumes unravelled and the big star the Three Kings were following fell half-way through the scene, but Daniel guessed that was part of the pleasure of a school nativity. And though he was admittedly a touch biased, he reckoned Simon, William and his car stole the show.

As the audience finally filed out Cindy took the opportunity to bend his ear back some more and it was a while before he could extract himself from her very friendly clutches. A few years back he'd have enjoyed her attention. Might even have considered asking for her number. Now all he wanted was to escape and find Melissa. A woman who was beautiful yet didn't know it. Whose cool exterior hid a centre so soft it was afraid of getting hurt again.

His progress out of the hall was hindered by a few parents wanting his autograph. Knowing it was the fans who'd helped make his career so memorable, he clamped down on his impatience and signed anything thrust under his nose. When he finally made it out of the hall and into the car park he found Alice and Melissa waiting for him.

'Why did those people want you to sign things?' asked the boy who, a few weeks ago, had hardly dared to look at him, never mind voice such a personal question.

'Damned if I know, William. Perhaps they thought I was somebody famous.'

'Are you?'

He laughed. 'Not as famous as you and Simon. At least not after tonight's performance. You rocked the place.'

'The car rocked,' Simon shouted. 'Did you see how surprised everyone was?'

'Yes, yes.' Alice clutched her son's arm. 'It was great, you were all great. But it's late and your dad's already in the car, waiting.'

'Goodnight Joseph,' Daniel bent to give his nephew a high five, whispering, 'I'd ditch Mary if I were you. She seemed a bit serious.'

'I hardly think you're the one to give my son relationship advice,' Alice mocked, looking pointedly at Melissa. 'Bye everyone.'

'I think it's time for us to go home, too,' Melissa said, hugging her coat around her.

'I'll walk you to your car.'

'Where's yours?' she asked as they set off towards her Golf. Then the penny dropped. 'Oh, it's in the hall, isn't it?'

'Yep. They asked me to wait until everyone had gone before driving it away. Obviously worried I'll run over a small child.'

She smiled. 'It was a lovely thing you did. Everyone got a kick out of it.' She smoothed a hand over William's hair. 'Especially this one.'

'It wasn't entirely altruistic. I got a kick out of it too.'

'Yes.' Her eyes darted over his shoulder. 'It seems Ms Stevens is one of your biggest fans now.'

'Jealous?' He asked softly, for her ears only.

'Hardly.'

But her reddening cheeks gave her away. Maybe he was getting to her, after all. 'You know, you needn't be jealous,' he whispered as they reached her car. 'I only have eyes for you.'

She slid him a glance and he grinned.

She shook her head, but smiled back.

A weary looking William climbed into the back seat. 'I think you've got one tired little boy on your hands,' he remarked, running a hand over William's rumpled looking hair.

'I think you're right.' Melissa helped him do up his seat belt. 'It looks like driving taxis is more tiring than I thought.'

Daniel said goodbye to William and closed the car door. 'Probably not the best time for me to push for an invite back to yours then.'

'No.' She hesitated, then surprised the heck out of him with her next words. 'You could come round tomorrow instead, if you like. I make a reasonable chilli.'

His heart bounced beneath his ribs and he opened

his mouth to accept, but then cursed. 'Damn. I finally get invited round for a meal and I can't make it.'

'It's okay.' She opened the driver's door, eyes downcast. 'Perhaps another time.'

Clasping hold of her shoulders, he turned her towards him. 'If I could be there tomorrow, I would. Believe me.' After checking William wasn't watching – his head was leant back against the seat, his eyes closed – Daniel lightly touched his lips against hers. It was the softest of touches, yet still it had his heart skittering. Before his baser instinct took over and he did what he really wanted to do – pin her against the car and take his fill – he stuffed his hands into his pockets. 'I've got to fly to America tomorrow. I'm committed to playing in a big charity tennis tournament. I don't usually take part in them abroad, too much time away from the academy, but the organiser is a friend, and I'm a sucker when a pal gets down and begs. I don't think they'll shift the date of the tournament, even for me.'

Her lips curved and his heart squeezed. 'Okay.'

'How about we make it the following Sunday? I fly in that morning so I might not be at my dazzling best, but after a week of hotel food, a home-cooked meal would go down a treat.'

She nodded, but Daniel had the feeling she was starting to regret her original offer. In a bid to remind her why she'd want to see him, he slid his arms around her waist and drew her against him. She was such a perfect fit – tall and willowy but soft and warm – he had to suppress a groan. 'Why are you looking so worried? You've only arranged to have me over for lunch.' Tilting his head back slightly he found her mouth again, nibbling at her lips before he slid his tongue between them and deepened the kiss.

She swayed with him, her arms moving to clasp his neck

and pull him further towards her. Reluctantly, while he still had some willpower left, he pulled away. 'Of course, you could decide to use me for sex.'

Laughter shot out of her. 'You're incorrigible. How can you make a woman want you, and then laugh with you, in the space of a few seconds?'

'That's only the beginning of my talents.' The sparkle in her eyes gave him all the encouragement he needed. With a quick check to confirm William was out for the count, Daniel dived back for another kiss. This time the need rose more forcefully and he pushed her back against the car, wedging her body against his.

'Goodbye, Melissa.'

One of the parents shouted out to them as they walked past. While Melissa gasped and uttered a croaky acknowledgement, Daniel regretfully took a step back. 'As a tennis player my timing was always impeccable. As a man, it's starting to suck.'

She seemed to be finding it as hard as him to regain her breath. 'Oh dear. Caught kissing in the school car park. My credibility is shot.'

'But look who you were kissing,' he reminded her, dragging her towards him for one last kiss. 'I'll see you in a week. Be good.'

'You, too. Don't go flirting with any more head teachers.'

He acknowledged her words with a wave of his hand. There was no fear of him doing that. He had a feeling he'd finally met his match.

Chapter Eleven

The week slid by slowly. On Monday Melissa bought a Christmas tree and, together with William, put up the decorations. The house seemed brighter with the festive trappings in place, but she still felt strangely flat.

On Tuesday she took William to his usual tennis lesson, but the flare of anticipation as she drove to the centre wasn't there. William, too, was more subdued than usual. It seemed both of them, in their different ways, were missing Daniel.

On Wednesday evening she found herself scanning through the sports channels, desperate to see if they were covering the charity tennis tournament Daniel was taking part in. To her disappointment, she couldn't find it anywhere.

Late Thursday afternoon she picked up the ringing phone with a thumping heart, only to have her hopes crash the moment she heard the male voice on the phone. Lawrence, not Daniel.

'Have you sorted a time when I can see my son yet?' he asked without preamble. 'Evangeline is keen to meet him.'

The thought of her son being in the same company as not only his overbearing father, but also a woman cold-hearted enough to sleep with the husband of a colleague, made her feel physically sick. 'If he sees you at all, it will be with me. Just the three of us.'

'Don't be ridiculous.' His tone was abrupt and dismissive. 'Of course Evangeline will be with us, too. She has a daughter around William's age. They can play together. Providing William has learnt the art of conversation, of course. Goodness knows what you're doing to the boy.

Young Sabine is far more confident. Very grown-up for her age.'

Melissa tried to ignore his nasty dig and focus instead on the irony of the situation. 'Has it escaped your notice that you made my life hell because you didn't want a child and yet here you are, marrying a woman who already has one?'

'Dragging you out of your ordinary life and into one of wealth and glamour was hardly making your life hell,' he countered mockingly. 'As for your other comment, a man my age doesn't have quite the same choices he once had ten years ago.' For a few seconds he broke off and she heard a rapid exchange of words before he came back on the line. 'I need to go. I expect you to email me some dates later this evening.'

Her hand tightened around the phone. 'You can expect all you like. It won't alter the fact that I'm not prepared to leave William alone with you or Evangeline. I have a lawyer now, Lawrence. One not in your pocket. If you want to discuss access to William again, you need to do it through him.'

Once she'd rattled off the number Daniel had given her for Peter Price, she threw the phone down and put her head in her hands. In the room next door she could hear Christmas adverts on the television, their upbeat jingles jarring with her mood, promising joy and happiness when her feelings were flowing fast in the opposite direction. With a sigh she rubbed at her eyes with the heels of her hands and tried to push out her dark thoughts.

Suddenly the sound of young laughter pierced the air. Slipping off the kitchen stool she peered into the sitting room. William was sprawled on the sofa, arms behind his head, a wide grin splitting his face as he watched a cartoon.

With a small smile – he looked like a pint-sized man – she went to join him, tucking his small body against her side. There she tried to let his presence, and the antics on the television, block out the memory of the phone call. Mostly she succeeded.

On Friday, determined to keep busy, she scoured recipes for a chocolate fruitcake and made it with William when he came home from school. On Saturday they iced it. As she swept up the escaped silver balls and wiped icing sugar off William's face, she felt an unexpected buzz of anticipation and convinced herself she was finally looking forward to Christmas. Her heart, though, knew the flutter in her belly wasn't for Christmas. It was for Daniel.

On Sunday morning, she woke up obsessing about what underwear to put on.

Following ten minutes of frantic searching through her drawers she finally sat on the bed and laughed at herself. She was making Sunday lunch for an attractive man, that was all. They were hardly going to have wild, passionate sex while William was around.

But if he hadn't been?

Refusing to answer her own question, she dressed – white matching underwear, pretty not sexy – then washed the kitchen floor and squirted bleach into the toilet, as she would for any invited guest. Finally she set about peeling the vegetables while William diligently laid the table.

'Have you sent that letter off to Father Christmas yet?' she enquired casually as she tried to chop the carrots into reasonably even slices.

'Yes.'

Mid-chop, her hand stilled. 'And are you still not going to tell me what was in it?'

'Nope,' he replied cheerfully. 'Father Christmas knows.'

'Where did you post it to?'

'Duh. Father Christmas. The North Pole.'

She searched for the right question to draw him out. 'I hope you haven't asked for too many things?'

'Just two.'

Crappity crap, crap. 'Two?'

'Yep.'

Wait till she saw Daniel. Still, surely the racket would be one of the things he wanted. She'd just have to hope his second wish was something she'd already earmarked to buy him.

'Will Daniel help with my Lego car?' William asked, carefully putting out the knives and forks, his tongue sticking out in concentration.

She didn't have the heart to tell him he'd put them the wrong way round. 'You'll have to ask him. Remember he's just flown in from America though, so he'll be tired. It might have to wait for another day.'

He nodded his head in acceptance, though Melissa knew he desperately wanted someone to help him. She'd tried, but it seemed she lacked the right chromosome when it came to Lego. Apparently it wasn't enough for the car to have four wheels and a steering wheel. The saddest part was that William did have a dad, but not one he wanted to play with. Or who'd ever wanted to play with him.

Until recently.

Before she could begin worrying again, the doorbell rang. 'I'll get it,' William shouted, scooting off down the hallway.

'Hey, champ, how have you been?'

Daniel's question was followed by a burst of schoolboy giggles. By the time she got there, Daniel had hoisted William over his shoulder and was tickling his feet remorselessly.

He caught her eye and though his grin remained, his eyes darkened. 'Missed me?'

'I may have,' she replied carefully, her heart beating wildly as her eyes drank him in. A tall, commanding figure dwarfing her small hallway. In faded jeans and a checked shirt, he exuded a vitality that even jet lag couldn't dim.

Slowly he lowered the squealing William to the floor. Then, his eyes never leaving her face, he leant forwards and kissed her softly on the lips. 'I've missed you,' he whispered. She opened her mouth to speak, but her words became entangled in her throat. Thankfully he filled the gap. 'So, what's your mum's cooking like?' he asked William. 'Should I be worried?'

'Yes,' her traitorous son replied with a laugh.

William was talking to him ten to the dozen. Daniel tried to pay attention to the little fella, but by God he found it hard to keep his eyes off Melissa. So far their relationship had been an exercise in self-control and his was slipping, fast. It had been a long week.

'Daniel?'

Guiltily he dragged his eyes back to William. 'Sorry, I was miles away. What did you say?'

'Do you like our tree? Mum and I put it up on Monday.'

Daniel glanced round the corner and eyed up the slightly wonky pine tree. It looked like it had barely survived a silver tinsel avalanche. 'It looks very festive,' he managed. 'Who did the decorating?'

'We both did.'

'Both?' Somehow he couldn't see designer Melissa having a tinsel fetish.

'Well, Mum did the lights and the baubles.' Which Daniel

could barely see. 'I did the tinsel. Mum didn't want it, but a tree has to have tinsel, doesn't it?'

'Obviously.' Across the table he met Melissa's eyes and they shared a smile. By the time he'd returned his attention to the once shy but now hard-to-shut-up William, Daniel's heart felt considerably fuller.

'Will you help with my car later?' William asked, shovelling in his last mouthful.

Melissa coughed lightly. 'Haven't you forgotten an important word?'

William grinned and damn if that gappy smile didn't do further funny things to his heart. 'Please?'

'I'll certainly try. What sort of car are we talking here? One in the garage?'

'Silly,' William chastised, wrinkling his nose. 'I'm not old enough to have a car in the garage. It's a car made of Lego.'

'Ahh, Lego cars. That just happens to be my speciality.' He sat back and lay his knife and fork down on his now empty plate. 'As your mum made the lunch, I guess it's only fair we help clear up first though, eh?'

'Okay.' William moved back his chair and started to help clear the table.

Feeling pleasantly full, Daniel slowly got to his feet. 'I hope there's a dishwasher hidden somewhere.'

Melissa raised her eyebrows. 'And if there isn't, are you going to withdraw your offer to help?'

Deliberately he rolled up his sleeves. 'Now what sort of man would that make me?'

'A normal one.'

He tutted. 'Very cynical. So tell me, you can cook and win awards for designing clothes. Is there anything you can't do?'

'Apparently I can't build Lego cars.'

'I'm sure you can.' William opened the dishwasher – Daniel gave a silent prayer of thanks for its existence – and while the boy loaded it up, Daniel attacked the greasy roasting tins in the sink. 'Your problem is the car you'll build will be very practical,' he continued, now up to his elbows in suds. 'A large boot, four doors, roomy interior. Zero style.' He shot her a teasing grin.

'The tennis player dares to say that to the designer?'

Her playful riposte almost made him forget what they were talking about. 'I think you'll find designing a car is quite different to a pair of trousers,' he countered when he'd unscrambled his brain. 'Though both should definitely have sex appeal.'

When he'd clattered the last roasting dish onto the drainer, he felt a tug at his arm. 'Come on, Daniel.'

As William darted up the stairs with all the exuberance of youth, Daniel let out a small sigh. 'There goes my post-lunch nap on the sofa.' Drying his hands he shouted, 'I'll be up in a minute, Will.'

Melissa – still sitting down at the table – gave a slight start.

'Sorry, doesn't he like his name shortened?'

'No, it's not that.' A shadow passed briefly across her face. 'Lawrence always insisted he was called William so I guess I stick to it out of habit. There's no reason you can't shorten it.' Shrugging her shoulders, she rose to stand next to him. 'He'll probably prefer it.'

Because he hated the haunted look she always got when she talked about Lawrence, and because he found it impossible to keep his hands off her, Daniel drew her against him, burying his nose in her hair. 'Mmm, you smell good.'

'I probably smell of chicken fat.'

'You smell of flowers, of sexy woman ...' He sniffed again. '... and maybe a little of chicken fat.'

On a laugh, Melissa pushed him away. 'Go play with the Lego. I'll bring you up a cup of coffee to keep you awake.'

He groaned as he let her go and turned to make his way towards the stairs.

'Wait.' She slipped her hand into his and squeezed. 'I know this is the last thing you need after a long flight, but I really appreciate you helping him.'

'Are you kidding? The chance to revisit my youth and build all those supercars I wanted to build at seven but didn't have the skill to? This is exactly what I need.'

After three sports cars were built, admired and put in pride of place on William's shelf, they looked out of the window in astonishment to find it was snowing.

'We can build a snowman!' William exclaimed.

Daniel surveyed the small dusting. 'I'm not sure it's thick enough, but I imagine if we go to the park we might be able to gather enough for a snowball fight.' He gave Melissa a wicked look. 'You guys against me. Last man standing ...'

She coughed. 'Or woman.'

If anything his expression became more devilish. 'That's not going to be the case, though for the sake of political correctness I'll rephrase. Last man or woman standing is the winner.'

Drawers were raided as they hunted for gloves and hats. Daniel refused her offer of a pink pair of woollen gloves and insisted he'd be fine. On the way to the park he set out the rules. If you received a direct hit, you lost a point. More than five direct hits against you resulted in elimination.

William was hesitant at first, but with Daniel's encouragement he got stuck in and his snowballs became bigger and his throws bolder. Despite that, and despite a fair amount of cheating from both her and William – the snow was so soft it was really hard to tell a direct hit – the winner was never in doubt.

'You could have let us win,' she complained as they walked back to the house.

'What?' he looked at her in amazement. '*Let you win?* Don't talk like that in front of a child. It'll give him all the wrong ideas.'

She shook her head, glancing down at his mottled blue hands. 'Surely you don't have to win *every* game you play. You're lucky not to have frostbite.'

'There's no luck about it. I knew I wouldn't have to throw too many snowballs to have you licked. Tennis isn't my only game, you know. I'm pretty good at cricket, too. My throws from the boundary are the stuff of legends. And anyway …'

'You always play to win,' William interrupted in a terrible imitation of Daniel.

They all burst out laughing. As she caught her breath, Melissa took in William's dancing grey eyes and Daniel's flashing white grin and knew her efforts to keep Daniel at arm's length had been a waste of time. Using a lethal combination of charm, patience and humour, he'd snuck into their lives anyway.

Daniel stayed downstairs while she supervised William's bath and helped him into bed. When she came back down he was stretched out lengthways on the sofa, arms behind his head, eyes closed. She caught a glimpse of tanned, flat stomach between the bottom of his shirt and the belt on his jeans and her heart fluttered. The desire to press her lips against his skin, to open his shirt and trail her fingers up his chest, was almost overwhelming.

But she wasn't that brazen. She'd only ever known one man and he'd done the seducing, not her, so instead she lightly touched Daniel's hand. His lids snapped open and she watched as his eyes slowly focused on her. She didn't need to be an expert on seduction to read the smouldering desire in their dark depths.

'Sorry.' Her voice came out alarmingly husky. 'William would like you to read him a story before he goes to sleep.'

To his credit, Daniel didn't sigh. He simply sat up and rubbed his eyes. 'No problem.'

She watched as he walked out of the room, drawn to his broad shoulders and the way his jeans hugged his hips. Lust was such a rare feeling for her but she recognised the signs very clearly now.

She ached. She wanted.

The sound of the phone burst into her erotic thoughts and reluctantly she went to answer it. The voice on the other end served as a bucket of cold water. 'Lawrence.'

'Melissa. You were going to send me some dates.'

Her heart beat frantically and she gulped in air, fighting for calm. 'I told you last time, if you want to talk about access rights to William you need to go through my solicitor.'

'How about on his birthday?' he said, bulldozing over her request. 'December twenty-ninth I believe.'

It was a measure of how little Lawrence had bothered with his son that Melissa was shocked he'd remembered the date. 'I can't. I'm planning a party for him.'

'Excellent. I'll come along.'

'No.' Damn, why had she mentioned the party? Inhaling deeply, she tried again. 'I don't want you at the party, and I don't want you calling this number again. If you want to see William you need to contact my solicitor, Peter Price.'

'That's ludicrous. I shouldn't have to go through a lawyer to see my own flesh and blood.'

'Neither should that flesh and blood be scared to see his father, but he is. Talk to Peter,' she reiterated before slamming the phone down.

Feeling shaky, she slumped onto the sofa and lay back against the cushion.

At the sound of a discreet cough, her eyes flew open. Daniel had squatted down in front of her, his expression concerned. 'It looks like the cook's wiped out.' He trailed his index finger down the side of her face. 'Is everything okay?'

She struggled to sit up. 'Yes, sorry. I'm just a bit tired and ... well, that was Lawrence on the phone.'

His face hardened. 'What did he want?'

'It's okay.' In a bid to soothe them both, she rested her hand on his arm and squeezed gently. 'He wants to see William after Christmas but I told him to go through my solicitor. He's called Peter Price and apparently comes highly recommended.'

'Ah, you've been in touch with him? Good.' He surprised her then by standing up. 'It's probably time I headed for home.'

'Oh.' She hadn't realised how much she wanted to be held by him, until now.

His large body stilled. 'Do you want me to stay?'

'Yes, no. Oh God.' Mortification shot through her and she jumped to her feet. 'Sorry. Of course you want to go. You're probably shattered.'

'I am tired, yes. But that's not the only reason I won't stay.'

She bit at her lip, her heart slowly shrivelling. He'd met someone else. How arrogant of her to expect him to wait for her to come to her senses. 'That's okay. I understand.'

'Do you?' Before she had a chance to answer he pulled her into his arms. 'If you only knew how much I want you, have wanted you, ever since I first saw you.' Relief flooded through her and as his hands ran up and down her back, she melted against him. 'But if I stay any longer, I'm not sure I can be content with just holding you. Are you ready for more?'

There was a rough edge to his voice that sent shivers through her. 'Yes.' A whisper mumbled against his shirt. A truth wrenched out of her even as her mind shouted at her not to be so stupid. She wasn't ready. Not yet.

Time seemed to stand still as she waited for him to take control. To seize the opportunity he was so clearly waiting for. Instead he kissed the top of her head and drew back. 'Do you really mean that? Here, now?'

She hung her head. 'I don't know. I want to, but ...' she trailed off, shaking her head. 'Oh God, I'm so out of practice. I'm scared of taking such a big step, and with William upstairs ... it doesn't feel right.' Staring up at him, she begged him to understand.

He smiled. 'The part I'm taking away from all that is that you want to. It's enough. When does William break up from school?'

'Wednesday. Why?'

'Would you come away with me next weekend? Both of you?'

Her heart skipped a beat. 'Away? Where?'

'I bought a place on the beach a few years ago, when I was trying to get my head round not being able to play tennis again. I found the sea really therapeutic. It's where I go to get away from everything.' He gazed down at her. 'I know December is hardly ideal for it, but I thought William might like a change of scenery.'

Her mind was racing as fast as her pulse. 'I'm sure he would.'

'And his mum?' Daniel ventured softly. 'Would she like to spend the day, and perhaps the night, with me?' He silenced her reply with a kiss. 'I want you to understand there's no pressure. There are four bedrooms, although in the spirit of openness and honesty it seems only fair to tell you I'm rather hoping you'll want to spend some of the time in mine.'

Melissa smiled against his chest. 'I think I might.'

'Good.' He planted another soft kiss on her lips. 'I'll rest a lot easier knowing I haven't blown my only chance.'

She followed him to the front door where he tucked his hand under her chin and drew her eyes up to his. 'I plan on catching up on my sleep over the next few days. You should do the same. If things go the way I'd like, you won't be getting much of it at the weekend. Good night.'

Chapter Twelve

The snow that had added the extra sparkle to his lunch date with Melissa and William began to melt over the next few days, though the memories of their fun in the park, and later of his time alone with Melissa on her sofa, lived on in Daniel's head.

He was becoming besotted with both of them.

By the time he next saw Melissa – at the tennis centre – he was ready to drag her off somewhere quiet and kiss her until neither of them could remember their names. As he wasn't sure she'd be a fan of such high-handed tactics he reined in his desire and settled instead for a highly possessive kiss on her mouth.

When he stepped back Alice, who'd been standing next to her, goggled back at him.

'Are we still on for the weekend?' he asked, fully aware of his sister's jaw dropping even further. 'No cold feet?'

'The weekend?' Alice blurted.

'Yes, the weekend.' Knowing it would frustrate her, he chose not to elaborate.

Melissa looked like she didn't know whether to run away screaming or stay and giggle. 'Yes, we're still coming,' she answered on a half laugh, her head bobbing briefly towards Alice before turning back to him. 'No cold feet.'

'Great. Shall I pick you up at nine? Not too early?'

Her eyes glinted with mischief. 'Well, you're the one who told me I needed to make sure I got in a lot of sleep.' Beside him, Alice spluttered so much he turned to check she wasn't choking. 'I'll make sure I get an early night, so nine is fine.'

'And just when were you going to tell me about this development?' Alice demanded, her voice still wheezy. 'I expect that sort of secrecy from my brother, but not from my friend.'

'Thanks,' he put in dryly.

'You were the one who started it,' Melissa protested. 'So it's hardly a secret. You kept badgering me about what a great guy your brother was and how I had to stop being so afraid of dating again.'

He whooped with laughter. 'She really told you I was a great guy?'

'She really did,' Melissa confirmed, grinning. 'She hammered it home to me all the time. Anyone would think you were destined for sainthood the way she's built you up.'

'That's enough,' Alice interrupted firmly. 'You're both very funny. Now put me out of my misery and tell me what's going on.'

He gave his sister a half smile, half smirk. 'I'm taking Melissa to the beach house. As it's December and not conducive to making out on the beach we'll probably try out the mattress in the master bedroom first. After that we'll move to the—'

Alice slapped her hands over her ears. 'You can stop right there. I really don't want to know about your sex life.' When she was sure he'd shut up, she lowered her arms. 'I admit it feels kind of odd, thinking of you both together, so I'm not going to go there. I do think you were made for each other though, and I'm desperately hoping this will be the start of something important. For both of you.'

A ball of emotion jumped to the back of his throat, surprising the heck out of him. He'd never been more relieved to see William and Simon returning from the changing rooms.

'Hey guys. Looking forward to breaking up from school?'

Simon let out a loud whoop. 'I'm going to watch TV and eat mince pies all day. When I'm not on the Playstation.'

As Alice muttered under her breath, Daniel gave his nephew a playful cuff. 'Good luck persuading your mum. And what about you, William? What are you looking forward to?'

'Going to the beach.' His grey eyes looked shyly into his.

And wham, the emotion was back in his throat again.

The forecast for the weekend was cold but sunny. Thank God. He'd been so desperate to get Melissa and William all to himself he hadn't considered how dull a weekend by the beach would be in the rain. After packing his case he dumped it in the car and then, with nothing else to do, sat in the driver's seat.

While his fingers drummed the steering wheel, he glanced at his watch. Still half an hour before he was due to pick them up. And only a twenty-minute journey to her house. Exhaling in frustration he slid his phone from his jeans pocket and checked his messages. Finding there was nothing new, his heart settled in his chest. She hadn't bailed on him.

God, he was twitchy. Already this morning he'd double-checked with his long-suffering housekeeper that she'd filled the fridge and put on fresh bedding. Then he'd rung her again and asked her to put up a small Christmas tree. With mountains of tinsel. He didn't feel he could phone her a third time, even if he could think of something else that needed doing. Which he couldn't.

Cursing softly, he turned on the engine and shot off down the road.

Despite taking a long way round, he pulled up outside her house at 8.52 a.m.

Stay and wait it out? Or knock on the damn door?

A curtain twitched and William's head peeped out from the window, a grin splitting his face. Daniel was out of the car and knocking on the door in ten seconds flat.

Melissa answered, looking fresh-faced and gorgeous in slim jeans and a bright fleece, her hair pulled back in a ponytail. Her eyes though, when they finally met his, betrayed her nerves.

Deliberately he placed a hand on either side of her face and bent to kiss her, very thoroughly, on the mouth. 'Good morning.'

He had the satisfaction of watching at least some of her nerves recede. 'Good morning yourself.'

Out of the corner of his eye he was aware of William watching them, though the little guy didn't look put out, only curious. 'Morning champ. Are you guys packed?'

'You bet!'

'William's been packed for four days now,' Melissa expanded, smiling fondly at her son. 'He didn't know how much Lego to bring so I told him to bring it all. I hope you brought the big car.'

'I'm not experienced with the packing habits of young boys, but I know enough about the habits of women to bring a big car.'

Melissa smiled, as she knew Daniel expected, though inside she was feeling sick with nerves. How many women had he brought to his weekend home, she wondered as he lifted their cases into his Range Rover. How many had he seduced there?

She bit at her lip, cross with herself. She wasn't going to ruin the weekend with thoughts about what had gone on in the past. This was about now.

'I'll have you know my packing was quite minimalist,' she remarked as she climbed into the passenger seat.

The hungry look he shot told her exactly how minimalist he was hoping she'd been.

Unlike William, her packing quandary hadn't been about plastic bricks, but about ... underwear. She knew he was planning on seeing her underwear this weekend, and she also knew, barring a major falling out between them, that she was going to let him.

And though the thought had her stomach knotting with nerves, a long forgotten thrill pulsed between her legs.

'It's going to take us about two hours to get down there,' Daniel announced when they were on the motorway. 'Do you think you can both make it without stopping? We'll have hot chocolate and a mince pie on the beach when we arrive.'

Melissa arched an eyebrow. 'I hope you've got that mince pie you're promising. There's nothing worse than a man who doesn't deliver on his promises.'

He shot her a slow wink. 'Honey, I never make promises I can't fulfil.'

The two hours sped by and as they finally turned in to a quaint, shingle lane, Melissa caught sight of what she knew must be his house. Standing away from others and perched right on the edge of the beach, it was made primarily of wood, with massive glass windows and balconies facing the sea. 'Oh, Daniel, it's beautiful,' she whispered, enchanted.

He turned off the engine and smiled. 'Yes, she is, isn't she?' His brown eyes smouldered down at her, making it quite clear it wasn't his house he was referring to.

Embarrassed, her pulse skittering, she fussed about undoing her seat belt. She'd never met anyone who could make her feel so comfortable, and yet so off balance, at the same time.

Climbing down from his seat, Daniel went to open William's door. 'Come on, young man. I believe I promised you a mince pie.'

Needing no further encouragement, William jumped out of the car and started towards the house before coming to a sudden stop.

'It's okay, Will.' Daniel walked over and gave him a gentle push. 'It's your house for the weekend. Go off and explore. See if you can find the sea. But for goodness' sake stop before you get to it or your mum will kill me.'

'No, not kill,' she corrected. 'Though I might torture you slowly.'

William shot down the path and Daniel grinned, a flash of white against the cool blue of the sky. 'I might just enjoy that.' Again her heart jumped, but before she'd struggled to form a reply he was pushing her, too. 'Go and join your son. I'll unload.'

She started off but had only gone a couple of feet when she turned back and flung her arms around him. 'Thank you, Daniel. Thank you, thank you, thank you.'

Surprise flickered in his eyes and it thrilled her to know that for once, she'd been the one to catch him off guard.

On a burst of happiness she gave him a quick wave and headed down to the beach, her boots making a satisfying crunch over the shingle. She found William watching the waves as they rolled over and ploughed up the beach, his expression part fear, part wonder.

'Don't stand too close,' she cautioned. 'You'll get your feet wet.'

He shuffled back a bit, though his eyes never left the sea. As she hugged his small body, guilt pulled at her, knocking aside her new-found joy. Since she'd left Lawrence the pair of them had just ... existed. Lurching from day to day, trying to kick-start their new life together. Yes, she'd bought a house, found William a school and set up her own business, but in the process of coping with all that she'd forgotten the important things in life. Fun days out. Trips to the sea.

Already she had a lot to thank Daniel for. He'd shown them how to live again.

The sound of feet on pebbles brought her out of her thoughts and she turned to find that very man walking towards them, carrying a tray. 'Hot chocolate and mince pie delivery.'

William shrieked. 'Awesome. This is way, way better than school.'

After wolfing down the mince pies they scrambled back into the shelter of the house. Though it didn't seem possible, Melissa thought the place looked even better from the inside, the sea making a superb backdrop for every room. When she went into the sitting room and saw the wide patio windows leading out to decking and the beach, she sighed with pleasure.

'Look Mum, a Christmas tree!' William exclaimed as he saw the tree she'd missed, too absorbed with the view.

She glanced at her rosy-cheeked son, and then over to Daniel, who looked smugly satisfied. 'How?'

'I have a fairy.'

'I can see it,' William interrupted, pointing to the dainty figure perched on top of the small pine tree. 'We have a star on our tree, but I guess a fairy is okay.'

Daniel burst out laughing. 'I meant I have a real-life fairy. She keeps an eye on the house and gets it ready whenever I come down.'

'And how often do you manage that?' she asked, trying

to ignore the prickle of unease. She wasn't going to think of the other women who'd stood where she was. She wasn't.

'Not as often as I'd like.' He paused, his eyes searching. 'Is everything okay?'

She forced a smile. 'Of course it is.' Shifting away from his watchful gaze she draped an arm around her son. 'Shall we go and unpack?'

Daniel carried their bags upstairs and showed William to his room. Diplomatically he left her bag in a pretty room next door before leaving them to it, though not before whispering in her ear. 'When you've finished here, why don't you join me in the room at the end of the corridor? You might enjoy the view so much you'll want to come back later.'

With the husky promise of his words echoing in her ears, she hastily emptied the contents of their cases into the drawers. Leaving William to unpack his toys, she stepped into the corridor. And even though it was broad daylight, and she was only going to see his room, not carry out a midnight assignation, her pulse hammered.

Once she stepped inside, her jaw dropped. She didn't see the white-washed floorboards or the massive oak bed covered in blue and white pillows, at least not at first. Her eyes were glued to the wall-to-floor glass windows opening onto a wide glass balcony overlooking the sea.

'What do you think?' he asked, taking her hand and leading her to the large easy chair by the window. There he pulled her onto his lap. 'Has it convinced you to share my room tonight?'

'I was convinced before I arrived.' Feeling wonderfully cherished, she rested her head against his chest and sighed softly. 'You have an incredible place here. I think if I owned it I'd be tempted to come down every weekend.'

'I'd love to, but life and work get in the way.'

The feel of his body surrounding her, and the steady thump of his heart beneath her, made her bold. 'Do you bring a lot of ... guests here?'

'Alice and her family come down quite a bit. My parents sometimes.' He tilted her chin, eyes smiling down into hers. 'But that's not the answer you're looking for, is it?'

She toyed with a button on his shirt. 'No.'

'You're the only woman I've brought here who wasn't related to me,' he told her, his gaze honest and direct. 'I bought it for the peace and quiet. A place where I could come to terms with the change in my career. Not as a babe magnet, or a place to hold wild orgies. Or whatever else it is you're imagining.'

Like a flower sensing spring, her heart slowly unfurled in her chest. 'I guess you hold those at home instead.'

He let out an exasperated huff. 'Jesus, I don't ...' He stopped when she started to giggle. 'Very funny. Now kiss me.'

Her breath caught. 'You're very demanding all of a sudden.'

'You haven't seen anything yet.'

His eyes darkened, focusing in on her mouth, and her heart did a slow somersault in her chest. Tentatively, because it had been a long time since she'd made the first move, she pressed her lips to his.

'Mum, did you see the bath? It's huge.'

She lurched backwards – she was pretty sure her seven-nearly-eight year old son shouldn't be seeing her smooch with a man who wasn't her husband – and tried to scramble off Daniel's lap. But his arm tightened around her, keeping her where she was.

The woman in his arms had gone from pliant to rigid in the blink of an eye. Or more precisely, in the time it took her son to run into a room.

Daniel knew Melissa was experiencing all kinds of worries at their blatant display of closeness, but he also knew he wasn't the type to hide away from things. If he was going to have a relationship with William's mum, which he sincerely hoped he was, then he had to make sure William was okay with it. He had no intention of skulking around behind the boy's back.

'It's a Jacuzzi bath,' he told William, running a soothing hand up and down her arm. 'Have you ever tried one? It's where jets of water come out from the side and make bubbles.'

'Cool.' His eyes flickered curiously round the room before settling back on them.

'You know there's room up here for a small one, if you want to join us.' He shifted, making space between him and Melissa.

After a moment's indecision, William smiled shyly and clambered up to join them.

'Umph, you're heavier than I thought,' he groaned as William climbed over him. 'What does your mother feed you? Rocks?'

'Sometimes her cakes are like rocks.'

They shared a man-to-man smile while Melissa let out an indignant shriek. 'So, what do you want to do today?' he asked a short while later. 'We can go for a walk along the cliffs, take the car out somewhere or stay here and play dare with the waves.'

Daniel's eyes followed William's as he looked out at the sea. It was a calm day and the waves were pretty small by December standards, but perhaps for a boy who wasn't used to the sea they didn't seem that way. 'I'm not sure,' he replied quietly.

'The waves aren't very big, are they? Just right for a game of dare, I reckon.'

'What's that?'

'We dare each other to get closer to the sea. The winner is the one who gets the furthest in before a wave comes, without getting wet.' Daniel almost laughed out loud at Melissa's expression of horror. 'It's okay, girls don't have to play. It's pretty much a game for men, anyway.'

William had been looking unsure, but now he was grinning. 'Let's play dare.'

Melissa fussed around before they set off, making sure William was wrapped up warm with his coat, gloves and scarf. When Daniel pointed out that he was going out there too, she huffed. 'You're big enough and daft enough to look after yourself. Besides, it's your game, so your silly fault if you get cold.'

Slightly miffed he went in search of his coat. Being an ex-scout, he also snagged a towel.

'Has he got a spare pair of shoes and trousers?' he checked as William dashed ahead of them. 'Just in case.'

'Yes.' She chewed that damn lip of hers again, a sign she was worried. 'But is this really a good idea? It is December and the sea can be really rough. What if a freak big wave drags him out to sea?'

'You're good at the what ifs, aren't you?'

'I can't help it. I'm a worrier.'

Because she looked so delightful with her uncertain grey eyes and pink nose, he kissed her. 'And I'm a big strong man who has been known to take a dip in this very sea, even in winter. Trust me. On a day like today the only bad thing that could happen is he'll get his feet wet. But he won't mind, because secretly he'll be hoping that happens.'

Melissa followed them down to the sea and watched from a safe distance while Daniel showed William how to dart in and out of the waves. At first he would only take one step forwards before running away but it wasn't long before the adventure of it began to sink in and he forgot to be scared. Daniel egged him on, encouraging him to go further and further in while always keeping right beside him, just in case.

Predictably, they took it one step too far.

'It's going to get me!' William shouted as he raced back to the beach. In his haste to get away he stumbled and though Daniel hauled him up, out of the water, the wave had already done its damage.

To both of them.

William collapsed onto the beach and for a heart-stopping moment Daniel froze. What if he'd pushed the boy too far, like he had the mother? What if he'd put him off the sea forever?

But then William raised his head, howling with laughter. 'It got us. My feet are squelchy.'

His heart beating once more, Daniel clutched William's hand and pulled him to his feet. 'Come on. Last one inside makes the tea. Let's make sure it's your mum.'

'I heard that, Daniel McCormick,' Melissa shouted after them but her voice was drowned out by the sound of scrunching pebbles as they raced to the house.

He'd delivered the challenge to make William laugh, but when he collapsed inside Daniel realised it had been a long while since he'd laughed so much, too. A long while since he'd allowed his inner child to break free.

It was exhilarating.

By the time Melissa arrived, they were taking off their soggy shoes and socks. 'Oops,' he said in a loud voice as she shut the patio door behind her. 'Looks like your mum lost.'

William sniggered. 'She's a girl. They're slow.'

He heard Melissa suck in a breath, but didn't give her a chance to retort. 'Still, at least tea will be good.'

A torrent of words tumbled out of her: *arrogant male, stereotypical attitude, she hoped she was bringing her son up better than that.*

When Daniel put his hands over his ears, William did the same. To her credit, Melissa stopped talking and burst out laughing.

'Okay, okay, you're both so funny. Why don't you boys get changed while I do the girl thing.'

William was half way out of the door when he suddenly stopped. 'Can I have a bath?'

Melissa frowned, obviously confused. 'Well sure, but usually I have to force you into one.'

When he didn't reply, just shuffled his feet, Daniel twigged. 'I'm guessing you mean in the Jacuzzi?' His grin was all the answer Daniel needed. 'Go and get it running. I'll be up in a minute to show you how the jets work.'

When he'd disappeared Daniel switched on the Christmas tree lights and popped his iPod into the music system, scrolling down to his one Christmas album. With the choir gearing up to sing 'Hark the Herald Angels', he strode over to Melissa and ran a hand over her ponytail. 'Don't fret about tea. It was a joke. My fairy housekeeper has left us a giant cottage pie which even I can manage to put in the oven.'

She let out a heartfelt sigh. 'Perfect.' Then she shocked him by reaching up and giving him a long, heated kiss.

'I'm not complaining,' he told her thickly when they came up for air, 'but what was that for?'

'For asking us here, for getting a tree.'

'Hey, it doesn't feel like Christmas without a tree.'

'Sometimes it doesn't feel like Christmas with a tree, either.' He cocked his head, encouraging her to expand. 'I used to think I was weird, because I've never liked Christmas. But now ...' She stared at the tree as the uplifting voices of the carol singers filled the room. 'Now I'm starting to understand what all the fuss is about.'

'Good.' He kissed the end of her nose. 'Magical things happen at Christmas time.'

'Maybe.' Her eyes dropped to his throat. 'And speaking of fuss, thank you for making one of William. He loves all the attention and it's so good for him.'

'No need to thank me. He's easy to like.' He cupped her chin and lost himself in her eyes. 'I could say the same about his mother.'

She blinked, slowly. 'You're easy to like, too.'

'I used to think so, but I was beginning to wonder if you'd ever realise it.'

She smiled, her lips curving against his throat. 'I liked you right away. It just took me a while to realise I shouldn't allow fear to rule me any more.'

He smoothed his hands over her shoulders and down her arms. 'You have nothing to fear from me, Melissa. I hope you know that.'

'I'm starting to.' Her eyes were wide and trusting. 'That's why I'm here.'

In that moment Daniel tumbled out of like. And straight into love.

Chapter Thirteen

William went to sleep as soon as his head touched the pillow. Kissing his hair, Melissa smiled gently down at him. What a day it had been, for both of them.

And for her, it wasn't over yet.

Her pulse picked up as she walked down the stairs. By the time she reached the entrance to the sitting room she could hear the thumping of her heart. Daniel was watching the television, his large frame bent as he rested his elbows on his knees, his eyes glued to the screen. Carols still played through the speakers and he'd dimmed the lights so the Christmas tree sparkled. The scene made her heart stir. Made her imagine a Christmas like the ones she'd seen in films. A Christmas where people laughed. And loved.

She shook off the sentimental feeling. Her son was the only person she needed to make her Christmas complete.

As she stepped into the room, her eyes strayed back to Daniel and she realised this wasn't quite the happy, Christmas scene she'd thought. He appeared uncharacteristically tense. Lost in his own thoughts as he stared at the screen.

That's when she realised he wasn't watching a festive film, but the repeat of an old tennis match.

On instinct she knelt down in front of him and wrapped her arms around his neck.

He leant into her on a sigh. 'Mmm, that feels good.'

'Are you okay? You look a little down.'

'Sorry.' He sat up, indicating for her to sit next to him.

136

Taking hold of the remote control he snapped off the television, then pulled her into his arms. 'It's nothing a cuddle with a gorgeous woman can't remedy.'

'You don't need to turn it off on my account.'

'I'm not. I'm turning it off for me. I watch the damn stuff out of habit.'

'Or because you miss it.'

He grunted. 'Maybe.' When she arched her eyebrows, he gave her a sheepish smile. 'Okay smart ass. Yes, I watch it because I miss it.'

'I can't believe you managed to find any on the television at this time of year.'

'It's pretty much always on, if you know where to look.'

'And you always look?' Another embarrassed smile. She decided she liked it almost as much as his cocky one. 'If you hadn't been injured, what tournament would you have been preparing for now?'

'The Australian open is in January.' His arms tightened around her. 'Instead I'm here, cuddling you. It's hard to feel sorry for me.'

But she did. He hadn't deserved such cruel luck. 'I never asked. How did it go in the US? It must be hard playing in charity tournaments rather than real ones.'

'Yes.' And in that single word she felt his loss. All this time she'd been the one moaning about being scared of loving and losing again, but he was right. He'd loved and lost, too. 'I used to enjoy playing in them when I was a pro, but it's tough knowing they're the only tournaments you're going to be taking part in.' He dropped a kiss onto her head. 'Enough about all that. How's William? Did he settle down okay?'

She smiled as she pictured her happy but exhausted son

flaked out on the bed. 'He went out like a light. Must be the sea air.'

'I hope it hasn't made you too sleepy,' he murmured, nibbling her ear.

Her pulse spiked, but this time it was more with nerves than desire. Wanting him was one thing. Actually having him, she was starting to realise, was something else entirely.

He must have felt her stiffen because he angled his head to look at her. 'Hey, what's wrong?'

One glance at his puzzled brown eyes and she knew she had to be honest. 'Please don't laugh, but I'm feeling nervous.'

He tugged her closer and she felt his lips smile against her hair. 'Me too.'

Laughter burst out of her. 'You? Never. I can't imagine you've ever been nervous about anything. Even match point at Wimbledon.'

'I was never nervous when I played,' he agreed, his fingers lightly toying with her hair. 'Excited, pumped up, but never nervous. I am nervous about how I'm starting to feel about you, though,' he told her softly, his lips warm on her face as he showered her with kisses.

Her throat closed and she shut her eyes, afraid of what her own might show if she opened them.

Silently he shifted them round so they were both stretched out on the sofa, her laying half on top of him. 'That's better. Now I can feel how well we fit together.'

They remained like that for a while, the only sounds those of the carols playing quietly through the stereo, the sea rolling up the beach and the reassuring thump of his heart. Slowly she began to relax.

'Nothing will happen if you don't want it to,' he said quietly, his hands stroking gently along her arms.

'But I do want it to.' She raised her head to look into his eyes. 'Very much.'

'Good. So do I.' Carefully he drew the hair from her neck and kissed her nape. 'Now all you have to do is to relax and trust me.'

She snuggled closer, drawing on his warmth. 'You make everything sound so simple, so easy. It must be wonderful to have such self-belief.'

He chuckled. 'It comes from knowing I'm loved. I've been exceptionally lucky. All my life I've known, no matter what I did, my parents loved me. From the sound of things, you haven't been that fortunate.'

'No.' He'd wrapped himself around her and she felt so secure the next words escaped without her thinking. 'I don't think my parents ever loved me.'

'Oh?' His arms tensed. 'When did you come to that conclusion?'

'It probably wasn't until my early teens. I was always a bit shy, but there was a time when I brimmed with as much confidence as the other girls I boarded with.' She slid him a glance.

'What?'

'I'm just checking you're not smirking.'

'Hey, I don't doubt for a moment that you have confidence. You seem to find it easily enough when you're arguing with me.'

She smiled. 'That's not confidence. It's just standing up for myself. I guess what I'm saying is I used to be a more positive person, but over time my parents' lack of interest chipped away at it. I can remember being excited about giving a ballet performance because it was a rare chance to see them during term time. Of course they didn't turn up.' His chest rose sharply, but he didn't say anything.

'There were other concerts, other occasions, and in the end I stopped hoping. It became easier to believe they wouldn't come. Then I wasn't disappointed.'

'And the glass became half empty.'

He understood. The realisation helped her to voice what she'd never told anyone. 'I'm pretty certain I was an accident. My parents were both devoted to their careers, probably even more than they were devoted to each other. Taking care of a child really got in the way so they palmed me off on nannies and boarding school. They never wanted me.'

'In which case they were stupid. And you're the most gorgeous accident I've ever met.' As he spoke her fingers ran idly across his chest, the pleasure of touching him helping to dull the painful memories of her childhood. When they meandered lower, he groaned. 'You're also going to cause an accident if you carry on doing that.'

She snatched her fingers away. 'Sorry.'

'Oh no. Don't ever be sorry for touching me.' In one swift movement he stood and lifted her into his arms. 'I think we should continue this upstairs.'

Carrying her as if she was weightless, he climbed the stairs and went into his bedroom, laying her carefully on the huge bed. 'Do you think you can stand me undressing you?' he whispered hoarsely. 'Because I need to do that. I need to do it very much.'

She nodded, trying to relax as he peeled off all her layers. 'I hope you won't be disappointed with what you find. Models tend to look better with their clothes on.'

'I'll be the judge of that.' With hands that were sure and confident, he expertly undid her bra.

Slowly, almost reverently, his long fingers touched her bare breast and she stifled a gasp. As his head bent to kiss her nipple, his tongue making clever circles around the sensitive peak, she couldn't prevent the strangled cry that escaped her, or the instinctive arch of her back as she silently urged him to continue.

'My God, Melissa, you take my breath away.'

His eyes found hers and he made no attempt to hide his feelings. She saw his hunger, his desire and, as his eyes travelled up and down her body, his frank and total admiration. And under that heated gaze, the girl with the awkward, misfitting features felt truly beautiful. 'Thank you. I think you'd take my breath away, too, if you took your clothes off.'

Smiling wickedly he quickly unbuttoned his shirt and unsnapped his jeans. Now it was her turn to watch hungrily as muscles rippled beneath tanned skin. A dusting of dark hair drew her eye from his chest to his stomach, and lower. Unable to resist, she smoothed her fingers over his hot skin. As the muscles tightened a thrill raced through her, dark and urgent.

'Lie down,' he urged, pushing her onto the mattress. She tried to keep her eyes open, not wanting to miss the sight of his powerful body as it moved over her. But then he touched her between her legs, and her eyes slammed shut. As his hands worked what had to be magic, she had no room in her mind for anything but feeling.

Her orgasm came quickly and gloriously, leaving her totally drained.

'Still nervous?'

Her eyes slowly came back into focus to find his face hovering over hers. There was a smugness in his smile, though the tension around the edges of it hinted at his continued control. She let out a sigh of deep feminine pleasure. 'I don't think I'll ever feel tense again.'

Capturing her mouth in his, he thrust into her in one lusty, fluid movement.

Daniel lay on top of her, totally spent. If a burglar burst in, he doubted he'd have the energy to raise his head, never mind chase the guy away. He knew he must feel like a lead weight but he couldn't move, not just yet. Not when she'd drained him of his last breath.

When he thought he could find his voice, he lifted his head. Her eyes were closed but her expression could only be described as serene. 'You slayed me, Melissa. Totally slayed me.'

Her lips curved and her grey eyes blinked open. 'Ditto.'

With a groan he eased himself off her and lay back against the sheets, dragging her body so it fit snugly against his side. 'I know I promised you a whole night of passion, but that was before you drained every ounce of energy from me.'

She curled into him. 'I only have Lawrence to compare with, but tonight was ... well ... wow. Just wow.'

Only Lawrence. It was a reminder of how far she'd allowed him in. 'Are you going to stay, so we can be wow again in a while?' He felt her smile against his skin and was amazed when his body stirred. Not dead, after all.

'I'd love to, but I want to make sure I'm in the spare bed before William wakes up.' She raised herself up, resting on her elbows. 'I'm not sure how he would take finding us in the same bed. I hope you understand.'

He did, though he couldn't pretend he wasn't disappointed. 'By my calculation that still gives us several hours to concentrate on exploring each other, to our mutual satisfaction.'

'I thought you were drained of energy?'

142

He shrugged and, quick as a fox, pulled her up so she was lying on top of him. 'What can I say? I was a professional athlete. We're known for our stamina.'

He then set out to demonstrate, time and time again, how good his stamina really was.

As dawn broke slowly on Sunday morning, Daniel carried her to the spare room and tucked her into bed.

When he returned to his own bed, he slept like the dead.

Chapter Fourteen

Daniel started the morning the second best way he knew how. He went for a run along the beach. As he pounded out the miles along the shingle – a serious work-out for the legs – he contemplated how he would have preferred to start the morning. Wrapped around a naked Melissa. She'd been fast asleep when he'd peeped in earlier, looking almost angelic with her blonde hair draped over her pillow like a halo. He'd checked in on William, too. A small figure almost drowned by the double bed, his thin legs had stuck out from the edge of the duvet like twigs.

His heart had stirred at the sight of them both.

An hour after he'd set off he collapsed onto the decking, peering through the patio doors to see if there was any life yet. Hmm, there was definitely movement. It came in the form of a small figure studying the Christmas tree. And moving the baubles round.

Daniel pushed open the door. 'Morning sleepy head. The tree not decorated to your standard?'

William jumped and took a guilty step back. 'Sorry.'

'Hey.' He draped an arm round his shoulders, hating that William still wasn't fully relaxed around him. 'That was a joke, not a complaint. You can touch it all you like. I got it for you.'

'You did?'

'Yeah. I don't bother with one just for me.'

'Why not? Trees are cool.'

'They are, if you've got someone to share one with.'

William nodded pensively and then turned his attention back to re-decorating the tree.

'Your mum up yet?'

'Nah. I tried to wake her, but she smiled and went back to sleep. I think she must be tired.'

Daniel fought hard to suppress a grin. He knew exactly why Melissa was so shattered this morning. 'Looks like it's you and me on breakfast duty then. What do you fancy?'

Following a quick sortie of the cupboards they decided on cornflakes.

'Did you send your letter off to Father Christmas?' Daniel asked while they munched. 'It's only a few days to go.'

'I did.' Eyes down, William continued to crunch through his breakfast.

'Okay, good. So if you get a racket from him, will you believe he exists?'

'I guess.' He paused for a moment and licked at his spoon. 'I added that second thing as well.'

'Right. And are you still not going to tell me what the second wish is?'

Finally William looked at him. 'Would you tell mum?'

No. The word was on the tip of his tongue, but a quick glance at William's trusting grey eyes and Daniel found he couldn't say it. 'I don't know,' he hedged.

'Then I can't tell you, 'cos then I wouldn't know if he exists, would I?'

It was hard to argue with his logic.

Melissa appeared a few minutes later, wearing loose-fitting pyjama bottoms and a fleece, her hair uncombed, her face make-up free. She smiled sleepily over at him and his heart cartwheeled.

'Sorry I'm so late. I couldn't seem to wake up.'

He gave her a knowing look. 'It must have been all that ... umm ... exercise yesterday.'

'It was the sea air,' she stated firmly, walking to the

breakfast bar and planting a kiss on William's head. 'Do I get any breakfast?'

'Oh yes.' He poured her a mug of the coffee he'd just made and placed a cereal bowl in front of her. 'I like to take care of my guests.'

Daniel's voice was low and flirtatious and Melissa felt a warm flush seep through her. How silly to have woken up worried there'd be awkwardness between them this morning. A man like Daniel probably didn't know the meaning of the word awkward.

'What do you want to do today?' His words flowed over her but Melissa found she was only half listening, her mind taken more with watching his biceps bunch as he spread butter onto toast. 'You've got choices. We can go to the pier where there's a Christmas fair.' *If he wanted her to listen, why didn't he throw a sweatshirt on over his running top? And put on some tracksuit bottoms?* 'There'll be rides and stalls and maybe the odd roasted chestnut thrown in. Or we can walk along the cliffs as we didn't get round to it yesterday.'

'Both,' William declared, grabbing at the offered toast.

'Is that okay with you, Melissa?'

Not fully certain what she was agreeing to, Melissa nodded.

'Good decision.' Daniel shoved his plate into the dishwasher and clunked the door shut. 'But that means we need to get a move on. Dressed and by the door in ...' He glanced at the clock on the wall. '... twenty minutes.'

He was walking away when she cleared her throat. 'Shouldn't that have been a question?'

'Nope. My house, my rules.'

'Bossy man,' she muttered under her breath as he disappeared off for his shower.

'Nice man.'

William's voice was so quiet she almost didn't hear him. Part of her wished she hadn't. Oh God, please don't let this ... whatever it was she and Daniel were having. Don't let it end up hurting her precious son.

With her heart feeling too full, she took a step back. It was easy, far too easy, to imagine everything she saw was real. That they were a family. William chomped happily on his toast at the breakfast bar, his Lego bricks scattered carelessly across the floor behind her. Her fleece from yesterday was draped over the back of the sofa. Behind that, the baubles on the Christmas tree blinked cheerfully in the weak winter sun as it shone through the patio doors.

But this *wasn't* their house, and her dream of having somebody to love her had led to a nightmare she was only just pulling out of. How could she risk diving headfirst into another one?

'Mum, can Daniel spend Christmas with us?'

She jumped, the coffee she was sipping scalding the back of her mouth. 'Why do you ask?'

He pointed over at the Christmas tree. 'He said he only put the tree up 'cos we were coming. He thinks trees are for sharing.' Serious grey eyes rested on her. 'He doesn't have anyone to share one with, does he?'

She started to feel hot, then cold. 'Not in his own house, no, but I can't imagine he'll spend the day there. I expect he'll be with Alice and Simon. Or perhaps with his parents.'

'But I want him to be with us.' There was a rare defiance in his eyes, and belligerence to his voice.

'You know *I want* doesn't get,' she remarked evenly, trying to hide her fear at the topic, though she felt a smidgen of relief, too, at the child-like normality of his reaction to not getting his way. 'Christmas Day is meant for families, not for friends. I'm sure we'll see Daniel during the Christmas period. Now, if you want to do … all the things Daniel suggested, you need to go and get dressed.'

Immediately he jumped off the bar stool and raced up the stairs, leaving Melissa with a strong feeling that this wasn't the end of the discussion. That perhaps, it was only the start.

The walk along the cliffs was invigorating. At least that's the word Daniel kept using when Melissa complained that the wind was going to blow them away. If it didn't freeze them to death first. She was exceptionally glad to see the beach house again.

'Can we say goodbye to the waves?' William pleaded, dragging on her hand.

'But you've seen them all the time we've been walking.'

'Not properly. Not up close.'

Daniel chuckled. 'I think your mum's a bit cold. I'll go with you while we leave her to warm up.'

Melissa gratefully left them to it and headed inside. From her vantage point on his armchair, away from the biting wind, she watched the two figures – one broad and incredibly tall, one slight and comparatively tiny – as they walked towards the sea.

Daniel picked up stones and showed them to William. A few seconds later he was whipping one across the waves.

Her heart lifted and filled. He was teaching her son to skim.

Leaving them to it she went to gather up their things, trying not to overthink as she found something of William's in practically every room of the house. He'd made himself at home. It meant he'd been relaxed and happy, which was good, wasn't it?

Leaving the bags stacked neatly by the front door she

settled back in the armchair ... and her heart leapt into her throat. Daniel had taken off his shoes and socks, rolled up his jeans and was holding William up by the feet, just like he'd done with Simon when they'd first met. Only this time he was dangling her son over the *waves*.

She stood quickly and jammed on her boots. Couldn't Daniel see that William was very different from Simon? Only yesterday he'd been scared to play with them. Now Daniel had him dangling over them, head first. Her body vibrating with alarm, she ran down to the sea.

'Daniel, what the hell do you think you're doing?' she yelled.

It was only as Daniel turned towards her that she caught sight of William's face. It wasn't the frightened expression she'd been terrified of seeing, but one alive with laughter. 'Look, Mum, I'm flying over the waves.'

Silently Daniel hauled William into his arms, before striding out of the sea and setting him down on the beach. 'I think your mum was worried I was going to drop you,' he remarked mildly. Without looking at her he sat on the pebbles and wiped at his wet feet with his socks.

Shame slapped straight into relief. 'I wasn't afraid you'd drop him.'

He glanced up, eyes guarded. 'You were afraid of something.'

'Yes. I didn't think William would enjoy what you were doing to him. It seems I was wrong. I'm sorry.' Her words sounded stiff and awkward. The fact that Daniel had understood her son more than she had compounded her embarrassment.

He pushed his feet into his boots and stood, surprising her by kissing her softly on the forehead. 'Hey, no harm done. You're his mother. It's your job to nurture and protect.'

'Maybe, but it's also my job to help him grow. To let him find his feet and make his own mark in life.'

'And you will.' His eyes filled with understanding as he smiled at her. 'Sadly holding a child up by the ankles isn't the answer to everything.'

They stopped off at the pier on the way home, as he'd promised William. The place had undergone a seasonal make-over and Christmas lights twinkled festively over all the usual rides. There was a Santa's grotto too, but it looked pretty shoddy so Daniel steered William away from it. If the guy was already unconvinced about Father Christmas, the sight of an overweight man in a poorly fitting red costume would seal the deal.

They were walking away from a session of trampoline bouncing when he realised Melissa wasn't by his side. Looking back over his shoulder he found her staring at the tacky booth of the palm reader advertising Christmas predictions.

He raised an eyebrow. 'You've got to be kidding.'

She sighed. 'Yes, you're right. I know it's nonsense.' But still she remained where she was, her attention fixed on the wild claims scrawled in gold paint across the booth. *Want to know what this Christmas has in store for you? Come inside.*

'Go on in,' he encouraged. 'I'll take William for a drink and you can meet us in the café. That way, when she tells you a tall, dark handsome man will whisk you off your feet this Christmas, she'll be right.'

'What's Mum doing?' William asked as Melissa mouthed thank you and darted into the booth.

'A woman inside that booth is going to charge her a silly sum of money to look at her hand and predict her future.'

'How can she tell the future from a hand?'

'She can't, and your mum knows that. She just enjoys the game. A bit like having a story read to you. You know it's not true, but it can still be fun to listen.'

After ordering – a coffee, hot chocolate and two fat, sugary jam doughnuts – they found a cosy corner in the café to settle down in.

'I asked Mum if you could spend Christmas day with us,' William announced, slurping at his drink and leaving a chocolate moustache across his mouth.

With his cup half-way to his lips, Daniel's hand stilled. 'Oh? What did she say?'

'She said you'd probably be with Alice or your mum and dad. Will you?'

Choppy waters. 'I'm not sure yet,' he hedged. 'I haven't made any plans.'

'Mum said Christmas day was a time for families, but if you marry her then we'll be a family, won't we?'

Oh shit. How had the waters gone from choppy to stormy in the blink of an eye? 'I guess, if that did happen, then we would be a family,' he agreed cautiously.

'Are you going to marry her?'

He'd entered the eye of the storm. As William stared back at him, quietly demanding an answer, Daniel knew there was no easy way back to safety. 'I don't know,' he replied honestly. 'It's early days, but I'm thinking that maybe, in a while, I might ask her. I don't know what her answer will be though.' He gulped at his coffee.

'Would that make you my dad?'

Christ. He'd navigated his way out of the stormy water, only to be hit by another huge wave. 'No, it wouldn't. You already have a dad.'

'I guess. But I'd rather have you.'

The breath left his lungs and Daniel had to fight to get the next words out. 'That's a really nice thing to say. I'd be proud to have a son like you.' Emotion clogged his throat and, damn it, filled his eyes. 'Maybe we can settle on being good friends.' Because he didn't know what else to do, Daniel held out his hand.

Solemnly William shook it.

With the tension now threatening to choke him, Daniel did the only thing he could think of. He grabbed at the remains of William's doughnut and started to eat it.

William's jaw dropped open and his eyes nearly popped out of their sockets. Then he burst into giggles.

And Daniel fell even further into love with Melissa's son.

It was early evening by the time Daniel parked his four-by-four outside Melissa's house. While Melissa went to open the door, he reached into the boot for their bags. In addition to the luggage they'd set off with, there was now a collection of pebbles and a giant inflatable snowman.

'I'm not sure we need the snowman,' Melissa stated as she came back to help him unload. 'You won it, so by rights it's yours.'

'Oh no you don't,' he returned quickly, pulling the plastic white object out of the car. 'I won it for William so it's his now. You know it's rude to turn down a gift, don't you?'

Melissa sighed and took the offending object from him. 'The palmist promised me tall, dark handsome men. Not inflatable snowmen.'

'I told you they know nothing,' he countered, hauling the last of the cases up her path and into the hallway.

All shy again – was this really the same boy who'd quizzed him about marrying his mother a few hours ago? – William thanked him for the weekend and trudged up the stairs. But once he'd reached the top he looked down and gave him a small wave.

A lump rose at the back Daniel's throat.

When he turned to find Melissa watching him with the same pair of quiet grey eyes, the lump grew larger. 'Do I get a drink or am I being kicked out?' he asked softly.

She didn't answer straight away and he could almost see the ease of the weekend ebbing away as she stepped into her home. His frustration made him want to shake her. Remind her that they were still the same people who'd shared a bed only a few hours ago. He settled for a truculent, 'Well?'

She swallowed. 'Of course you can stay for a drink.'

Chapter Fifteen

Melissa's hands shook a little as she made both her and Daniel a coffee. Thankfully the cause of her unease had gone upstairs to say goodnight to William, giving her a few moments to compose herself.

It wasn't as if there was one thing she could pin her emotional jitteriness on. It was a whole raft of feelings and thoughts that had flooded to the surface when she'd watched William solemnly wave down at Daniel. There was the reality of coming home after a wonderful weekend away. The adoration she'd seen in her son's eyes. The reading from the palmist who'd told her love was staring her in the face this Christmas. If she was brave enough to reach out for it.

Overriding everything was the knowledge that, like her son, she didn't want Daniel to go home.

It was that last thought that made her hands tremble. Relying on someone else for her emotional happiness again terrified her.

She jumped as Daniel came up behind her and slid his arms around her waist, warm and steady. 'Hey, it's only me.' He lifted her hair and planted a soft kiss on her neck.

'Sorry, I was miles away.' She drew in a deep breath, picked up the mugs and turned round. 'Shall we take these into the sitting room?'

He accepted his mug but didn't move. 'Are you okay?'

'I'm fine.' Because she knew he wouldn't leave it at that, and because she was a terrible actor, she gave him at least part of the truth. 'Just, you know, that feeling of coming back down to earth. It was a pretty amazing weekend.'

His lips curved. 'It was, wasn't it?'

She led the way and went to sit on the sofa. Daniel placed his mug on the coffee table and sat down next to her.

'So, only a few days until Christmas. Have you solved the William second wish puzzle yet?'

'No. I'm just going to have to hope he's satisfied with the racket, which does presume that was the first item on the list.'

'Oh, it was,' he asserted with his usual confidence.

'And you know that because you've seen the letter?'

'Well, no, not exactly. William told me he'd asked for it though, so I'm pretty certain he will have done.'

'I see, so that's one item I'm *pretty certain* my son wants and another I haven't a clue about. It's not exactly a ringing endorsement for your idea of convincing him about Father Christmas, is it?'

She was rewarded with his full on sheepish grin, complete with twinkling eyes. 'Oops.'

'Exactly.' Though it was hard to be cross with someone who could grin like that. 'I suppose getting half what he wants will simply mean the jury is still out on the concept, so no harm done.'

'And Father Christmas has chosen a fantastic racket.'

Since Daniel had picked it out for her, she couldn't deny that. 'He has.'

'I'd love to be there when he opens it.'

She tried not to flinch. Tried to sip at her coffee as if he hadn't just thrown a live hand grenade into the conversation. But she might have known he wouldn't simply leave it at that.

'So what are your plans for Christmas?' he asked into the silence. 'Do they have any room for me?'

'I know William wants you to come over on Christmas

day,' she stated carefully, grinding to a halt as her mind couldn't work out what it wanted to say next.

'But you don't.'

That wasn't it. 'That's not true. You know I enjoy your company, but Christmas Day is too ...' Oh help, she couldn't finish her sentences.

'Too what? Too early? Too special? Too hectic?'

'It's certainly not the last one, not with just me and William.' How did she explain that seeing him on Christmas Day made their relationship seem too important, too permanent?

He shifted his long legs and she felt both his tension and his disappointment. 'When do I get to see you then?'

'I don't know.' She lowered her lashes. 'I don't want to rush into anything. For William's sake, we need to be careful.'

He sighed heavily. 'You're not just thinking about William, are you?'

'No,' she admitted.

'How about Boxing Day? Or is that too ... as well?'

There was an edge to his tone that had her eyes flying up to his face, but where she'd expected to find irritation, she only found hurt. 'Please don't be upset. It's not that I don't want to see you. Just that I want to take things slowly. Christmas Day is for families, not for lovers.'

She watched as he leant forward and threaded a hand restlessly through his hair. 'And Boxing Day?'

There was a tightness to his features and to his voice that she'd rarely seen. She found she didn't have the heart to tell him she thought that was a family day, too. 'Boxing Day would be fine.'

He exhaled loudly. 'Okay then. Cold turkey it is.'

To his credit, though it clearly wasn't the outcome he'd

wanted, he gave her a smile. A little forced, a little tired, the fact that he tried at all meant more than she was prepared to admit. 'I'll look forward to it,' she stated softly, running her hand down his arm.

He sat back, letting out a half laugh. 'I suspect not half as much as I will.'

For a pulsing moment his eyes held hers and she could almost feel his hunger. Then he dipped his head and sank into her mouth, his lips hot and eager. For a while he drove them both mad, pushing them further and further towards the brink of no return.

Moments before she fell over the cliff, Melissa pulled away, her breathing ragged. 'We need to stop.'

Cursing, Daniel flopped back against the sofa, fighting for air. Waiting for his heart and the rest of him to calm. No woman had ever made him lose control like Melissa did. 'I want to stay the night.' He sounded truculent and hated himself for it.

'I don't think that's a good idea.'

'Why not?' Frustration made his voice sharper than he'd intended.

'Because it's too much, too soon. Like Christmas Day.' Her eyes begged him to understand. 'We've already spent the weekend together. It's too much to have William waking up in his own home, finding a man in bed with his mother.'

'It wouldn't be a man,' he countered. 'It would be me. And I could be long gone before William wakes up.' When she didn't reply he heaved out a sigh. 'But that isn't the only issue, is it?'

'Daniel, please stop pushing me,' she pleaded. 'I want to be with you again but you need to give both me and William time and space to get used to all this.'

Frustration mixed volatilely with thwarted desire. 'Hell, this is so damn hard.'

'I'm sure there are plenty of women out there who'd be happy to make it easy for you,' she snapped.

'Is that what you want?'

Her hesitation nearly undid him. 'No,' she finally replied. 'It isn't what I want.'

The breath he'd been holding rushed out of his lungs though he found he was too unsteady to form a reply.

'I warned you at the beginning that I didn't want a relationship,' she continued, and he would have believed she was unaffected by the conversation were it not for her hands twisting in her lap. 'Yet you pushed and pushed and now it appears we're in one. A fabulous weekend by the sea doesn't suddenly make this easy for me though.'

'No.' He made himself take a breath, remembering all she'd told him about her marriage. How she'd spent most of her life bending to someone else's tune. Trying to force her to bend to his wasn't just stupid, it was guaranteed to lose him the two people he was fast discovering he didn't want to live without. 'Will you hit me if I say I'm glad I'm not the only one having a tough time?' He softened his words with a wry smile.

Her light eyes studied his face and he wondered what they saw. 'I do want you.' She spoke the words slowly, as if they were being dragged from her. 'I just don't want that desire to take over, to overwhelm me. I need to know I'm in control. That the choices I'm making are mine. I've had somebody run my life already. I won't ever let that happen again.'

'You think that's what I'm trying to do?' Fear trickled up his spine. He'd ballsed this up, big time.

He must have looked as terrified as he felt because

her eyes softened and she trailed gentle fingers across his jawline. 'No, I don't. You're determined and supremely confident but not controlling or ruthless.' She gave him a small smile. 'At least not away from the tennis court. I just need you to ease your foot off the pedal a little.'

The soft light from the lamp behind her shone onto her face, accentuating the clarity of her eyes and the fullness of her lips. She had the look of a porcelain vase, a delicate, almost fragile beauty, but that was deceptive. She was, in fact, incredibly strong. Certainly she held him in the palm of her hand, though she didn't even know it.

Because his instinct, when pushed into a corner, was to come out fighting, he deliberately bent down for another kiss. He was gentler this time, more in control. And when he eventually pulled back, it was her who looked utterly undone. 'If you don't want me to make love to you,' he whispered, 'you shouldn't look so damn sexy.'

Her eyes shot open and the last remnants of tension slipped from her face as she started to giggle. 'Oh God, how am I ever going to resist you?'

'You seem to be doing a good job of it tonight,' he muttered, giving in for a moment and nuzzling her neck.

He heard her gentle sigh. 'Only at considerable personal cost.'

'Good.' Abruptly he jumped to his feet before he ended up going back down a track he knew wouldn't end the way he wanted it to. 'I'll see you Boxing Day. Come to my house and plan to stay the night.'

'I ... umm.' He could almost see her mind trying to think up excuses, but thankfully coming up empty. 'Okay.'

Settling for the small victory, he gave her one final kiss before letting himself out.

*

159

The next few days went by quickly for Melissa. With just her and William to worry about, there was no pre-Christmas day urgency, so they took time to enjoy the small things. Making mince pies, watching Christmas films on the television, choosing the turkey. Along with Alice and her children, they also went to see Father Christmas in his grotto, complete with reindeer. Unsurprisingly, Simon dashed straight in, breathlessly reciting all the things he wanted for Christmas. William hung back, shaking his head when she asked if he wanted to go in next. Still, the fact that he couldn't take his eyes off the jolly round man in the red jacket was enough.

Two days before Christmas Lawrence decided to upset the happy spirit that had lingered since their weekend away, by knocking on their door.

This time he was with Evangeline – and Sabine.

'I'm not prepared to go through some lawyer to talk to my ex-wife,' he declared as she opened the door. 'It's time my son met soon-to-be members of his family. William, this is my fiancé Evangeline and her daughter, Sabine.'

A wild-eyed William, who'd dashed to the door with Melissa, clearly hoping it would be Daniel, immediately clutched at her hand.

Melissa was torn between wanting to slam the door shut, yet not wanting to appear rude to Evangeline's daughter. Lawrence and Evangeline, she had no problem being rude to.

Before she'd made up her mind how to handle the situation, Lawrence pushed his way in, taking over as usual. 'Coffee seems to be in order. Evangeline has hers black.'

Figuring it was less stressful for William if she bit back her anger and accepted the situation, Melissa strode into the kitchen and started to make the drinks. An awkward silence seeped through the house and she struggled for something to say.

'Perhaps you'd like to show Sabine your room, William,' she suggested. That way he would be out of the way from the father he kept darting nervous glances towards.

William nodded and immediately raced to the stairs, clearly relieved. Sabine flicked back her long dark hair, let out a theatrical sigh and trooped out after him.

'Sabine is wonderful with other children,' Evangeline declared pompously. 'I'm sure she can persuade poor little William out of his shell.'

Melissa levelled her a look. 'You respect my son, and I'll respect your daughter.'

Evangeline's eyes shot into her hair-line at Melissa's tone, but thankfully she made no further comment, accepting the drink and following her through to the sitting room where she sat next to her fiancé on the sofa.

'So, isn't this nice.' Lawrence spoke into the stilted atmosphere, his expression telling her he knew exactly how annoyed she was with him and was enjoying it.

'I would have appreciated the courtesy of some warning.'

'But we're spontaneous.' He turned to his fiancé. 'Aren't we darling? Next time we'll take William out to the park.'

Melissa stiffened. 'If this is part of your strategy to see William without me, you can think again. He's a long way from being ready to do that.'

'We'll see.' Lawrence stirred sugar into his coffee, his long slim fingers gripping the spoon in a way that seemed effeminate to her now, after the muscular athleticism of Daniel.

The strained conversation moved on to something they all had in common – fashion – though thankfully it wasn't long before Sabine swept back into the room and declared

William boring, and the house too small for games. 'I want to go home.'

Evangeline glared at Lawrence, who let out a dramatic sigh and rose to his feet, clattering his coffee cup onto the table. 'Fine.'

Seeing her bombastic ex forced to bow to the bidding of an eight-year-old-girl, Melissa had to bite on the inside of her cheek to stop from smiling.

Once she'd shown them out, Melissa raced upstairs to check on William, who was playing with the Lego cars Daniel had made him. 'So, what did you think of Sabine?'

He angled his head to catch her eye, his nose wrinkling. 'She plays like a girl.'

Melissa laughed, relieved he seemed none the worse for his encounter. 'That's probably because she is one.' Deciding two days before Christmas wasn't the time to talk any further about the situation, Melissa hunkered down next to him and joined in his game. While trying not to be too much like a girl.

Christmas Eve was quiet and blessedly free of uninvited guests. As she watched William carefully hang his stocking up on the fireplace though – not bad for a boy who didn't believe in Father Christmas – Melissa couldn't help but think of a guest she wished she had invited.

Daniel would have been with her now, if she hadn't turned him down. If she hadn't run scared again. He'd have shared, and no doubt added, to William's excitement over setting out the mince pies and carrots for Father Christmas.

And later, snuggled down in her bed together, he'd have added to her own pleasure.

Instead she lay alone in her bed on Christmas Eve, wishing she'd been able to see spending Christmas day with Daniel as simply a logical next step in their growing relationship, like he did. And not the race to a finish line she was terrified of crossing again.

Wishing too that she didn't have the memories of her first failed relationship snapping at her heels, reminding her sharply that when it came to men, her judgement couldn't always be relied on.

Chapter Sixteen

Melissa woke up on Christmas morning to the sight of William's small body standing next to her bed. When he clambered up next to her, excitedly telling her there were presents in his stocking, the worries and loneliness of the previous night began to recede. Here in this bed, she had all she wanted in life. Sure she might wonder how it would feel to share in the excitement of watching William unwrap his presents, but now wasn't the time to dwell on it. She would look forward to seeing Daniel tomorrow, but today ... today she had all she needed.

This was going to be a good Christmas.

'It's not snowing,' William complained when he ran to the window, though his disappointment was soon forgotten as he attacked his presents with all the exuberance a seven-nearly-eight year old should. Amid the tearing of wrapping paper she heard the occasional exclamations of, 'wow, a Lego bulldozer,' or, 'chocolate rules'.

When he unwrapped the inflatable chair she'd bought on impulse, he snorted with laughter. 'I'll get Simon to sit on it and pull out the stopper.'

His favourite present was his racket. Daniel had managed to obtain a smaller version of the racket he'd won Wimbledon with. Melissa knew William didn't understand the significance of it, but she'd realised it immediately and had barely been able to choke out a thank you when he'd smuggled it into the house for her.

'Did Father Christmas get you everything you wanted?' she asked finally as she stuffed all the discarded wrapping paper into a black bin bag.

'Almost.' He grabbed at a ball of paper and started hitting it with his racket.

She peered closely at him. 'What was the thing he didn't bring then?'

'Oh, he couldn't bring it. Just …' He swatted another ball of paper. '… make it happen.'

'I see,' which was a stupid thing to say because she didn't. 'And has it happened?'

'Not yet, but maybe.'

As tiptoeing round the subject was getting her nowhere, she went for the direct approach. 'What do you want to happen?' He either didn't hear her because he was having too much fun playing paper tennis, or he was ignoring her. 'William? What did you ask Father Christmas to make happen?'

Mid-way through picking up another paper ball, he paused and shot her a cheeky grin. 'I told you. That's between me and him.'

Melissa had no option but to laugh. Whatever it was, it clearly wasn't upsetting him, so she decided to let the matter lie.

The phone rang just after they'd finished Christmas lunch. She didn't need to look at the caller ID to know who it was. He might not have been there in person, but Daniel had been in her mind all day. By the look on William's face when he dashed to talk to him, he'd been in her son's, too.

She let them talk while she cleared up the dishes, then took the phone back as William settled down to watch *Ice Age*.

'Regretting not inviting me yet?' Daniel asked when she told him what film they were about to watch. 'You could have been cuddling up to me while you watched the mammoth and the sloth squabble.'

'You've watched it then?' she asked, slightly surprised.

'You can't beat a good film animation. Plus I do have a nephew.'

'Of course.' In her more cynical moments, when she wondered if Daniel was just being kind to William to get to her, she conveniently forgot the bond he already shared with Simon. 'What are you doing now?'

'Recovering from the monster turkey Alice forced down my neck and trying to duck out of the game of charades she seems determined to make us all suffer. Dad's fallen asleep, so I guess that's one way out.'

Melissa felt a pang of longing. His Christmas sounded so normal. The type of Christmas she'd always longed for but never had. Siblings, parents, love and laughter. Her eyes slid to William, his small body focused on the television. She had a lot to be thankful for.

'Hey, are you still there?'

His voice brought her back. 'Sorry, yes, I'm here.'

'Are you nodding off like my dad? Maybe it's not the turkey. Maybe it's me.'

'Serve up something different from cold turkey tomorrow and we'll find out.'

She could almost hear him smile. 'Is that a culinary challenge Ms Stanford? If so, I gladly accept it. I'm even more glad to hear you're still coming.'

'I don't think William would speak to me again if we didn't.' His silence told her he'd hoped for something else, so she added, 'I'm looking forward to it, too.'

She heard the slight whoosh of exhaled breath. 'Not as much as I am. Come as early as you want. And stay as long as you want,' he finished softly, before putting down the phone.

It was a while before her heart rate returned to normal.

*

Boxing Day arrived sunny and crisp. An overnight frost covered the ground making everywhere look silver and magical in the weak morning sun. Whether it was that causing her spine to tingle with anticipation, or the fact that they were on their way to see Daniel, Melissa didn't dare to guess.

Though the frost certainly added a sparkle to everything, she suspected the sight of Daniel's house would still have left her overawed on a dull, rainy day. She knew he was wealthy – he'd been a major tennis star so his winnings and endorsements must have run into millions. Then there was his tennis academy, which Alice had proudly informed her he was planning to repeat in other centres around the country. Even so, she hadn't been prepared for *this*. An elegant Georgian mansion house, nestled down a quiet leafy lane in the best part of town. As she edged her car towards the wrought iron gates they opened regally and she turned into the long gravel drive. Words like classy, handsome and immaculate sprang into her mind. They remained there as she stared at the man walking down the steps to greet them.

Daniel opened the door for William, who scrambled out of his seat with the enthusiasm of a dog knowing it was going for a walk. After giving him a few hearty high-fives, Daniel turned his attention to Melissa, taking her hand as she stepped out of the car.

'Did you find it okay?' he asked, planting a soft kiss on her lips.

'Thanks to the powers of satellite navigation, yes.' She glanced up at the house. 'It's stunning.'

'Thanks. I bought it after winning my first grand slam. Figured it was a nice way to spend the prize money.' He gave her a searching look. 'Any bags?'

She smiled coyly. 'Perhaps.' But then put him out of his misery by clicking the boot open.

He eyed up the luggage with a satisfied smile. 'Excellent.'

With a bag in each hand, he led them up the marble steps and into the hallway.

The decor was a mixture of traditional and modern. He'd kept faith with the period of the house, making the visitor very aware they were in a Georgian home, but he'd furnished with a view to comfort and modern day necessity. As William darted off to explore, Daniel dropped the bags on the floor and took her in his arms.

The kiss was hungry and proprietary. 'Are you going to tell William about us, or shall I?' he asked when he finally drew back.

His eyes sent her a clear message. Tonight he wanted her in his bed. She'd learnt he was an easy-going man, but push him too far and he dug in and pushed right back.

'I'll tell him.' And though she resisted being pushed, she was coming to understand there was a difference between Daniel's determined nudges and the bulldozing approach taken by Lawrence.

'Good.' Daniel led the way upstairs, calling for William so he could show him his room.

'Here it is, buddy.' He placed the small holdall in a pretty blue room that wasn't fussy enough to offend a boy but was stylish enough to please the designer in her.

William rushed inside and jumped on the bed. 'Awesome. And I get my own bathroom.'

Tactfully Daniel slipped out and Melissa moved to join her son on the bed. 'I'm going to be sleeping in Daniel's room tonight,' she told him, and braced herself for the avalanche of questions.

There was a moment's pause while he studied her, and she held her breath. 'Where's that?'

The air left her lungs in a rush and she laughed softly. 'Let's go and find it shall we?'

They walked past two further bedrooms, neither of which looked lived in, so they carried on down the corridor. The final bedroom was dominated by two things. A massive walnut bed and a sixty-inch plasma screen television on the wall. Daniel emerged from the bathroom and swung William up, throwing him onto the bed. 'What do you reckon, Will? Springs bouncy enough for you?'

William shrieked, scrambling to his feet so he could throw himself onto the bed again. 'It's a trampoline.'

Daniel slipped behind Melissa and put his arms around her waist. 'Do you think it'll see that much action tonight?' he whispered in her ear.

She smiled, enjoying the feel of his strong arms around her. How lovely to lean back and know she would be supported. It made her wonder, what if that support wasn't just physical, but emotional, too? She knew Daniel was capable of supplying both, yet still the doubts niggled. The more she relied on someone, the more vulnerable it made her.

Behind her, Daniel drew back. 'If you've finished wearing out my bed springs, Will, why don't we go and see what we can find under the Christmas tree?'

He flopped back onto the bed, eyes wide with delight. 'You got a tree?'

'Of course I did. This year I have someone to share it with.'

Daniel couldn't explain to anyone how he felt watching William and Melissa scramble under the gigantic tree he'd lugged from the garden centre. It was the first he'd ever bought for the place and as he surveyed the poignant scene – baubles dancing on the branches as the two people he'd come to love tried to find their presents – he realised the place didn't feel like his house today. It felt like his home.

'You shouldn't have bought us so many,' Melissa exclaimed as she sat back on her heels, shaking pine needles out of her hair.

'Oh sorry. I didn't realise there were rules about that.'

She put her hands on her hips and gave him a mock glare. 'As if you'd have stuck to them anyway.'

'Don't listen to her,' William declared, coming out from under the tree with his arms laden. 'I like lots of presents.'

'Spoken like a true Christmas lover. Hey, I almost forgot, did the big man bring you what you wanted?'

'I had loads of things.'

'Including both the things you put on your list?'

'Nearly.'

Daniel met Melissa's eyes and she shrugged, giving him an *I haven't a clue either* look.

'Well you need to say if you're bored with opening presents now.' William shot him a look of such disgust, Daniel burst into laughter. 'I guess you should open these then.'

William sat cross-legged on the floor and poked at the red and gold wrapped gifts, clearly deciding where to start.

'I hope you haven't spent too much money on him,' Melissa whispered as she slid onto the sofa next to him, her face turning anxious before his eyes.

Irritation pricked. 'Will you just relax and trust me?'

Sure he'd eyed up all the toys he'd *wanted* to buy William. A digital Scalextric set had been first on his list, closely followed by the full Star Wars Death Star Lego set, complete with Superlaser control room and Imperial conference chamber. While he'd had no problem picturing the glee on William's face as he opened them, it had been just as easy to picture the horror on Melissa's. She was already wary of their relationship; bombarding her son with expensive gifts would only scare her more.

Regretfully he'd toned down his shopping list.

As William tore his way through the presents he'd painstakingly wrapped, grinning as each one was revealed, Melissa noticeably relaxed. There was the compulsory football, a sports bottle with William's name on it, a tennis shirt with the tennis academy logo sprawled across the back. Jumbo tennis rackets for the garden.

'There seems to be a theme,' Melissa murmured next to him.

He shrugged. 'I'm a guy. We do sports or cars.'

'Awesome!' William exclaimed when he ripped open the final present. 'It's just like yours.' As he eyed up the gleaming red remote control Ferrari, Melissa giggled beside him.

'Something funny?'

'Nope. It's just that you weren't wrong with the sports and cars thing.'

'There was a ton of other stuff I'd rather have bought,' he returned a trifle sulkily.

He was rewarded with a soft kiss on his cheek. 'I know, and I'm grateful as much for what you didn't buy as for what you did. Thank you.'

Mollified, he pointed to the presents she'd found with her name on them. Two smaller ones, one that still looked suspiciously racket shaped, and one large rectangular one. 'Feeling relaxed enough to tackle yours now?'

He'd had restless nights deciding what to buy her.

His instinct had been a fat diamond ring – even now he broke into a sweat thinking about it. Not the ring, but the implications. This was the woman he wanted to marry.

'Look how fast it goes!' William's squeal knocked him out of his trance and he watched as the Ferrari raced across the floor and careered into the skirting board.

'William!' Melissa scolded. 'Be careful. I don't think the sitting room is the right place for you to be playing with that. It should be outside.'

Immediately William looked contrite and Daniel's heart went out to him. 'It's only a skirting board,' he reminded her gently. 'They're there to be knocked. It's their purpose in life, like car bumpers. Besides, it's cold outside.'

William's mouth twitched with the beginnings of a smile and Melissa sighed. 'Okay. Carry on, but if all your furniture has dents in it after this, don't say I didn't warn you.'

William picked up the car, turned it round, and shot it down the hallway. At the inevitable sound of the car crashing against another solid object, Melissa flinched.

'Hey, lighten up.' He ran a finger down her tense face. 'No harm done.'

'No.' Her breasts rose and fell as she let out a long, slow breath. 'Sorry. It's a hang-up from my marriage. Lawrence went mad if William played with his toys anywhere but in his room. And if he knocked anything over ...'

'I'm not Lawrence.' Bloody hell, didn't she realise that already? 'I won't shout at William for knocking chunks out of my furniture. But I will shout at you if you keep implying I'm anything like your damn ex.'

'Okay.' Her lips curved. 'Point well made.'

'Now open your flipping presents.'

With her expression relaxed again, she bent her head

and set about tackling her gifts with all the decorum and neatness William had lacked. After carefully peeling back the sellotape she slid off the paper, folding it neatly before her eyes focused on the contents.

Having gone through the torture of watching her open two this way – some Molton Brown shower gel, and a Jo Malone scented candle – Daniel grabbed at the next one and tore the wrapping off himself. 'The phrase *they ripped open their presents* exists for a reason.'

She giggled at the tennis racket he presented her with. 'I had a suspicion I knew what this was. I guess now I've got no excuse not to play.'

'Please open the last one quickly. I've watched paint dry with more excitement than you opening your presents.'

In truth he was a little nervous about the last gift. Not the large one, but the small one he'd taped to it.

'Oh Daniel, that's perfect,' she exclaimed as she studied the large black and white print of William playing tennis that he'd had framed. 'Thank you so much.' Her eyes fell on the small envelope attached to the frame. 'What's this?'

'Open it and find out.'

His heart thumped in his chest. While it wasn't the ring he'd wanted to give her, he hoped it conveyed the sentiment.

'Oh my goodness,' she gasped. 'It's stunning.' Her face paled and she started to shake her head. 'But it's too much Daniel. I can't accept this.'

'Why not?' He could feel himself getting annoyed. 'Don't you like it?'

'Of course I do.' Her slender fingers trailed over the brooch he'd had made. It was of a needle and thimble and was covered with diamonds.

'Then please accept it.'

*

Melissa saw the rigid way Daniel was holding himself and knew if she did anything other than thank him for his beautiful, and incredibly thoughtful, gift, he would be really hurt. So she pushed away her concerns about how much it must have cost and flung her arms around him. 'It's absolutely gorgeous. I love it. Thank you so much.'

Beneath her hands, his shoulders relaxed. 'My pleasure.'

But now she had another problem. 'It makes my gift to you look terrible though.'

He bent to pin the brooch to her blouse and then drew back to admire his handiwork. 'If it's from you, I'll love it. Guaranteed.'

'Remember that when you've opened it.' Rummaging in her handbag she retrieved the small parcel she'd lovingly wrapped in gold paper, tying it with a gold and silver ribbon. At least it looked good from the outside.

In under a second he'd shoved the bows aside and torn off the paper. 'Hey, wow, a tie. That's great.'

'It's not just any tie.' She turned it over so he could read the label. *Melissa designs*.

He seemed genuinely chuffed. 'I shall wear it with the utmost pride.'

Their eyes caught and he raised his hand to her face, trailing his fingers sensuously over her cheek. 'Thank you.' He was bending down for a kiss when the sound of a radio-controlled car shattered the peace.

Ruefully Daniel drew back. 'Anyone for cold turkey?'

Melissa let out a small shriek of horror. 'You promised—'

'It was a joke,' he interrupted, helping her up. 'You know I always deliver on my promises.'

Chapter Seventeen

'Best day, ever,' William declared as she settled him into bed.

Melissa laughed. 'You always say that.'

'This time it's true.'

'Better than the day we had on the beach?' Daniel quizzed from his position in the doorway.

'Umm.' William's brow furrowed in concentration. 'Maybe not better. As good as.'

'So it's the best day ever, except for the day on the beach?' Daniel pushed, his eyes twinkling with amusement.

'Yes. Oh, and Christmas Day,' William added quickly.

'I think you'd better stop there, before it starts to tumble any further down your list. Goodnight, champ.'

He eased out quietly and as Melissa bent to hug William, she suffered another pang of disquiet. How simple it had been to play happy families again today. Daniel slipped so easily into the role of father, it was hard to believe he wasn't one.

Even more terrifying was how easy it was to see him in the role of husband.

Taking a deep breath she pushed the thought from her mind and went downstairs to where Daniel was sitting on the sofa, idly scanning a magazine.

His head shot up when she entered. 'Did he go to sleep okay?'

'Yes. He's one tired but happy little boy.' As she settled onto the sofa next to him, she noticed the replica Wimbledon trophy on the mantelpiece. 'I can't believe I didn't see that earlier. I thought all your trophies were at work.'

Daniel followed her eyes and smiled. 'I have to admit to vanity on that one. It was the trophy that meant the most to me, so it seemed to belong here rather than the office.'

Melissa took a moment to study his strong, handsome profile. It had to hurt, knowing what he'd missed out on, but he hadn't let the experience make him bitter. He'd used it to make himself stronger. As an unexpected ball of emotion rose inside her, she squeezed his hand. 'What was it like, being a professional tennis player?'

'Not as glamorous as it sounds, that's for certain.' Lying back against the sofa he pulled her against him. 'Sure there were parties and screaming girls.' He levelled her a cocky grin. 'Lots of screaming girls. But there were also hours and hours of practice. In the gym, on the court, every day. Don't for one minute think it's an easy life.'

'I used to love to watch you play,' she told him, nestling against his chest. 'I couldn't believe the control you had over the tennis ball. You seemed to be able to place it exactly where you wanted it. I was always lucky just to get the damned thing over the net.'

'It takes a modicum of inherent skill, a massive amount of practice, fierce determination and a dollop of luck.' He shifted so she was lying almost on top of him. 'I'll tell you one thing. I bet you can play tennis better than I can make a pair of trousers.'

The laugh burst out of her. 'Somehow I can't picture you sewing,' she admitted.

'Too right. When I lose a button, I have to buy a new shirt.' He undid her ponytail, allowing her hair to escape over her shoulders. Casually he started to trail his fingers through it. 'Have you any idea how much I want you?' he murmured huskily.

As if he'd turned on a switch, she felt herself melt against him.

Shifting further down the sofa he captured her mouth while his hands ran hungrily down her blouse, undoing buttons and working it free. Soon her bra was thrown aside too, quickly followed by the rest of her underwear.

She'd never felt so aroused, so alive. So wanted.

Reaching out she snapped open his jeans and he groaned. In one fluid movement he stood and tugged them down, along with his boxers. Before she knew it he was lying back on top of her, thrusting into her in one powerful motion.

Melissa had never felt anything like it. It was fierce and frenzied. Hot and passionate. Mind blowing. When she cried out her release his came straight after, his body arching stiffly before collapsing in a heap on top of her.

'Oh, God,' he muttered, levering himself off. Dragging on his jeans he sat on the floor, back against the sofa, his head in his hands.

'Hey, are you okay?' Her jumbled mind raced over what had just happened. 'Did I do something wrong?'

He snapped his head up. 'You?' he asked incredulously. 'Jesus.' He rubbed at his hair. 'Did I hurt you?'

'Of course not.' She moved to drape her arms around his neck. 'It was wonderful,' she whispered.

'Being pinned to a sofa by a man acting like a hormonal teenager was wonderful?' He shook his head in disbelief. 'Not to mention that I didn't use a condom. I could have made you pregnant.'

Her arms tightened around him. 'I've never had anyone need or want me as much as you did just now. So yes, it was wonderful.' She kissed the top of his head. 'And I'm on the pill now, so relax.'

Scrambling to his feet, he dragged her into his arms.

'Christ, Melissa.' He buried his head against her neck, his breath hot and ragged against her skin. 'I've fallen in love with you.'

Her heart took off inside her chest, beating frantically. The only person to have ever told her he loved her was her son. Her parents had never said the words, no doubt because they hadn't felt them. Lawrence had told her he desired her, he wanted her. Never that he loved her. But as much as Daniel's words caught at her heart, fear of being hurt again, of hurting her son again, coiled in her chest, threatening to crush her. 'Daniel, I … I …' Panic caused her to stutter over whatever words she was trying to formulate.

He placed a finger over her lips. 'I'm pushing again. I know. Please, don't say anything.' Bundling her up in his arms, he lay them both back down on the sofa. 'In a while I'm going to take you upstairs and show you my softer, gentler side. For now though, can we just stay here and rest? I need to get my breath back.'

Slowly her body relaxed and a warm contentment seeped through her, drowning out the cold fear. *I feel safe*, she thought. *Here, in his arms, I feel safe and happy.*

He wasn't going to force her anywhere she didn't want to go. If she could just learn to trust him then maybe, just maybe, in time there would be a future out there with all of them in it. Together.

The following morning Daniel woke to the feel of his mattress bouncing up and down and the sound of his television being played far too loudly.

'Somebody shut that stupid mouse up.' He opened a sleepy eye and glared at the set. 'Some of us are trying to get some sleep around here.'

From his position at the foot of the bed, William grinned. Then re-focused his attention back on the cartoon.

Next to him, Melissa attempted to smother a giggle. 'We always watch Mickey Mouse in the morning.' Amusement danced in her eyes. 'You should try it some time. It keeps you young.'

Daniel growled, snaking his arm around her under the duvet. 'I can think of better things to do when I wake up.'

Letting out a small sigh of pleasure she leant against him and closed her eyes. As his hands started to wander though, her eyes flew open and she stared pointedly at William's back.

He gave her a wry smile. 'Okay, I get the picture.' He pushed back the duvet and climbed out of bed. 'It looks like I'm going to have to get rid of my energy some other way.'

After dressing quickly in his tracksuit bottoms and running vest he darted a look at the two occupants of his usually quiet bedroom. The boy, mesmerised by the large TV, his eyes wide and his grin goofy. The woman, flushed from a night of loving. The swell of his heart only confirmed what he already knew. He loved them both. Somehow he would have to find a way to keep them.

They spent the morning playing with William's presents in the back garden. Following an energetic session of football and soft-ball tennis, Daniel wondered why he'd bothered to go for a run.

He threw together some cold turkey sandwiches for lunch – courtesy of Alice who'd shoved a huge plastic container at him as he'd left on Christmas day.

'I see I didn't escape the turkey after all,' Melissa commented, giving him one of her wide-eyed looks.

They always made him want to kiss her, so he did.

William made a noise that sounded like a variation of yuck, but when Daniel glanced over at him his expression wasn't disapproving. It was ... knowing. As if he understood something nobody else did.

Taking their sandwiches into the lounge, they lay across the floor and got stuck into a game of Monopoly.

As Daniel steadily accumulated property, built hotels and raked in his earnings, William got bored and went to play with his Ferrari.

The day slowly faded into dusk, and Melissa reluctantly got to her feet. 'As you can't even let us win at Monopoly, I think we might as well go home.'

It was on the tip of his tongue to ask her to stay another night, but he clamped down on the impulse. He'd pushed his luck enough recently. When she started to gather up the plates, he touched her arm. 'I'll do that. You go and collect your things together.'

He was in the kitchen, slotting plates into the dishwasher, when he heard Melissa out in the hallway, giving William his five-minute warning.

'We have to go home soon. Can you start to tidy your things?'

'No.'

Out of sight of the pair of them, Daniel winced.

'Don't talk to me like that. This is a warning. You need to gather your toys up because we have to go home.'

The boy who'd been as good as gold all day yesterday and today suddenly turned sulky. 'I don't want to go home.'

Because he felt like he was eavesdropping, Daniel edged out of the kitchen and stood in the doorway so they could both see him.

'There's no choice, William. This is Daniel's house. We need to get back to our own.'

Suddenly William bolted across the hall and clutched at Daniel's legs. 'We don't have to. Not if Daniel marries you.' William yanked at his arm. 'You said you were going to ask her, didn't you? Then we could live here, with you, couldn't we?'

Daniel didn't know who was more startled, him or Melissa. Helplessly he stared over at her, not knowing what to say. As he read the fury in her face, his heart almost stopped beating. Only a few hours ago she'd looked at him with tenderness. Now he felt like something she'd found stuck to the bottom of her shoe.

'William,' she said in a voice colder than he'd ever heard her use. 'Go and get your bag packed and wait by the front door.'

'I don't want to.' His small body remained glued to Daniel's side. 'I want to stay here. With my Dad.'

Her face had drained of all its blood. 'What did you say?'

'I want Daniel to be my dad.' William's face stared up at Daniel, his eyes pleading. 'I know you said if you got married it wouldn't make you my dad, but it would feel like you were, wouldn't it?'

As his heart suffered emotional overload, Melissa's eyes slammed into his, spitting fire. 'William, go and bring your bag down here. Now.'

Her anger was palpable. As William shot away Daniel stood frozen to the spot, the sound of his heart pounding in his ears. Fear ripped through his chest and as it zinged up his spine he had a crazy premonition that this was it. He'd lost her.

'What, exactly, did you think you were doing, talking about marriage to *my son*?' With deceptive calm she strode up to him, took her hand back and slapped him round the face.

He didn't see it coming. As he took the full force of her wrath, the smack of flesh on flesh echoed round the hall. At least it achieved one thing. It jarred him out of his trance. 'Now wait a minute.' He grabbed at her hands, just in case she was planning a second ambush. 'What the heck was that for?'

'For talking to my son behind my back. For getting his hopes up.' Her voice wobbled as she tried to wriggle free from his clutches. 'And damn you. For arrogantly assuming I want to marry you.'

He could see tears welling in her eyes and his heart lurched. She reminded him of a lioness, defending her cub at all costs. 'Calm down.' Keeping a firm hold of both of her hands he tried to reason with her. 'I didn't mention anything about marriage, William did.'

'But you answered him, didn't you? You discussed it with him without my permission. Without my knowledge. You had no right to do that. He's *my* son.'

He flinched. 'I'm sorry. I didn't think.' His own voice was far from steady and he inhaled a deep breath. 'Isn't it the way we're heading though?' He risked letting go of her hands and used his own to cup her face. 'You already know I'm in love with you. Will you make me the happiest man alive and marry me?'

She recoiled faster than a striking snake. 'No.'

Melissa whirled away, not wanting to look at him as the first clutches of panic clawed inside her.

'No, what?'

Feeling trapped she marched to the front door, grasping at the handle. She needed to get away from here, away from him. She wasn't just afraid of what he was offering her, she was afraid of her desire to accept it. 'I can't marry you.'

'Is that I can't marry you now, or I can't marry you ever?'

With rising hysteria she turned to face him. 'Why won't you understand? I've been married before. I can't go there again. Not for you. Not for anyone.'

'People remarry all the time,' he replied quietly.

'Not me.'

'I see.' He stood motionless, as if unsure of his moves. 'You're right. I have been arrogant. I assumed at least some of my feelings were being returned. Tell me, just what do you think is going on between us?'

'We're having a ... dalliance. An affair.' She caught a glimpse of the raw hurt that flashed in his eyes before he slammed them shut.

Her heart shattered. Oh God, this was such a mess. She should have stuck to her guns and never got involved. She'd worried about the effect on her and William; she hadn't bargained on hurting Daniel, too.

'So I've just been a means of getting you back into dating again?' He folded his arms across his chest, as if trying to protect himself from her answer.

'Yes.' It was an answer uttered in self-preservation, not in truth but the moment she'd said it Daniel's shoulders hunched and his head dropped into his hands.

Pain tore through her heart. He didn't deserve what she was doing to him. But while she wanted more than anything to tell him she'd been stupid, that of course she loved him, of course she would marry him, she couldn't.

She was still trying to untangle both her and William from the effects of the last time she'd made that promise.

It didn't mean she had to be cruel though. Letting go of the door handle, she walked up to him and, ignoring his rigid stance, wrapped her arms around his waist. 'That was a lie. I always said I would never have anything to do with another man, but despite my good intentions, you got under my skin. I care for you, Daniel.'

He pulled her hands off his waist and took a step back, torment swirling in his eyes. 'Obviously not enough to marry me. Just what are you so afraid of, Melissa?'

'You know the answer to that,' she shot back, widening the space between them.

'So you're going to let one bad experience sour the rest of your life? I thought you were more sensible than that.'

Anger bubbled inside her once more. 'What is it about me that makes men want to tell me what to do, or how to feel?'

'I wasn't aware I was doing that,' he replied stiffly.

'Well you are.' She swung away, exasperated. 'You push and push, Daniel. I've already been in a relationship with a man who did that. I don't want another one, thanks.'

Daniel swore, thrusting a hand through his hair. 'Damn you, I've told you before. I'm not your bloody ex husband.'

'Then stop behaving like him.'

A muscle twitched in his jaw. 'I apologise. I didn't realise telling you I love you, and want to marry you, would be so abhorrent.'

Melissa threw her hands to her face in anguish. When he put it like that, it made her sound harsh and ungrateful. 'Oh God, it isn't, of course it isn't. It's just too much and far too soon.'

He nodded, though his face was grim. 'I get the message, loud and clear. I'll back off.'

She waited for the relief to surge through her. That was what she wanted, wasn't it? Space to breathe, to think. But all she felt was an impending sense of dread. 'You make it sound so final.'

'Isn't it?'

No. The word stuck in her throat. She wasn't ready to

say goodbye – she was only just getting used to having him in her life, to being happy – but was it fair to encourage when she wasn't ready to give him what *he* wanted? When she didn't know if she'd ever be ready?

Her heart weighing heavy, she ignored his question and picked up her bag. 'I've had a lovely few days. We both have. Thank you.'

'I won't see you out, if you don't mind.' His voice sounded so raw, compounding her misery. 'I think it's best for William if you tell him I said goodbye.'

He turned on his heel and walked away from her down the hallway.

On a sob Melissa dashed up the stairs to find her son.

Chapter Eighteen

The following day passed uneventfully and Melissa managed to reassure an upset William that she and Daniel were still friends. She'd even managed to convince herself of that fact. He understood that she cared for him, but that she needed more space, more time. It wasn't the end, just a minor blip.

On the twenty-eighth she drove William to the tennis academy. She'd have been happy to duck out of it, but William had stomped his feet and insisted he wanted to go. As he so rarely played up, and as she'd been the one who'd encouraged him to take up the sport in the first place, she'd acquiesced. Where she'd once felt a lovely sense of anticipation driving there though, now she was agitated and anxious. She wanted to see Daniel. She was dying to see him.

But now she was going to find out whether her take of their situation was the same as his.

William rushed up to Daniel as soon as he saw him, and her heart lifted at the mutual affection between man and boy. High-fives were exchanged, William's new racket admired and laughter filled the air.

When Daniel looked in her direction though, Melissa received only the slightest of nods. There was no casual kiss on the cheek. Certainly no kiss on the lips when nobody was looking.

His coolness hurt; the signal it sent was even more painful. Where she'd said slow down, he'd heard stop.

Slowly the reality of the situation began to sink in. She and Daniel were over.

Catching sight of Alice and some of the other mothers arriving, Melissa fled to the changing rooms. She couldn't face them. Not at the moment. Not when the new world she'd been so carefully building had come crashing down on her. And all she wanted to do was cry.

While Melissa was regaining her composure in the ladies' changing room, Daniel wasn't faring much better on court. Never had he been so grateful for the distraction of a bunch of boisterous kids. His one consolation was that Melissa didn't look any better than he did. He wanted to believe she was regretting turning down his, admittedly half-cocked, proposal so swiftly, but he'd already made enough arrogant assumptions.

At the end of the coaching session he hung back, pretending to need a talk with one of the other coaches. At some point he had to find a way back to being friends with Melissa – he couldn't lose her totally, it would destroy him – but at the moment it was all too raw.

When he thought the coast was clear he walked slowly back towards the locker rooms, only to find the crowd of kids and parents still there.

'What's going on?' he asked his nephew, who was at that moment ripping open an envelope.

'William's giving out his party invitations.' Simon looked down at the card he'd pulled out. 'Sick.'

Daniel tried not to squirm at his nephew's term. To an old fogey like him, sick would always mean carrots swimming in a smelly liquid. 'When's the big day then, Will?' he asked.

'Tomorrow.' He stared down at the two envelopes he had left. 'I forgot to write you one, but I want you to come, too.' A grin split his face. 'Please.'

Daniel's heart thumped and he glanced quickly over at Melissa. Her expression – startled, bordering on horrified – told him all he needed to know. How the heck did he get out of this one without hurting the boy's feelings? 'That's really kind of you, but you don't want an old man like me there. A party is for your friends.'

William frowned. 'You are my friend and I want you there.'

Help. Again he looked over at Melissa, this time for support. He knew damn well she didn't want him there. 'Look mate, I'm just not sure …'

'We'd both like you to come,' she said evenly, nodding in confirmation at his unspoken *are you absolutely sure?*

Okay then. He inhaled slowly, taking time to remind his heart that this wasn't about her wanting to see him. This was about her making her son happy. 'Well, with an invitation like that, how can I refuse?' he replied, ruffling William's hair. 'I'd be honoured to come.'

He made his escape quickly, anxious to avoid any further contact. Seeing the pair of them was too sharp a reminder of what he was missing, and one he hadn't flaming needed. His mind was doing a good enough job on its own.

What he *did* need was to go and get quietly drunk somewhere.

He strode towards his office with renewed intent, though hopes of a speedy exit were dashed the moment he opened the door to find Alice sitting on the end of his desk. Her arms were crossed, her expression fierce. Both were a stark contrast to the worry in her eyes.

'You look like hell,' she told him bluntly. 'What's going on?'

'Thank you,' he returned sourly. 'You're not looking too marvellous yourself.' Cuttingly he let his eyes wander over her ill-matched combination of tracksuit bottoms and bright green silk blouse.

She glanced down and her expression softened. 'Yes, well, I was in a rush and this was all I could find quickly. I blame husbands who come home demanding their tea just when you need to leave. What do you blame?'

'Myself,' he replied bitterly, sitting down heavily in his chair.

'Oh.' Alice studied him for a few moments and then edged off the desk. 'Let me go and check Simon is okay. This conversation sounds like it might take a while.'

'What conversation?' But he found he was talking to an empty room. Needing something to take his angst out on, he read the first letter in his in-tray. The bathroom company reminding him he hadn't settled the bill for the shower refurbishment yet. With a muttered oath he scrunched it into a ball and threw it into the bin. He'd pay up when they came back and ironed out the snags.

His office door burst open and Alice swept in again. 'Okay, we're good. I've asked Hank to watch Simon for a bit.'

Daniel barely contained his grimace. 'I'm sure the centre's deputy manager has more important things to do than take care of my nephew just so you can grill me.'

'Tough. As the older sister, I get to boss you around.' She sat opposite him, plonked her handbag on the floor and fixed him with her steely glare. 'So, what's the cause of this sullen mood?'

'I asked Melissa to marry me.'

Alice stared at him wide-eyed for a few seconds, and then let out a long deep sigh. 'Oh dear. I take it from your surly behaviour that she said no?'

He ran a hand through his hair, wanting to rub away the

dull ache he could feel starting at his temple. 'Of course she said no.' Knowing it was nothing his sister hadn't heard before, he let out a ripe oath. 'I played it all wrong. I've only got myself to blame. You warned me she didn't want a relationship, Melissa herself warned me, but did I take any notice? Of course not.' Emotion pressed on his throat and he had to force the next words out. 'I wanted the dream too much,' he admitted hoarsely. 'Melissa and William, a future together. I tried to rush her, to push her where I wanted her to go. In the end she dug in her heels and refused to budge.'

'Hey, don't be too hard on yourself.' Before he knew it Alice was standing over him, hugging him tight. 'You just followed your feelings. It must be a McCormick family trait. I mean, look at me. I wouldn't be onto marriage number three if I hadn't gone with my heart.'

'Or if you hadn't been in so much of a rush to jump into marriages one and two.'

She let out a short laugh. 'Okay, point taken, but who's to say our way isn't right? If you'd let Melissa go at her pace you'd still be dancing round each other now.'

He allowed himself a glimmer of a smile. 'Maybe. But at least I'd still be thinking we had a shot at a future together. I've just blown that out of the water.'

'How do you know you've blown it? Perhaps if you take a step back and start again more slowly.'

He shook his head, the action causing the dull ache to shift into a sharp throb. 'Melissa wants a friend and occasional lover. I want a wife and family. The two will never come together.'

Alice squeezed his hand. 'You should never say never. You taught me that.'

He laughed, but his heart wasn't in it. 'Sometimes I talk the biggest load of bollocks.' Sighing, he crossed his legs and sat back in the chair. 'I have to face it, Alice. I asked her to marry me. She didn't say maybe, or ask me again in a few months. She said no.'

'Then she's a bloody fool,' Alice replied staunchly. 'Did she tell you why?'

His head felt as if it was about to explode and the last thing he needed now was to go back over old ground. 'The brief version is that she'd already been in a relationship with a man who bossed her around and she didn't want another.' Rubbing a hand over his forehead, he heaved out a sigh. 'Can we leave it there? Please? I know you're only trying to help but I've had enough.'

Her eyes swimming in sympathy, she bent to kiss his cheek. 'Okay, I'll leave it there,' she agreed. 'I can't promise I won't interfere, though. You two are made for each other. Any fool can see that. You might be pig-headed at times, but you sure as hell aren't anything like Lawrence.'

He smiled wanly. 'On that we can agree, though I'm not sure she does.' He winced as a sharp arrow-like pain pierced his skull. 'Bugger, I've got a splitting headache. There goes my plan for getting quietly wasted.'

Alice reached into her handbag and pulled out two tablets. 'Here, take these before you get into that lethal car of yours. Then get home and get some sleep.'

'Yes boss.'

Melissa kissed William goodnight and walked slowly down the stairs. The lights from the Christmas tree in the sitting room winked over at her, taunting her. Reminding her of a time a few days ago when she'd felt happy. When she'd dashed down the stairs with a bounce in her step, not lead in her heart.

Seeing Daniel again had been more traumatic than

she'd bargained for. And now, thanks to William's shock invitation and her big mouth, she would have to see him again tomorrow. Endure an awkward afternoon together playing happy families. Just what she needed. She turned into the sitting room and was about to flop onto the sofa when she heard a knock at the door.

No peace for the wicked. And damn it she *felt* wicked. She was hurting both Daniel and her son. Never mind what she was doing to herself.

'Alice.' She gasped in surprise at the woman on her doorstep. 'To what do I owe this honour?' Though she had a sinking feeling she already knew.

Refraining from any of their usual greetings – the kiss on the cheek, the hug – Alice walked quickly into the sitting room. 'This won't take long. I think you know what it's about.'

'I guess it's about Daniel.'

'Too right it is.' Alice sat stiffly on the sofa. 'Look, I don't want us to argue. We were friends before you met my brother and I hope we can still be friends.'

'So do I.' They were both acutely aware how much her voice trembled.

Alice's expression softened. 'You warned him all along that you didn't want a relationship, so in a way he only has himself to blame. Which is something he's well aware of,' she added quickly.

Not knowing what to say, Melissa sat in the armchair opposite and prepared to listen.

'He's hurting, Melissa, and I hate to see my brother in pain. He's been through enough already with his injury, the loss of his career. He doesn't deserve this.'

'I know,' Melissa replied sadly. 'He deserves someone who'll love him, marry him and make him happy.'

'But it won't be you?'

Her heart tightened, making it difficult to breathe. It was so easy to picture her standing beside Daniel and William, happiness shining in their eyes. But hadn't the picture of her and Lawrence begun like that, too? 'I'm sorry. I didn't want any of this to happen. I didn't want to hurt Daniel. I just can't get married again.'

'You don't love him?'

'Please don't ask me that,' she begged, her voice faltering. 'All I know is whatever I feel for him, I can't marry him.'

With a sad smile, Alice rose to her feet. 'Then it's time for me to leave.' She walked quietly to the front door and had opened it by the time Melissa caught up. 'It might take a while for us to get back to normal, but I promise you we'll get there. You will still come to my New Year's Eve party?'

'Yes. If you want me to.' She shook her head, misery dragging her at. 'Not that I'm going to feel like celebrating.' It looked like she was destined to have bad Christmases.

'Oh, Melissa.' Alice moved to give her a light hug. 'When I leave, I want you to think on this. Daniel is nothing like Lawrence. And you are nothing like the naïve young girl you were when you first got married.'

The words stayed with her as Melissa wearily made her way back upstairs. After undressing she climbed into bed and curled into a ball, feeling every bit the lonely, sad, young girl Alice believed she'd moved on from.

Chapter Nineteen

It was the day of William's birthday. Though she'd been horrendously late giving out the invitations – leaving it till the day before, unbelievable – her foresight in telling everyone well before Christmas had thankfully paid off and eight of William's friends were coming. In two hours. So far she'd blown up balloons and iced the cake. Looking down at her handy work, she tried not to feel too guilty over the fact that beneath her decorative drawing of a sports car, was a shop-bought cake. But it was a chocolate cake, and it would have eight candles on it, which was probably all William really cared about.

'William, will you get that?' she called as she heard a knock on the door, quickly sliding the candles into the icing.

A few seconds later there was a scuffle of feet racing up the stairs. 'William?' Sighing she washed her hands and walked towards the door. Then came to an abrupt halt.

Lawrence.

Wearing a long dark overcoat, his greying hair tied back in a ponytail and his eyes unsmiling, he looked just one step short of sinister.

'What are you doing here?' she asked coldly.

'I've bought a present for William. It is his birthday today, isn't it?' He held out a carefully wrapped gift.

Her pulse racing, she told herself not to let Lawrence upset her today. Nothing was going to spoil William's party. 'Thank you,' she replied quietly, taking the gift from him. 'I'll see that he gets it. Now if you don't mind, we're getting ready for his party.' She took a step back, her hand shaking as she reached to close the door. But Lawrence put his foot in the way, blocking her movement.

'Can you spare me a few minutes?'

'Exactly why should I do that? What have you done for me recently that makes you think you deserve any of my time?'

Lawrence looked at her oddly. 'What happened to the warm and soft girl I married?'

'She turned older, wiser and more prepared to stand up to you.'

He nodded. 'Yes, I can see that. How about if I say can you spare me a few minutes, *please*?'

It wasn't a word she was used to hearing from his lips. Reluctantly she led him into the sitting room. 'Okay, but five minutes, no longer.'

Lawrence sat and placed his hands on his knees, his actions slow and deliberate. 'I take it William is still scared of me?' he asked finally, seconds before her nerves threatened to shred. 'The way he shot up the stairs as soon as he saw my face would seem to suggest that.'

'Is it any wonder? You spent the first five years of his life shouting at him and the next three ignoring him.'

'Not exactly father of the year, am I?' he replied wryly, then sighed. 'Look, I didn't come to cause trouble. In fact I came to say I won't be troubling you again. I've talked it through with my lawyer and I realise I can't just see William by himself, not after all this time. He'd hate it and ...' He trailed off, staring at his hands.

'You'd hate it, too.'

His eyes jerked up to hers and he finally gave her a small smile. 'Yes.'

Melissa stared at him, too afraid to hope. 'Why did you demand to see him then?'

His eyes darted back to the floor and for once the supremely confident Lawrence looked embarrassed. 'I wanted a playmate for Sabine. She's always moaning, wanting Evangeline's attention. I figured if William was with us now and again during the school holidays, we'd get some time to ourselves.'

A bubble of hysterical laughter flew out of her. 'But Sabine went and ruined your plans by not getting on with William.'

He gave her a small smile. 'Something like that. Plus my lawyer made it quite clear it would take a lot of time and effort on my part to show that I was a fit enough father to be left alone with William. I don't have the time or inclination for that.' Finally he looked her in the eye. 'He said you'd hired the meanest lawyer in town to fight me.'

'I hired someone recommended to me.' And unlike her divorce lawyer, who'd come courtesy of Lawrence, Peter Price had come recommended by someone who really cared for her. Who said he *loved* her.

Slowly Lawrence stood up. 'I won't be causing you or William any more grief. You have my word. Have a good life, Melissa.'

Her heart dancing beneath her ribs, Melissa instinctively went to kiss him on the cheek. 'You, too.'

'What was that for?'

She pressed a hand to her chest where her heart was now doing cartwheels. 'For giving me my son.'

After seeing him out she sagged against the door, trying to collect herself. It was a truce. She and Lawrence had finally worked out a truce. On a burst of happiness she flew up the stairs to find William.

He was in his room playing with his cars, his face looking

far too solemn for a boy on his birthday. 'Are you okay, sweetie?'

His eyes remained on the cars. 'I don't want him to be my dad.'

Her heart aching for him, Melissa bundled him into her arms and hugged him tight. 'It's okay, my darling. You won't ever have to see him again. Not if you don't want to.' Blinking away the tears, she smiled down at him. 'He bought you round a present. I know he was a mean father to you, but he's not all bad.' Clearing a space on the floor she sat and took his hand. 'The problem was, he didn't know how to be a father. He came round to say that he's not going to try any more. If you want to catch up with him again when you're older, you can do that. It will be up to you.'

Buried in her arms, his little body relaxed against her. 'Okay.' A moment later he popped his head up. 'When does my party start?'

Melissa chuckled and looked down at her watch. 'In one hour, big boy, and we've still got a lot to do. How about you come downstairs and help me?'

As he rang the bell on Melissa's front door, Daniel could hear the sounds of young kids having fun. Shrieks, giggles, thumping noises. It looked like the party was in full swing. He was running late, his meeting with a journalist taking longer than he'd planned. Still, she'd promised a good article on the tennis academies, though he wasn't altogether sure whether that was because she believed in what he was doing, or because she fancied a date with an ex- player. He'd managed some half-hearted flirting in response, figuring it might further his cause. It wasn't as if anyone in his life was going to be jealous.

Melissa opened the door with a flourish, her lips curved in a ready smile. The second she registered who it was, the smile froze.

'Daniel,' she murmured, backing away so she could let him in. 'We assumed you weren't coming.'

Stung, his grip tightened on the present he was carrying. 'I said I would. I'm a man of my word.'

'Yes, I know. I'm sorry.' Her eyes fluttered closed and when she opened them again she smiled awkwardly. 'I didn't mean it to come out like it did. We thought something had come up, that was all.'

'My meeting took longer than I'd anticipated.'

He received another stiff smile. 'Okay.'

Exhaling deeply, he told himself to stop being so damn sensitive and followed her inside. The usually tidy sitting room looked as if it had been ransacked. Balloons were strewn everywhere, mixing colourfully with the discarded wrapping paper and cards. Birthday banners fought for attention alongside Christmas decorations. 'Where's the birthday boy?'

'He's showing his friends his room.' She raised her eyebrows to the ceiling. As if on cue, there was a series of loud thumps, followed by a scream of laughter. 'He'll be pleased to see you.'

Numbly he nodded, grasping at the chance to escape. He was an easy-going man, but right now he couldn't seem to find his equilibrium. It was too painful to look at her and know he had no right to kiss her. To touch her.

Cautiously he made his way up the stairs and knocked on William's door. 'Is there an eight year old boy in there?'

'Daniel!' William almost fell through the door and into his arms. 'You made it. I told Mum you would.'

'How does it feel, being right all the time?' he asked, hanging him up by his ankles.

William giggled and tried to punch him on the arm. 'You're just in time to see the magic man. He's going to show us some tricks.'

'Excellent. I could do with knowing how to make things vanish. Young boys in particular.' Carefully he put William down and handed him the present he'd dropped by the door when he'd come in. 'Happy Birthday, champ.'

William tore open the wrapping paper while his friends gathered round. Daniel recognised all but two of them from the academy.

'Wow! A tennis bag just like yours,' he exclaimed. He looked at the signature scrawled across the side. 'It's got your name on it.' He threw his arms around Daniel's waist. 'Thank you.'

'I didn't know whether to get you that or Lego. I figured you'd already had a load of Lego from Father Christmas and this might be more useful.'

William stroked the side of the tennis bag, the last of the personalised bags from his playing days, when sponsors had clamoured for his endorsement. 'It's cool. Maybe you can get me the Lego next year.'

Next year. His heart lurched painfully but he was saved a reply as Melissa's voice carried up to them. 'The magic man has arrived. Do you want to come down and see some tricks?'

There was a stampede to the door and Daniel stood back as they flew past him and down the stairs. Simon gave him a fleeting grin, but was obviously in too much of a hurry to say hello to his uncle.

Following them down at a more sedate pace, Daniel eased into the back of the dining room where they were huddled.

The table and chairs had been pushed to the side, out of the way, and the kids sat on the carpet, mesmerised, as the magician began his routine. After a short while Melissa came to join him. 'A moment's peace,' he whispered.

She turned to him and smiled. It was a genuine smile; the first he'd received since that fateful day when he'd cocked everything up and proposed. For a moment, just the briefest of moments, they shared that special connection again. The one that had his heart lifting and his hopes rising.

But then she shifted her gaze back to the magician.

Melissa tried not to be too hurt that Simon, the last of their small guests, was collected by his father, not his mother. Maybe Alice was busy, as Richard claimed. Or maybe she was finding it hard to be her friend. Brushing her worries aside, Melissa focused instead on how much William had seemed to enjoy his party. If she was honest, she had, too. It had been lovely having the house filled with mischievous laughter.

One rather large guest still remained and was currently helping William pick up all the rubbish in the living room. How stupid that the only anxious moments she'd experienced all day had been caused by Daniel, and not the children. Not that she could blame him for them, because actually he'd been an enormous help. Thanks to the air of authority he carried, her young charges had known they could have a laugh with him, but not push him. A look, a quiet word, and they were quickly back on track.

So no, it wasn't Daniel's fault that her heart raced whenever he accidentally touched her, or their eyes met. Also not his fault that in his low slung jeans and a steel-grey linen shirt he looked outrageously attractive. Or that whenever she looked at him all she could think was what a cowardly fool she was for turning him down.

'You didn't need to do that,' she protested as she entered the room.

'No problem.' He tied up the bag and dropped it by the back door. 'As your last remaining guest though, I think it's time I made tracks, too.' He glanced over at William, who'd stretched himself out on the sofa. 'It looks like the birthday boy is ready for bed.' Bending down, he ruffled his hair. 'Great party, Will. See you next week at tennis training.'

'It was very kind of you to come,' she told him as she followed him into the hallway, her heart lurching wildly as he halted by the door. Oh God, she shouldn't be so incredibly aware of him. His fresh, sporty cologne. His big, muscular body.

'My pleasure.' His deep brown eyes sought hers and once again she felt the full force of his magnetic attraction. And a sharp, painful tug on her heart.

Who moved to whom? Who cared? All she knew was his lips were finally touching hers and her body was aflame with wanting. Instinctively she returned his kiss, hunger to hunger, heat to heat.

'Mum, can I put the telly on?'

William's words burst into her consciousness and she pulled away, breathing hard. Not daring to look at Daniel, she gulped for air and tried to calm her racing pulse. 'Of course you can, darling. I'll be there in a minute.' Was that really her voice? Good Lord, she sounded like Marilyn Monroe with a sore throat. Awkwardly she coughed. 'I forgot William was there for a moment.'

'For once I wish he hadn't been.' Daniel's look was loaded with meaning. 'Though perhaps it's for the best that he was.'

'What do you mean?'

Briefly he closed his eyes. 'Come on. You know what I mean. This is hard enough to come to terms with, without complicating things.'

'But it doesn't have to be this way between us,' she whispered, desperation making her brave. 'Why can't we carry on as we were?'

'What, the casual love affair? Meeting up and sleeping together when our diaries allow?'

It wasn't how she'd have put it. There seemed to be no room for caring in his version. No room for love. But if it meant they could be together again? 'Yes, if you like.'

He cursed under his breath. 'Christ.' Leaning against the front door, he rubbed a hand over his face before laughing softly. 'You know there was a time in my life when I'd have jumped at that type of offer, but not any more.' Intense brown eyes focused on hers. 'I want to lay down roots. I want marriage and a family. If we get back together, and I don't piss you off too much, would you marry me eventually?'

Melissa snapped her eyes shut, afraid that if she continued to look at him she'd give the answer that was in her heart, not in her head. Before she could think of a reply that wasn't a yes, but wasn't a definitive no, he was opening the door.

'I thought not.' He stepped outside. 'Goodbye, Melissa.'

Without a backward glance he strode down the path and into his Ferrari. A tall, athletic figure. A gorgeous, kind, charming, *honest* man.

A man who'd said he loved both her and her son. That he wanted to have them both in his life, permanently.

A man she'd turned down. Not once, but twice.

She hung her head, tears flooding down her cheeks and splashing onto the doorstep. Today had been a good day up until now; her relationship with Lawrence had taken a positive step forward, her son had never looked happier.

Yet here she was, seemingly still stuck in the past as her chance of a future roared off down the street. Regret, sharp and bitter, flooded through her and the tears fell more quickly.

It was a long while after the Ferrari had disappeared from view that she wiped her eyes, sucked in a breath and went to join her son.

Feeling utterly miserable, mixed with two parts frustrated and five parts hurt, Daniel let himself into his house. Going to William's party: bad idea. Kissing Melissa in the hallway: bloody stupid idea.

To take his mind off his misery he snapped on the television. Festive cheer screamed back at him, people with silly hats laughing with each other in front of a jolly, over-the-top Christmas tree. He turned the damn thing off again.

He was starting to hate Christmas.

Shrugging off his jacket he was about to slump into his armchair with a large whiskey when his phone rang.

'What?' he snapped, seeing his sister's number flash up. 'I'm in a foul mood so if this is another one of your pep talks I suggest you put the phone down now.'

'This is a New Year's Eve party invite. And you have to come.'

His heart sank to his socks. 'Since when was it written in the sibling rule book "thou shalt attend your sister's party whenever she asks"?'

'Since your sister is planning the party around you,' she replied in an annoyingly smug tone.

'Did I miss something? Is it my birthday? Have I won an award I didn't realise I was entered for?'

'Very funny. This is serious business. Do you still want Melissa to marry you?'

If his heart had been able to sink any lower, it would have. 'What has that got to do with anything?' he countered, trying to keep the exasperation out of his voice. 'Of course I want her to marry me, but she doesn't want to. Short of drugging her and dragging her up the aisle, I don't think there's anything either of us can do about it.'

'You never used to give up so easily.'

Irritated, he raked his hand through his hair. 'If this was a tennis match, I'd know what to do, how to win. It's not and I don't.'

'Well I have an idea and as long as you play your part, it should work.'

'Hell Alice, this isn't a game. This is my life.' Slipping from irritated to angry, he began to pace.

'I know, and I'm not trivialising it, honestly. I hate to see you hurting, and I think I've found a way to nudge things in the right direction.'

To say he was sceptical was an understatement. But what did he have to lose, that he hadn't already lost? 'Go on then. Tell me the plan.' He let out a short laugh. 'It can't make things any worse than they already are.'

'Well, it centres round the party. I was always planning to have one, but now I'm changing tactics a little and as well as the couples I'd originally asked, I've invited all the single, attractive women I know. Women who fancy you like mad. Personally I find it hard to believe, but apparently you're sex on legs.'

204

'I'm not comfortable with the way this conversation is going. And if you're paying me compliments, I know the ending won't be pretty.'

'No, the end will be spectacular. All you have to do is be yourself.' She paused. 'And by that I mean the man you were before you met Melissa. Do you remember him? The charmer who flirted with any woman in a skirt.'

'You make me sound like a total philanderer,' he protested. 'I wasn't that bad.'

'I'm not saying you were. Just that I need you to be that man again on New Year's Eve. When Big Ben chimes, Melissa will be so jealous she'll be begging you to marry her.'

Daniel raised his eyes to the ceiling. Of all the harebrained ideas Alice had thought up over the years, this had to take the prize. 'I'm happy to flirt with some attractive women ... you did say they were attractive, didn't you?'

'Stunning.'

'Okay. I'm happy to play my part, but you know it won't work.'

'Come on little brother. Where's your fighting spirit? What happened to the famous McCormick optimism?'

'It vanished with my sense of humour,' he replied gloomily.

'Well, you've got two days to find them.'

Chapter Twenty

Melissa's heart pounded as she walked up Alice's drive. Why had she agreed to go to her New Year's Eve party? Daniel was bound to be there and she wasn't ready to face him again so soon.

'Mum!'

Melissa halted, belatedly realising she'd stepped on the sleeping bag William was dragging. 'Sorry, darling.'

Two seconds after she'd rung the bell, Alice opened the door and immediately enveloped her in a hug of old. The sort of hug they used to give each other before Daniel had told Melissa he wanted to marry her ... and panicked her so much she'd ruined everything.

'Bye Mum!' Melissa just had time to glimpse the back of William's head as he raced up the stairs to where Simon was waiting for him.

'I guess that's the last I'll see of him until tomorrow.' Alice had offered a sleep-over for William and though Melissa knew it made sense, right now she didn't actually want to stay at the party until midnight. In fact right now she felt like turning round and heading home.

'Ah, but just think, now you get to spend time with the grown ups,' Alice reminded her, taking her jacket. Her eyes flickered quickly over the outfit Melissa had spent hours agonising over. 'You look stunning, by the way.'

In the end her desire to dazzle Daniel had pushed her into choosing a short, hot-pink dress that clung to her like a second skin. In a bid to make the outfit look less *woman trying too hard* and more *sexy but sophisticated*, she'd thrown one of her sheer diaphanous blouses over the top. 'Thank you. You're looking very glamorous yourself.'

'How kind. I must give you the name of the hot new designer who made my trousers.'

She gave her a quick twirl and Melissa laughed. Alice did look pretty amazing in the deep purple silk trousers she'd made for her.

'Let's go and find one of those lovely young waiters I hired and get ourselves a drink.' Alice hung her jacket in the hallway before zeroing in on a dark-suited man carrying a tray. She whisked two glasses of champagne from him, handing one to Melissa. 'Here's to a good party. May it achieve what it set out to do.'

Melissa glanced at her quizzically. 'What is that, exactly?'

'To make sure everyone brings the New Year in with a smile on their face.'

Melissa could have sworn there was a touch of mischief in Alice's eyes but before she had a chance to quiz her, the doorbell rang again.

As Alice went to greet the arriving guests, Melissa hung back. It was only when the couple came into the hall that she realised she'd been holding her breath, waiting to see if it was Daniel. Of course it wasn't. No doubt he would arrive fashionably late. By which time she'd be totally strung out if she carried on like this.

An hour went by and though she made a determined effort not to listen and not to watch, each time the doorbell rang her damn heart lurched in her chest. How ridiculous to feel this crazy mixture of anticipation and dread at the prospect of seeing the same man who'd been at her son's party two days ago.

This time there were no children to distract though. This time they might be able to manage some time alone.

Perhaps in a dark, intimate corner. With slow music in the background.

She swigged back the last of the champagne in her glass. She had to stop thinking like this. She'd turned him down. He wasn't going to come running back to her now. The best thing for her to do was accept and move on.

Another ring of the bell, and once again Melissa felt the fluttering of her heart. This time it didn't slow when she took a look at the new arrival. This time it sped up so much she worried it might crash out of her chest.

Daniel couldn't have looked more handsome. In common with most of the men at the party, he'd opted for a jacket and matching dark trousers. Unlike any of the other men, he wore them with a panache that had her drawing a sharp breath. So great was his heartthrob appeal that he had every woman in the room ogling at him, herself included.

For the umpteenth time she asked herself, *why had she turned him down?*

Daniel hadn't wanted to come. Not that he didn't enjoy a good party. He did. He just didn't enjoy them when he knew there would be a woman present who would knot his insides so hard he would have trouble concentrating on talking to anybody else.

The instant he walked into the hallway, he saw her. She was hard to miss. Not because she was wearing a vivid pink dress, but because she was the most beautiful woman in the room. God, how he longed to rush over to her and run his hands over that willowy body. Kiss those full, pink lips.

Deliberately he walked in the opposite direction, towards the temporary bar Alice had set up in her dining room. God bless his sister for that, at least.

After he'd helped himself to a glass of champagne, he

wandered into the sitting room where he was flattered to find there was no shortage of women who drifted in his direction, giving him the eye, chatting inanely to him. Having been rejected by the one woman he wanted, it was a welcome ego boost to be flirted with, even though his mind couldn't focus on what they were saying. It was too full of wondering what Melissa was doing.

'Daniel?'

A woman with long blonde hair and an eye-popping cleavage looked up at him, clearly waiting for an answer he'd failed to provide. Failed even to listen to her question. He gave himself a silent shake. Time to focus on what was in front of him. What he could have, rather than what he couldn't. 'Sorry, I didn't quite catch that.' He smiled apologetically.

'I asked if you wanted another drink?' The blonde pointed to his empty glass and smiled at him from beneath her lashes.

'Please, allow me. I'll go and hunt down a bottle. Champagne all round?' He smiled at the gaggle – or should that be giggle? – of women surrounding him before darting away, welcoming the chance of a few minutes' peace to get his game head on. He wasn't going to let Melissa ruin the rest of his life. Or even this damn party. He was going to go back to his female admirers, focus on their conversation and bloody well enjoy himself. He just needed another drink first.

After ordering a whiskey from the bartender Daniel nipped round the back and grabbed another bottle of fizz. The whiskey slipped easily down his throat, burning then mellowing.

Feeling marginally better he set off back to his harem. Which was when he bumped into her.

'Melissa.' His scrambled brain could manage no more.

'Hello, Daniel.'

He was renowned for his easy charm, so why was he now tongue-tied? 'You look ...' Words that used to trip so easily off his tongue vanished from his memory. 'Well, you don't need me to tell you how fabulous you look. You just have to watch the stares from the salivating men as you saunter by.'

She smiled, relieving some of the tension he'd seen in her face the moment she'd caught sight of him. 'Not true, but I thank you anyway.' She looked down at the bottle he still held. 'Feeling thirsty?'

'Ah, it's not all for me.'

'No, I didn't think it was.'

Had she been watching him? 'Melissa ...'

'It's okay,' she cut in. 'I mean, we're not together any more, so you don't owe me an explanation.' She glanced over at the group of waiting women. 'Enjoy your evening.'

With that she walked away, leaving him effectively dismissed. Given permission to go and chat up anyone and everyone he chose.

He no longer felt the burn of the whiskey he'd drunk. Instead he felt cold and hollow. Clenching tighter onto the bottle he marched back to the women who were interested in him.

Away from the woman who wasn't.

Melissa felt the tears sting her eyes as she walked away from Daniel. The fact that she only had herself to blame made the whole situation that much worse. She wasn't sure how much longer she could bear to watch him chatting with those women. Every time they made him laugh, she felt sick.

As the evening wore on, the party crowd grew more

and more vocal and watching Daniel grew more and more painful. By now the blonde had successfully manoeuvred the others out so it was just her and Daniel. Could she position herself any closer to him?

'Melissa, are you okay?'

Alice glanced at her curiously. Melissa blinked and tore her eyes away. 'Yes, I'm fine. Sorry. You were saying about that boutique?'

As the conversation between Alice and the other mums from the tennis academy resumed around her, Melissa felt like a woman apart. Why didn't she have the sense to stop looking over at Daniel? And why did it hurt so much when she saw the blonde placing her hands on his arms, running them slowly, sensuously, up and down? What the heck had she expected? That he would go crying off into a cave and not come out again until she'd decided she was ready to marry him? If she'd learnt one thing about Daniel, it was that he was strong and determined. He wanted to get married. If he couldn't have her, he'd go and find himself someone else.

'Only forty-five minutes to go before midnight,' Alice gushed. 'I'd better go and find that husband of mine and see if he's sober enough to sort out the fireworks.'

Melissa didn't take in any of the following conversation. She was too busy watching in horror as the blonde moved her hands from Daniel's arms and placed them, quite deliberately, on his chest.

That was it. Pain seared through her as the green-eyed monster trampled all over her heart.

Excusing herself, Melissa fled from the sitting room. Not even stopping to pick up her jacket, she stumbled out of the house and down the path. It was only when she reached the road that she realised she didn't have her car here. She'd come by taxi so she could have a drink. Shuddering with cold, she dialled the cab firm number. Better to be outside, alone in the dark, than inside the house watching the man she'd fallen in love with move onto another woman.

Daniel was fast discovering that it was one thing to have his ego soothed by a flirtatious woman, but it was another thing entirely to be treated as a piece of meat. When her hands moved from his arms, where she'd been making a show of feeling his muscles, to his chest, it was the last straw. He clasped her by the wrist and pulled her hand away. Time to move on to another group. Perhaps, with luck, he could catch up with Melissa later. Hopefully by then he'd have drunk enough to anaesthetise the pain.

Walking through to the kitchen, he found his brother-in-law sitting at the table, poring over some instructions, a huge box of fireworks sitting next to him. 'All set to go off with a bang?'

'Maybe. Just figuring out how to make sure the bang happens in the sky, and not in my face.'

'Ah.' Daniel sat down next to Richard and together they worked out where to set the fireworks to maximise the chance of the former and minimise the chance of the latter. They were coming in from the garden when Alice accosted him.

'The eagle has landed.'

Daniel halted. 'What flipping eagle?'

'It's a saying, dumbass. It means the mission is completed.'

He rubbed at his forehead. 'For goodness' sake, stop talking in riddles. You're making my head hurt.'

'I'm just saying Melissa is no longer at the party. Apparently she left fifteen minutes ago, looking pretty upset.'

His heart lurched. 'God, is she okay? Is she sick?'

Alice thumped him on the arm. 'Of course she is. She's sick of seeing you flirt with Annabel.'

But Daniel didn't hear what his sister was telling him. He was too busy dialling a cab to take him to Melissa's.

Thirty minutes before midnight on New Year's Eve.

Chapter Twenty-One

Melissa scrubbed off every inch of her make-up, undressed and crawled into bed.

She was going to bring in the New Year alone. Exactly as she deserved.

When she'd first dreamt of falling in love, it had never felt like this. As a young girl she'd imagined love to be warm and beautiful; a fierce, protective hug that would never let her go.

What she felt now hurt more than anything else in her whole life. More than her parents not being around in the school holidays. Even more than the way Lawrence had treated her. When she thought of Daniel with another woman, it broke her heart.

It turned out being in love was painful and raw. A gaping hole in her chest that would never be filled.

Tears gushed from her eyes and Melissa was helpless to stem the flow. She was onto her second pack of tissues when she heard a knock at the door.

'Melissa.' She recognised the voice instantly. 'If you're there, please open the door.'

Startled, she sat bolt upright. Instinctively she checked herself in the mirror. Bad idea. Puffy eyes and a clown red nose. Then her mind jumped in a panic to William. Oh God, what if Daniel had come round to tell her something was wrong? Grabbing a dressing-gown, she fled down the stairs. 'Is it William?' she yelled, struggling with the locks on the door. 'Is he ill?'

The moment she threw the door open she was bundled into a strong pair of arms. 'Shh, it isn't William,' Daniel reassured her. 'He was fast asleep last time I checked.'

Instantly she relaxed, her body remembering how good it felt to be held by him. How warm and safe. But then she remembered who'd last been in those arms, and jerked away. 'What are you doing here?' she asked sharply.

Hurt came and went in his eyes. 'I came to check you were okay. You left the party before midnight.'

'I felt tired,' she replied stiffly. 'I had the beginnings of a headache so I thought I'd better leave.'

Daniel studied her with narrowed eyes. 'You've been crying,' he stated. Gently he drew a finger down her cheek and she jolted backwards. His eyes darkened. 'Christ, Melissa, is my touch so distasteful to you?'

Nothing could have been further from the truth. At the realisation, her eyes filled with more tears. 'Go home, Daniel,' she sobbed. 'Leave me alone.'

He let out a ripe oath. 'How can you expect me to leave you like this? I'm not going anywhere until you start to talk to me.' As if to prove it, he stalked into the living room and sat on the sofa, crossing his legs and stretching out his arms behind his back. 'I've got all evening,' he continued, his dark eyes quietly assessing her. 'So if you want to go back to bed, I suggest you start by telling me why you've been crying.'

He left her with no choice. Besides, she owed it to him to be honest. 'I was jealous,' she muttered, sitting as far away as she could from him.

'Good.'

Her head snapped up. 'You bastard. Is that all you can say? You go cuddling up with another woman right under my nose and now you sit there, pleased as punch that it hurt me.'

'First off, if you were watching, it was her who was doing

215

the cuddling up, not me. Heck Melissa, you have to know I'm not attracted to her.' He let out a slow, deep breath. 'How can I be, when I'm in love with you?'

Briefly she closed her eyes, allowing the warmth of his words to penetrate her heart. 'And the second point?'

He moved from the sofa to sit on the edge of the coffee table, his eyes level with hers. 'I have to admit to being pleased you were jealous. At least it shows you have some feelings for me. I know they aren't strong enough to make you want to marry me, but my ego takes some consolation from knowing you care enough to be jealous.'

'Of course I care,' she mumbled, afraid to let him look into her eyes. Afraid he'd see that she'd moved way beyond caring, and straight into love.

He took hold of her hand, startling her. 'Seeing you and not being with you, it's killing me,' he said softly. 'I don't know what to do any more. I've tried to call it off, but I can't seem to live with that.' Carefully he kissed her fingers. 'I want you in my life, however you'll have me. If you won't marry me, that's fine. I'll learn to live with it. One thing I can't do is live without you.'

For an instant Melissa's heart seemed to stop beating. When it started again, it beat so fast she almost felt dizzy. *So this was love*, she thought, stunned. This man cared so much for her... *loved* her so much ... he was willing to give up on his dream of marriage just to be with her. No longer pushing for what he wanted, Daniel was stepping back and giving her what he thought *she* wanted.

A few days ago promising herself to him had seemed a risk too huge to take. Another gamble on love, when she'd failed so miserably the first time.

But what she and Lawrence had shared hadn't been love, she realised, not really. Their relationship had been based on need – he'd needed her looks, her willingness to bend to his bidding. She'd needed his security.

Daniel had just unselfishly proved how much he *loved* her.

Was promising herself to this man really the huge risk she'd convinced herself it was?

Reaching out, she carefully touched his face. The sharp cheekbones, the chiselled jaw. 'I want you in my life, too,' she admitted hoarsely. 'It wasn't until I saw those women fawn over you, I realised how stupid I'd been.' She put her arms around his neck, holding him tight. 'You're mine, Daniel, and I'm yours.' He let out a low groan as her lips sought his but before he could deepen the kiss she drew back. 'Will you ask me to marry you one final time?'

'Really?' His voice was thick with emotion.

She smiled, nodding once.

'Third time lucky?'

She nodded again.

'Melissa, will you marry me? Please?'

And this time she didn't feel fear or panic. This time all she felt was utter joy. 'Yes, Daniel. Yes, yes, yes.'

His face split into a grin and he lifted her into his arms. 'I thought I'd never hear you say those words,' he murmured into her neck. 'I promise we'll have a long engagement. Time for you and William to get used to the idea. But, oh God.' He buried his face in her hair. 'You're actually going to marry me.'

Just then the grandmother clock in the corner of her room started to chime, signalling midnight, and they both started to laugh.

'Happy New Year,' she whispered.

'It will be now,' he replied, his lips seeking and finding hers again. 'It's going to be the happiest year of my life so far.' His eyes settled on hers. 'This is really happening, isn't it?'

Grinning, she kissed him back. 'Yes.'

'I have this mad desire to run through the streets, announcing it to the world before you change your mind.'

'I won't change my mind,' she countered firmly. 'So why don't you put all that boundless energy to some better use?'

He needed no further hint. Taking the stairs two at a time, he carried her up to the bedroom.

'Do you want to tell William by yourself?' Daniel asked as they pulled up outside Alice's house the following morning.

She shook her head. 'We'll tell him together.'

Tears shot into his eyes and it was only through sheer force of will that they remained there and didn't escape down his damn cheeks. 'I appreciate that,' he said when he finally had a handle on his emotions. 'But don't you think it would be better if you told him on your own? I mean, he'll need time to think about it. To get used to the idea. Me being there ... well ... it might crowd him.'

Her beautiful grey eyes scrutinised him. 'Why Mr McCormick, I do believe you're nervous.'

He wiped his slightly clammy hand down his trousers. 'Perhaps.'

To his chagrin, she started to laugh. 'You've faced championship points without batting your eyes, but you're nervous about telling a boy who adores you that he's going to get what he wants after all?' She shook her head, still laughing.

How could she be so calm when his heart was thumping against his ribs? 'This time it's real. He might not like the idea so much when he knows it's actually going to happen.'

'I thought you were a glass half full kind of guy?'

'Not when it comes to matters of the heart,' he muttered.

She stopped her laughing and took his face in her hands. 'Then this is where I tell you to trust me. Do you really think I would suggest doing this together if I had any doubt about his reaction? My son loves you as much as I do. Relax.'

Feeling better, though still unbelievably jittery, he allowed her to drag him up the path and towards the house.

Alice opened the door, took one look at the pair of them, and beamed. 'Well, well. Look what we have here.' She gave him a none-too-subtle wink. 'Isn't it galling to know your sister is always right?'

He took the crowing on the chin, figuring anyone who'd managed to achieve the seemingly impossible and get him and Melissa together deserved a boast or two. Still, it was his brotherly duty to pull her down at least a couple of pegs. 'One occasion doesn't equate to always.'

Melissa looked from him, to Alice and back to him, her face puzzled. 'What's going on?'

Oh no, he wasn't getting into that now. He wanted all his ducks lined up before he told that one. 'It's a long story which I'll share over a glass of celebratory champagne. Once we've told William.'

Right on cue, William bounded down the stairs to join them. 'Mum!' He did a double take. 'Daniel!' Racing up to them, he put his arms around them both. 'Does this mean you're friends again?' he asked, taking in the fact that they were holding hands. 'I know you said you were, but then you didn't talk much so I guessed you weren't, not really. You just said you were to keep me happy.'

Melissa rolled her eyes at him. 'You think you're pretty smart, eh?'

Daniel could feel the weight of his sister's stare, but right now he had something more important to do than satisfy her curiosity. Thanking her for the party, he shepherded William and Melissa away from her prying eyes and back into his car.

'How was your evening, Will?' he asked as they did up their seat belts. 'Did you stay awake till midnight?'

'Nearly.'

'What did you and Simon get up to? Did you watch a film?'

Melissa slid him a look. 'Seriously? You're going to spend the drive back to our house having polite conversation?'

'Well, yes. I mean it doesn't have to be too polite, but ... yes.'

'So we're not going to say anything till we get back to our house?'

'Say anything about what?' William piped up from the back seat.

Melissa's lips began to twitch and she looked like she was trying really hard not to laugh. All vestiges of tightness had left her face and she looked carefree and happy. 'God you're gorgeous,' he blurted.

'Thank you.' Tugging his hand, she pulled him towards her. 'You make me feel gorgeous,' she whispered. Then she turned round to William. 'We've got something to tell you, but Daniel wants to wait till we get home.'

In his rear-view mirror, Daniel watched as William's eyes bulged. 'You're getting married, aren't you?'

He'd wanted to wait until William was in his own home, but then again nothing about this proposal had run to plan so far. Daniel shifted his body so he could face the boy in the back. 'Yes. I've asked your mother to marry me, and she's said yes. Is that still okay with you?'

William's eyes filled with delight. 'Yippee! That's the best news ever. Father Christmas rocks.'

'Father Christmas?' Daniel asked, feeling a bit put out. 'Why does he deserve any credit?'

William shot him a dazzling grin. 'My second wish, remember? I asked Father Christmas for a new dad, and now he's given me you.'

And that was it. The tears in Daniel's eyes were no longer content to stay put. As he fought to stop them flooding down his cheeks he slid a look at Melissa.

It didn't help.

She was half laughing, half crying.

Almost simultaneously they opened their doors and jumped into the back seat, enveloping William.

And there, surrounded by his new family, Daniel gave a silent thank you to the big guy with the white beard and the red suit.

Perhaps he did exist, after all.

Thank You

Thank you so much for taking the time to read *Second Wish*. Unlike the boy in this story, if you were to ask me what my two Christmas wishes were, I'd tell you! My first wish would be that you'd enjoyed this book. My second wish would be that you'd leave me some feedback. Authors love feedback – it can inspire, motivate, help us improve. So if you feel inclined to leave a review on Amazon, Goodreads or any of the retail sites, or simply contact me through Facebook or Twitter, that would fulfil my Second Wish (without any need to hassle the guy with the white beard and red suit ☺).

Kathryn x

About the Author

Kathryn was born in Wallingford, England but has spent most of her life living in a village near Windsor. After studying pharmacy in Brighton she began her working life as a retail pharmacist. She quickly realised that trying to decipher doctors' handwriting wasn't for her and left to join the pharmaceutical industry where she spent twenty happy years working in medical communications. In 2011, backed by her family, she left the world of pharmaceutical science to begin life as a self-employed writer, juggling the two disciplines of medical writing and romance. Some days a racing heart is a medical condition, others it's the reaction to a hunky hero...

With two teenage boys and a husband who asks every Valentine's Day whether he has to bother buying a card again this year (yes, he does) the romance in her life is all in her head. Then again, her husband's unstinting support of her career change goes to prove that love isn't always about hearts and flowers – and heroes can come in many disguises.

A Second Christmas Wish is Kathryn's fifth novel published with Choc Lit.

For more information on Kathryn:
www.twitter.com/KathrynFreeman1
www.kathrynfreeman.co.uk

More *Choc Lit*

From Kathryn Freeman

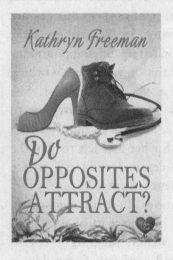

Do Opposites Attract?

There's no such thing
as a class divide – until
you're on separate sides

Brianna Worthington has
beauty, privilege and a very
healthy trust fund. The only
hardship she's ever witnessed
has been on the television.
Yet when she's invited to see
how her mother's charity,
Medic SOS, is dealing with the
aftermath of a tornado in South America, even Brianna is
surprised when she accepts.

Mitch McBride, Chief Medical Officer, doesn't need the
patron's daughter disrupting his work. He's from the wrong
side of the tracks and has led life on the edge, but he's not
about to risk losing his job for a pretty face.

Poles apart, dynamite together, but can Brianna and Mitch
ever bridge the gap separating them?

Available in paperback from all good
bookshops and online stores. Visit
www.choc-lit.com for details.

Too Charming

Does a girl ever really learn from her mistakes?

Detective Sergeant Megan Taylor thinks so. She once lost her heart to a man who was too charming and she isn't about to make the same mistake again – especially not with sexy defence lawyer, Scott Armstrong. Aside from being far too sure of himself for his own good, Scott's major flaw is that he defends the very people that she works so hard to imprison.

But when Scott wants something he goes for it. And he wants Megan. One day she'll see him not as a lawyer, but as a man … and that's when she'll fall for him.

Yet just as Scott seems to be making inroads, a case presents itself that's far too close to home, throwing his life into chaos.

As Megan helps him pick up the pieces, can he persuade her that he isn't the careless charmer she thinks he is? Isn't a man innocent until proven guilty?

Search for the Truth

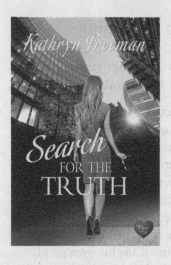

Sometimes the truth hurts ...

When journalist Tess
Johnson takes a job at Helix
pharmaceuticals, she has a
very specific motive. Tess has
reason to believe the company
are knowingly producing a
potentially harmful drug and,
if her suspicions are confirmed,
she will stop at nothing to make
sure the truth comes out.

Jim Knight is the president of research and development at
Helix and is a force to be reckoned with. After a disastrous
office affair he's determined that nothing else will distract
him from his vision for the company. Failure is simply not an
option.

As Tess and Jim start working together, both have their
reasons for wanting to ignore the sexual chemistry that fires
between them. But chemistry, like most things in the world
of science, isn't always easy to control.

Before You

When life in the fast lane threatens to implode …

Melanie Taylor's job working for the Delta racing team means she is constantly rubbing shoulders with Formula One superstars in glamorous locations like Monte Carlo. But she has already learned that keeping a professional distance is crucial if she doesn't want to get hurt.

New Delta team driver Aiden Foster lives his life like he drives his cars – fast and hard. But, no matter how successful he is, it seems he always falls short of his championship-winning father's legacy. If he could just stay focused, he could finally make that win.

Resolve begins to slip as Melanie and Aiden find themselves drawn to each other – with nowhere to hide as racing season begins. But certain risks are worth taking and, sometimes, there are more important things than winning …

Read a preview at the end of this book.

Nice boys don't kiss like that!

Too Damn Nice

Do nice guys stand a chance?

Nick Templeton has been in love with Lizzie Donavue for what seems like forever. Just as he summons the courage to make his move, she's offered a modelling contract which takes her across the Atlantic to the glamorous locations of New York and Los Angeles. And far away from him.

Nick is forced to watch from the sidelines as the gawky teenager he knew is transformed into Elizabeth Donavue: top model and the ultimate elegant English rose pin-up, seemingly forever caught in a whirlwind of celebrity parties with the next up-and-coming Hollywood bad boy by her side.

But then Lizzie's star-studded life comes crashing down around her, and a nice guy like Nick seems just what she needs. Will she take a chance on him? Or is he too damn nice?

Available as an ebook on all platforms.
Visit www.choc-lit.com for details.

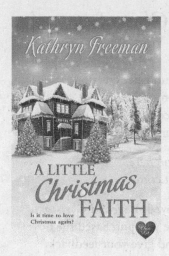

A Little Christmas Faith

Is it time to love Christmas again?

Faith Watkins loves Christmas, which is why she's thrilled that her new hotel in the Lake District will be open in time for the festive season. And Faith has gone all out: huge Christmas tree, fairy lights, an entire family of decorative reindeer. Now all she needs are the guests …

But what she didn't bank on was her first paying customer being someone like Adam Hunter. Rugged, powerfully built and with a deep sadness in his eyes, Adam is a man that Faith is immediately drawn to – but unfortunately he also has an intense hatred of all things Christmassy.

As the countdown to the big day begins, Faith can't seem to keep away from her mysterious guest, but still finds herself with more questions than answers: just what happened to Adam Hunter? And why does he hate Christmas?

Available as an ebook on all platforms.
Visit www.choc-lit.com for details.

Introducing Choc Lit

We're an independent publisher creating
a delicious selection of fiction.
Where heroes are like chocolate – irresistible!
Quality stories with a romance at the heart.

See our selection here:
www.choc-lit.com

We'd love to hear how you enjoyed *A Second Christmas
Wish*. Please leave a review where you purchased the novel
or visit: **www.choc-lit.com** and give your feedback.

Choc Lit novels are selected by genuine readers like yourself.
We only publish stories our Choc Lit Tasting Panel want to
see in print. Our reviews and awards speak for themselves.

Could you be a Star Selector and join our Tasting Panel?
Would you like to play a role in choosing which novels we
decide to publish? Do you enjoy reading women's fiction?
Then you could be perfect for our Choc Lit Tasting Panel.

Visit here for more details…
www.choc-lit.com/join-the-choc-lit-tasting-panel

Keep in touch:
Sign up for our monthly newsletter Choc Lit Spread for
all the latest news and offers: www.spread.choc-lit.com.
Follow us on Twitter: @ChocLituk and Facebook: Choc Lit.

Where heroes are like chocolate – irresistible!

Preview
Before You

by Kathryn Freeman

CHAPTER ONE

Aiden sucked in a deep breath, plastered the required smile onto his face and strode into the press room. Flashes went off as he took his seat, all eyes in the packed room aimed his way, but his smile didn't waver. He knew racing drivers were no longer simply men who drove fast around a track. They were a commodity, a brand with an image that had to be maintained, no matter how they were feeling inside.

Today the press assembled in the Delta HQ wanted to meet Aiden Foster, the new Delta driver. So that's what he'd give them.

'So, Aiden, the start of a new racing season. Is this the year you're finally going to follow in your father's footsteps and win a World Championship?'

'I wondered when that question was going to rear its head.' He glanced down at the sleek, expensive watch on his wrist. 'Hey, and it's only two minutes into the press conference. Must be a record.'

There was collective laughter. 'Come on, you can't blame us for making the comparisons,' the journo protested. 'It's not often a son follows his father into the world of motor racing. Especially when that father was such a legend in the sport.'

'My father was a brilliant driver,' Aiden agreed amiably. 'The day he died was a sad one for the sport. However, I'm not my father.'

'Well, no, by my reckoning by the time he was your age he'd already won three of his five world championships.'

The jibe hit its target and Aiden imperceptibly flinched though his lips remained fixed in a polite smile. 'Actually, I was thinking more along the lines of me being taller and better looking than him, but hey, you've got a point, too.'

Again there was laughter; all part of the game he played with the press. He was the laid-back playboy; the joker and charmer. It was what the public wanted him to be. What *he* wanted to be. And some days he was. It's just some days he was also a screw up.

'Does it feel strange, racing for the same team as your father?'

Strange? It's bloody terrifying, he wanted to shout, but of course that didn't fit his image. 'Strange isn't the right word. I feel honoured to be racing for the team that brought my father such immense success. If I can emulate just a fifth of that success, I'll be very happy.' One World Championship. It was all he asked.

'Any regrets about your move from Arrows to Delta?'

Grateful for the shift in focus away from his father, he flashed the reporter a more genuine smile. 'Delta are a fantastic team to work for. I loved my time at Arrows, but now I have the chance to race in *the* fastest car in motorsport, so no. No regrets.' He rested back on his seat and gave the room a glimpse of the devilish grin he was famous for. 'But be sure to ask me again at the end of the season.'

'Is that before or after you lift the World Championship trophy?'

He turned to the female voice asking the question. Cute, blonde and with a glitter in her eye that suggested she might be hitting on him. 'Better ask me before. Leave it till after and I'll be too drunk on champagne to be coherent.'

'Is that a promise then, Aiden?' asked the balding man to her left. 'You're actually going to win this year?'

Aiden resisted the impulse to roll his eyes. As if there were any guarantees in this game. Even if he was in the fastest car, driving the fastest lap, he could still end up mangled against the wall. Like his father.

'The only promise I can make is that I'll be trying my hardest. I've got the backing of a great team and I'll be driving the best car. With a few dollops of luck, this could be my year.'

He smiled again, hoping it came across as gracious and confident though inside his gut squirmed like a bag of snakes. This *had* to be his year. He'd been racing in this, the highest level of motorsport, for six years now and had yet to secure a title. Joining Delta wasn't only the best chance he'd ever get to win the championship, it would likely be his last. At twenty-eight he wasn't a veteran – but he wasn't going to get any better. This was the year he could finally put the past behind him. Stop people talking about Aiden Foster, son of Sebastian Foster, former five times World Champion, and get them talking instead about Aiden Foster, current World Champion.

Shit, just the thought sent shivers up his spine.

The conference wrapped up and as Aiden stepped away from the microphones he found himself face to face with the cute blonde.

'Hi. I just wanted to introduce myself.' She stuck out a slim, well-manicured hand. 'I'm Devon, from *Just for Ladies*.'

Laughing, he shook the offered hand. 'Sorry, that's not a publication I've heard of.'

She giggled coyly, capturing her bottom lip with her teeth; a flash of white against the vivid pink of her lipstick. 'No, I don't suppose you have. We're a woman's magazine, targeted towards the yummy mummy set. We don't usually follow racing but I've been asked to write an article on glamour, sex and the world of motorsport and ... well ...' She licked her dewy lips. '... I thought maybe I could start with you?'

He smiled, wondering again whether she was coming on to him. For some reason – the money, the danger? – women were attracted to racing car drivers. It was a side benefit he'd enjoyed over the years, though lately he found himself becoming ... he hardly dared admit it, but a bit *bored* by the whole thing. Mind you, Devon did have an ID badge around her neck, so perhaps there really was an article and it wasn't her letting him know she wanted to have sex with him.

'Where, exactly, were you thinking we might ... err, *start*?' he asked with a smile.

She lowered her lashes a fraction. 'Maybe we could set up a time when you're less busy? I'm happy to interview you at home, if you'd prefer. You know, somewhere more relaxing. More private.'

Aiden did know. And though sex delivered on a plate, no matter how attractively dished up, was starting to lose its appeal, she *was* cute. 'Have you got a pen?'

Quick as a flash he was offered a sparkly pink biro.

Feeling faintly ridiculous, he scrawled his mobile number across her ID badge. 'Give me a call and we'll sort something out.'

With a broad smile and a coquettish little wave, she thanked him and left the room, swinging her hips in a way he couldn't help but notice.

'Don't tell me. She works for some mindless women's mag and she wants to interview you somewhere private.'

Aiden turned to find Melanie Hunt, one of the Delta press officers, giving him one of her looks. Since joining Delta a month ago he'd learnt that Melanie could convey a world of messages through just one glare from her pretty hazel eyes. Today's message was *did you really just give that woman your phone number?*

He grinned, ignoring the mixture of disgust and incredulity that spread across her pleasantly attractive face. She was more girl-next-door than beach babe, though both had their merits. 'I thought you were all about me raising my profile, making sure everyone knows which team I'm on now?'

'As long as your *profile* is the only thing you'll be raising when she lures you into her satin pink boudoir.'

A laugh erupted out of him. With her casual, no nonsense clothes, make-up free face and wickedly sharp sense of humour, Melanie was a long way removed from the highly polished, pushy, ultra confident press officers he was used to. Thank the Lord.

She gave him a brief smile, her dimpled cheeks magnifying the wholesome, fresh-faced, farmer's daughter image. Then her attention dropped to her phone – the essential press officer's equipment. She had that in common with the others, at least.

'So tell me,' she asked eventually, having finished whatever vital phone business she'd been conducting. 'What insightful, thought-provoking article is your bunny boiler planning on writing?'

'What makes you think she's a bunny boiler?'

'What makes *you* think she isn't?'

He shrugged. 'Maybe I like my women a bit crazy.'

'Maybe you just like women,' Melanie murmured. 'So, the title of the piece?'

Aiden tried to stifle a smile. 'Sex in motorsport. Or something along those lines. I can't quite remember the full title, though I do remember the sex and motorsport bit.'

Mel found her stomach flipping as she watched amusement flare in Aiden's clear grey eyes. She'd like to bet the bunny boiler had every intention of finding out about the subject of sex in motorsport by doing her own personal, in-depth analysis.

'It's good to know women's magazines aren't dumbing down the sport, or their readers, in any way.'

He quirked an eyebrow. 'Touchy.'

Realising he was right, she sighed. 'A little, sorry. But sometimes … doesn't it piss you off, the assumption that you're stupid enough to fall for every pneumatic bosomed, bleached blonde with laser enhanced white teeth that pouts in your direction?'

'Err …'

'And that the sport seems to think the only place for women is smiling emptily behind the sponsors' logos, dressed in a skimpy skirt and low plunging top?'

'Personally I don't have any objections to women wearing a skimpy skirt and low plunging top.'

His flashing grin told her he was teasing. At least she thought he was, though she found Aiden pretty hard to read.

'Sorry, you've caught me on a bad day. I usually try to keep off the soapbox during daylight hours. So, this cutting edge interview that's going to get to the very heart of motor racing. Do you *want* to do it?'

'You mean do I want to have sex with a cute blonde in a pink boudoir? Or do I want to get embroiled in a fight to the death with a bunny boiler?'

A laugh bubbled out of her. Aiden in full flow, like he had been earlier in front of the press, was sharp and funny. 'I mean, do you want to give up a few hours of your valuable time to help produce an article that bored housewives in the southern counties will spill their lattes over?'

He regarded her quizzically. 'I'm getting the sense you don't want me to do it.'

'Put it this way, there are far better, more serious, professional platforms we can, and will, use to raise your profile in Delta. So the only reason for you to do this article ...'

'Is if I fancy the sometime bunny boiler.'

'And even then, I'm pretty sure you can get what you want out of the meeting, without actually having to open your mouth.'

Once again he chuckled and, just as she had earlier, Mel found she daren't look at him. If she did her tongue might hang out and she'd lose any professional respect she might have earned in the month since he'd joined Delta. But because she was still a woman first, and a press officer second, she allowed her eyes to briefly rest on the grooves at the side of his wide, laughing mouth. To flicker over the straight white teeth and up to his brilliant silver grey eyes. Then she forced her attention back to her phone.

'Actually,' he said as she pretended to check her messages, 'I think you'll find that in order to get the absolute most out of any such meeting, I really do need to open my mouth.'

Shocked, she snapped her head up and nearly drowned in his glittering, highly amused eyes. 'Point taken.' She coughed to ease her suddenly tight throat. 'I've got a schedule of far more suitable opportunities I could do with running by you when you've got a free moment.'

'Sure, I'm happy to meet up, though I'm not really fussed who I talk to.'

She noticed his attention drift away from her then and onto his teammate, Stefano, who'd just entered the room. Mumbling something about duty calling, Aiden gave her a quick smile of apology and strode over to join him.

Mel couldn't help but watch his retreating back. A tall, lean figure dressed in jeans and a dark navy jacket, dark hair curling slightly over his jacket collar. He had an easy stride, one that exuded authority and self-confidence. His whole body language screamed yes, he was incredibly rich and good-looking. And yes, he was aware that people watched him wherever he went.

'You wouldn't be admiring our new driver's backside, would you?'

She swung round to find Frank, race engineer for Aiden, grinning at her.

'A woman's got to get her kicks where she can find them.'

He shook his head in mock disapproval, though she couldn't mistake the hint of seriousness in his next words. 'I advise caution with that one.'

'Do you really think you need to tell me that?' Mel looked askance at the man who'd become a surrogate father to her since she'd joined the Delta team six years ago. 'I mean, apart from the very obvious fact that he wouldn't look twice at me, anyway.'

Frank furrowed his brow, deepening the lines that fifty-five years of living had already put there. 'Why not? You're very nicely put together.'

A sound very much like a snort fled her mouth and Mel glanced down at her sensible flat loafers, comfortable chino trousers and efficient cotton blouse complete with Delta team logo. 'That's exactly what someone like Aiden is looking for in a woman, isn't it? Someone *nicely put together*? Not a blonde bombshell, or a sexy hot bird?'

A slight flush crept over Frank's weathered face. 'There are some men who don't like the obvious. Who appreciate the more natural.'

Realising she'd embarrassed him, Mel threaded an arm through his and gave it a quick squeeze. 'Then that's the type of man I'll need to find. And it clearly isn't Aiden Foster.'

Together they walked past the slick reception area of the

Delta HQ, buried deep inside the Surrey countryside, and out into the sunlight.

'Out of interest, why the warning about Aiden? Are you two not getting on?'

Frank halted, his eyes squinting slightly. 'I wouldn't put it as strongly as that. Obviously it's early days and we're still tiptoeing round each other.'

She sensed the race engineer's hesitation. 'But?'

Chuckling, he ran a hand over his thinning grey hair. 'Okay, yes, there is a but. He has all the right attributes for a brilliant driver: great reflexes, mentally quick, physically strong and in fantastic shape. Plus he has an understanding of the aerodynamics and engine capabilities that, frankly, sometimes puts mine to shame. But,' he added, smiling at the emphasis, 'he's, I don't know, I think *tense* is the word for it. Sure he can act cool and laid-back in front of the cameras, but when he's in the garage or on the track ...'

'He turns into a wrench throwing monster?'

'No, not that bad, though he doesn't mind shouting to put his point across. A keen desire to win is a fundamental attribute for any driver, but it's almost as though he wants it too much.'

'Maybe he's just finding his feet. He'll calm down once he feels more settled.'

'I'm not sure that's the answer. I really don't think being calm is what he needs. When he's behind the wheel, I actually think he needs to let go more.'

'I guess watching your father die after slamming into a wall makes it hard to do that.'

Frank turned to look at her, his sharp blue eyes missing nothing. 'Something tells me you're no longer thinking about Sebastian Foster's crash.'

Mel smiled sadly. 'You're right. I'm thinking about Mum and Dad's. At least I didn't have to watch them die.'

Frank took her hand in his large, reassuring one. 'Come on, sweetie. How about I give you a lift home? Or even better, why not come and have dinner with us? It would make Nancy's day. Plus it might put me back in her good books. I've been late home the last few nights. If we'd had a dog, he'd be three pounds heavier now.'

Mel giggled, grateful for the turn of conversation. 'So, let me get this right. I help smooth out the relationship between you and your wife *and* I get a delicious meal. How can I say no?'

CHAPTER TWO

Aiden stared regretfully at Devon. It had been a while since he'd been stupid enough to let his libido rule his head but after the press conference he'd felt out of sorts, thanks to all that talk about his father. Not wanting to spend yet another evening at home with his own thoughts he'd accepted the dimpled blonde's invitation.

This morning he regretted it. Devon was talking about meeting up again, when all he wanted to do was push her out and get on with his day. He had a plane to catch. The first race of the season was just over a week away, in Melbourne, and he really, really needed to get his head into the right place.

'Look, Devon, we've been through this. What we had last night was great sex. Please don't start thinking it was anything more.'

'But you enjoyed it, didn't you?'

Her lips came together in what he guessed was meant to be a sexy pout, though to be honest she reminded him a little of a hungry goldfish.

'Of course I did, but I enjoy lots of things, like white water rafting and surfing. It doesn't mean I want to do them every day.'

He tried to soften his words by kissing her on the cheek but she lurched away from him, her eyes flashing with temper. Thankfully whatever outburst she was about to have was curtailed by the sound of his intercom.

With a shrug of apology, he went to answer it. 'Hello?'

'Aiden, it's Melanie. We have an eleven o'clock?'

Bugger. He'd totally forgotten. 'Sure, come right up.' At least now he had an excuse to get rid of Devon.

He turned to find the blonde putting on her strappy stilettoes with tight, jerky movements. 'Devon, I'm sorry, but I've got a meeting with the Delta press officer now, so I need you to go.'

'And that's it, is it?' she asked, standing so she could glare at him eyeball to eyeball. 'I was just a cheap shag?'

The remark was so close to the bone, Aiden winced. She had a right to be angry with him. Sure he'd made no promises, but a woman was entitled to think a man who took her to bed was at least interested enough to see her again.

Clasping her hand in his, he twined his fingers around hers. 'No, you weren't a cheap shag. You were a beautiful way to spend an evening. If you get to one of the races, maybe I can buy you a drink.'

'I'll be in Melbourne,' she admitted.

'Your magazine is sending you all the way to Australia?' he asked in disbelief, certain she was winding him up. 'There'll be plenty of other races far closer to home.'

'I know, but we're running a series of articles on young Australian fashion designers so I'm mainly going for that.' She looked up at him hopefully, smiling as if he'd just promised her a dream holiday instead of the shallow offer of a drink. 'So, can we meet up?'

He felt a rush of shame. This was the absolute last time he was sleeping with a woman he had no intention of seeing again. 'Look, I'm going to be a bit busy, it being the first race of the season. I can't make any promises.'

A sharp knock on his door indicated the press officer's arrival and, with great relief, Aiden went to let her in.

'Hi, sorry I'm a bit late, the traffic getting into London was hellish and ...' Melanie trailed off as she caught sight of Devon. 'It looks like my being late was a blessing in disguise.'

Awkwardly Aiden made the introductions. 'Devon writes for the *Ladies Only* magazine—'

'*Just for Ladies*,' Devon interjected, rolling her eyes at him.

Melanie gave the blonde a guarded smile. 'Hello, I'm Melanie, one of the Delta press officers. I take it you've just interviewed Aiden for a piece in your magazine?'

As the women shook hands, Aiden squirmed silently, wondering what the heck Melanie was up to. She knew damn well Devon hadn't spent the night interviewing him.

Devon let out a flustered sounding laugh. 'To be honest, we haven't got round to the interview yet.'

'But we'll try and catch up in Melbourne,' Aiden finished firmly, desperate to take control before the whole fiasco blew up in his face. 'Thanks for coming by Devon.' He gave her a chaste kiss on the cheek. 'I'll see you around.'

Ignoring her miffed expression, he all but pushed her out of the door.

Behind him, Melanie coughed. 'I take it you got what you wanted out of that particular interview?'

He turned to find her staring at him, pretty hazel eyes filled with an emotion that looked a lot like disappointment. As he wasn't particularly pleased with his own behaviour, he really didn't need the sharp edge of her disapproval. 'Yes, thanks,' he replied tersely.

For a second she looked wounded, and instantly he regretted taking his self-disgust out on her. Fixing a smile on his face he motioned over to his large cream sofa. 'Please, take a seat.'

She nodded coolly – he didn't blame her for the attitude – and he studied her as she went to sit down. Again she was wearing a pair of nondescript trousers and utilitarian blouse – he couldn't remember ever seeing her in anything else. If he had to guess he'd say they probably hid a really neat figure, which made it all the more confusing why she chose to downplay her looks. Either she was an absolute sex bomb outside work, or she was … what? Too scared to put herself out there?

'Can I get you something to drink?' He glanced at his watch. 'Eat?'

A small smile hovered around lips that were full and pink but unadorned with lipstick. 'Well, if you're offering, a lightly whipped omelette with salad garnish would go down a treat.'

Relieved she wasn't going to give him a hard time over his shitty behaviour, he relaxed enough to laugh. 'Ah, you have me there. I can boil a kettle to make you a cup of instant coffee, or crack open a pack of chocolate biscuits. The omelette is outside my skillset, I'm afraid, whipped or not.'

She cocked her head to one side and seemed to consider him. 'How about a cup of tea and a chocolate digestive?'

'That, I can manage.'

Mel was relieved when Aiden disappeared into his kitchen. It gave her a chance to get her head around what she'd just seen. She thought they'd been joking when they'd talked about him seeing the blonde journalist, so it was one heck of a shock to find he'd done exactly what they'd laughed about – had a meaningless one night stand with a woman who'd come on to him at a press conference. She felt oddly let down. She'd been hoping to find there was more to the man than the flippant persona he presented to the press.

Sighing at her foolishness, she placed her bag on the floor by her feet and sank back into the expensive leather sofa. It was hard for women not to like Aiden Foster. Even she – used to being around racing drivers so much she was supposedly unfazed by them – had to admit when it came to Aiden, she was no different to the rest. How could she be when the man had film star looks, charisma, a dry, playful sense of humour and a swagger just the right side of arrogant?

So, yes, like millions of women round the globe she, too, had a crush on him. It was the reason she was now sitting here feeling so desperately disappointed. Aiden Foster was exactly the playboy the media purported him to be.

'One cup of tea.' He sauntered back in and planted a snazzy black and white mug directly onto the glass coffee table. 'Plus biscuits.' With a flourish he produced a white china plate containing several chocolate biscuits of various types, all neatly laid out.

He went to sit on the opposite sofa, casually crossing one barefooted, jean clad leg over the other and Mel found she couldn't stop looking at his feet. Long and narrow, they were actually pretty sexy ...

'So, you're here to discuss my image, huh?'

She dragged her gaze from his feet, past his slightly crumpled white shirt and up to his face with its flashing cheekbones and mesmerising grey eyes. It certainly was quite an image. Taking a gulp of tea she pushed her brain out of fan mode and into professional press officer. 'It's not your image I wanted to talk about. Delta have no issue with it and it would seem you have no problem living up to it,' she couldn't resist adding.

There was a subtle stiffening in his body language. 'I

presume that's a veiled reference to finding Devon here when you arrived?'

'It was and you're right to glare at me. It's none of my business.'

'True, so why do I get the feeling you're annoyed with me?'

'I'm not annoyed,' she corrected him. 'Not really. I guess, I just … I know it sounds silly, but I was hoping you'd be one of the good guys. A racing driver who's more than just a walking penis.'

His sharp, startled laugh filled the quiet room. 'Did you really just say penis?'

'Why, should I have used another word instead?'

'No, please. Penis is fine.' He laughed again, softer this time. 'Now there's a sentence I never thought I'd say. So, tell me, is that all you think I am? A man who likes to drive fast cars and have sex?'

'I'm sure there are a lot more strings to your bow. I mean, you made me a cup of tea, so there's one, for a start.'

'And now you're just trying to avoid the question.'

He was right, and though she spent a lot of her working life advising people how to skate round a difficult question, it didn't seem fair to avoid this one. Not when she'd been the one to bring it up.

'Truthfully, I don't know you, so I can't comment, but I think that's part of the problem. You don't allow anyone to know you, so we're left to speculate. Draw obvious conclusions from what we *can* see, like the fact that we rarely see you with the same woman twice. You're very good at giving interviews, always smooth and charming, but your answers don't actually say anything about *you*. The man behind the sexy driver.'

'So now I've got a penis and I'm sexy,' he drawled. 'It's getting better.'

She began to laugh, but halted when she realised what he was doing. 'That's exactly what I'm talking about. Once again you cleverly tried to divert the conversation with a quip, a line. Anything that means you don't have to talk about you.'

'Maybe that's the way I prefer it.'

'Which is fine, but unfortunately that attitude doesn't help when you're working with the media. If they're left with a lot of gaps, they tend to fill them in their own way. Hence my comment about the walking penis. It might sound like a joke, but that's how some of the press refer to you. From what I've seen from archived interviews, your father had a very different style. He tended to wear his heart on his sleeve—'

'I'm not my father,' he cut in, his cool grey eyes now glacial. 'Don't compare me to him. Please.'

So she hadn't just imagined it at the last press conference. It seemed he did have a huge chip on his shoulder with his father's name engraved on it.

'I guess you get pretty fed up with people doing that, don't you?' she asked softly.

A muscle twitched in his jaw. 'Yes.'

'Did the pair of you get on?'

His lids lowered over those stunning eyes. 'My father was a risk-taker, a hellraiser and the best driver of his generation. What's not to get on with?'

Frustration coiled in her belly at his obvious fob off but there were times to push and times to stop. This was the latter.

'Okay, have it your way, but you're going to have to get used to a lot of questions about him.'

'You think that's a change from the normal?' He threw her a casual smile though the gesture was ruined by the clenched muscle in his jawline.

'I'm well aware you're used to fielding questions about your father, but now you've joined his old team, the interest in that relationship is only going to escalate. I've been bombarded with interview requests since the announcement was made.'

'You must be really cursing my arrival then, huh?'

An image flashed through her mind of her and Sally, the other press officer, jigging up and down with glee when they'd been told of Aiden's signing. 'Not at all. It actually makes my job easier when people come to me wanting interviews rather than the other way around.' Reaching into her folder, she passed him a sheet of neatly typed paper. 'And that's what I came here to discuss with you. I've drawn up a list of interviews scheduled for the next few months. They'll take place mainly after test sessions or practice sessions. I know it's a bit of a bind—'

'It's fine,' he cut in, not even glancing at the piece of paper.

Because he still appeared tense, she tried to lighten the mood. 'I can't guarantee all the journalists will be hot-looking blondes, but I'll do my best.'

Instantly he was on his feet, swiping a hand through his hair. It sprang back, making him look rumpled and more sexy than she wanted him to be. 'Look, Devon was a mistake, I admit it. Despite what you're thinking, I don't make a habit of hooking up with women in that way.' His chest rose and fell as he sighed. 'At least I don't any more.'

She sensed the anger was directed at himself rather than her but still, annoying their star driver wasn't going to help her do her job. 'I'm sure you don't make a habit of it,' she placated. 'Even if you did, as I've already said, it really is none of my business so please, just ignore me. You'd be amazed how many people find that's pretty easy to do.'

Melanie gave him a small smile and Aiden calmed down

enough to study her. She did look quiet, like he imagined a librarian might look if he'd ever ventured inside such a place. Appearances could be deceptive though, and he had a strong feeling this press officer would be impossible to ignore. She seemed to have a way of seeing past the facade and right into the core of a person. Heck, she'd already worked out he hadn't got on with his father. Nobody else had ever made that connection.

It made him wish even more he hadn't invited Devon over last night. Bad enough disappointing himself, but for some reason he found disappointing his fresh-faced press officer even harder to stomach.

'Anyway, back to the interviews.' Her eyes flitted away from his gaze and down to her notes, allowing Aiden to continue his study. Her hair was a deep chocolate brown with curls that struggled to be contained in the haphazard ponytail she usually shoved it into. What with that and her make-up free face, Aiden reckoned she must have spent all of two minutes getting dressed this morning.

'Your first interview is scheduled to take place after the Malaysian Grand Prix,' she told him, following her statement with an apologetic smile. 'It's with a guy from *Motorsport* magazine who was insistent that he wanted to explore what it was like for you following in your father's footsteps and coming to Delta. Consider yourself duly warned.'

He covered his unease with a wry smile. 'Duly noted.'

She smiled back and he realised he liked making her smile, enjoying the way her brown eyes warmed and her dimples winked. All too quickly her eyes focused back on her notepad. He tried to pretend that he cared as she talked through the rest of her list.

'Well, that's all I have for now.' She closed her notepad and tucked it into her oversized brown handbag.

Small animals, maybe even small children, could probably

live in there quite happily without ever needing to see the light of day.

The thought must have made him grin because she halted in the process of heaving the bag onto her shoulder and eyed him suspiciously. 'What are you smiling at?'

His lips twitched. 'Nothing.'

Her glance turned into a glare. 'It might have been only a month since you joined the team, but I know you, Aiden Foster. You reserve most of your smiles for when you're in front of the cameras, so to be smiling now you must have found something really funny.'

That successfully wiped the smirk off his face. 'What do you mean by that?'

She chewed on her bottom lip. 'You mean the bit about what you found funny, or ...'

'The bit about me being a grumpy git?'

Her cheeks reddened slightly. 'Sorry, I didn't mean to be rude. I have a tendency to speak what's on my mind without filtering it first, which probably isn't an ideal trait for someone in my role.' Her fingers fiddled with the straps of her bag which she still hadn't put on her shoulder. 'It's been an observation of mine that ... well ... maybe Aiden Foster the racing driver and Aiden Foster the man aren't quite the same person.'

He stilled, surprised ... no, more than that, shocked. 'How do they differ?'

She was still finding it hard to meet his eyes. 'Well, I guess Aiden Foster the driver is charming, funny, laid-back and a bit of a womaniser.'

He could live with all of those. 'And the man?'

Shaking her head, she finally looked at him. 'I don't know. He keeps himself very hidden, but I think he's much more serious.'

Her ability to see through him made the hairs on the

back of his neck start to prickle. 'So you don't think I can be funny and charming without a camera lens being poked into my face?' He raised his eyes in mock despair. 'And there was me thinking you liked me.'

'I think both of you can be charming, and, yes, even though I'm sure it doesn't matter to you, I do actually like you.'

Having dropped her bombshells she hoisted her bag onto her shoulder and made her way towards the door. For a few seconds he remained rooted to the spot, trying to assimilate everything she'd just said. It was only when her struggles with the door resulted in a muted curse that he was finally knocked out of his trance sufficiently to open it for her.

She gave him the full dose of her pretty eyes. 'Thank you. You know I actually think I'd prefer the real Aiden Foster, if he ever dares to come out and show himself.'

With that she slipped out. He was left staring at her small, retreating figure as it walked towards the lift, his mouth slightly agape, probably resembling a ruddy carp.

At least he hadn't had to tell her he'd been laughing at her handbag, he mused as he finally shut the door. Mind you, considering the psychoanalysis she'd subjected him to instead, that might have been a blessing.

Available to purchase in paperback and as an eBook on all platforms. More details at www.choc-lit.com.

Where heroes are like chocolate – irresistible!